EX LIBRIS

THE SONG
OF THE NIBELUNGS

THE SONG OF THE NIBELUNGS:
A BOOK THAT INSPIRED TOLKIEN
- With Original Illustrations -

Book #1 of 'The Professor's Bookshelf'

Cover images by W.B. MacDougall

Uniform Title: Nibelungenlied. English.
The song of the Nibelungs illustrated = das Nibelungenlied
Margaret Armour, translator;
W. B. (William Brown) MacDougall, illustrator;
Cecilia Dart-Thornton: introduction.

Revised edition.
ISBN: 9781925110036 (pbk.)
First pub. as The fall of the Nibelungs:
London, J. M. Dent & Co., 1897.

Subjects: Epic poetry, German--Translations into English.
Mythology, Germanic--Poetry.
Germanic peoples--Poetry.
Middle Ages--Poetry.
Nibelungen--Poetry.

Copyright (C) 2018 Leaves of Gold Press
ABN 67 099 575 078
PO Box 3092, Brighton, 3186, Victoria, Australia

THE SONG OF THE NIBELUNGS

- A Book That Inspired Tolkien -

INCLUDING A GLOSSARY OF TERMS

Translated by Margaret Armour
Illustrated by W. B. MacDougall
Introduced by Cecilia Dart-Thornton

www.professorsbookshelf.com

THE PROFESSOR'S BOOKSHELF

Welcome to The Professor's Bookshelf, a collection of books that inspired the imagination of Professor JRR Tolkien, author of The Hobbit and The Lord of the Rings.

All our titles have informed the professor's writings in one way or another. In most cases the man himself has revealed their influence in his essays or interviews; in others, his biographers and researchers have uncovered the evidence. Some were widely obtainable and popular in his literary circles, so that he certainly knew of them and there is little doubt he read them.

Tolkien's own drawings adorn the pages of The Hobbit and it is easy to imagine him as a boy, long before the invention of television, poring for hours over the images in his favourite volumes - images that helped shape his creation of Middle Earth.

Where possible we have selected illustrated editions available in his lifetime. Both texts and pictures have been reproduced, and our books are mostly copies of the editions the professor held in his own hands.

Like the celebrated nineteenth century English textile designer, artist and writer William Morris, we at The Professor's Bookshelf reject the notion that illustrated materials are unsuitable for adults. To Morris, who was one of Tolkien's favourite authors, illustrated books for adults presented an opportunity to integrate literature with design and art. In essence, a book is itself an artistic creation. The Professor's Bookshelf celebrates this by embellishing our 'Illustrated' series with the original plates (whole page illustrations printed separately from the text), cuts (illustrations printed within the text), borders, fonts, miniatures, and ornamental capital letters, in addition to our own 'endpapers' and bookplates.

Each Professor's Bookshelf classic opens with an introduction by fantasy author Cecilia Dart-Thornton, about whose acclaimed Bitterbynde Trilogy Grand Master of Science Fiction Andre Norton wrote: 'Not since Tolkien's The Lord of the Rings fell into my hands have I been so impressed by a beautifully spun fantasy.'

Literary scholars have studied the texts in the Professor's Bookshelf collection, finding threads and motifs linking them to the professor's famous works. On reading them you will be awakened to that vast library of myth, magic, legend and fantasy whose legacy inspired the great English writer, poet and philologist, J.R.R. Tolkien.

~ SOME TITLES IN THE SERIES ~

1. The Song of the Nibelungs (illustrated)
Translated by Margaret Armour, previously published as 'The Fall of the Nibelungs', illust. W. B. MacDougall, pub. 1897

2. The Poetic Edda (illustrated)
Translated by Olive Bray, previously published as 'The Elder or Poetic Edda', illust. W. G. Collingwood, pub. 1908

3. The Story of the Glittering Plain (illustrated)
By William Morris, illust. Walter Crane, pub.1894

4. The Red Fairy Book (illustrated)
By Andrew Lang, illust. H. J. Ford and Lancelot Speed, pub. 1907

5. The Princess and the Goblin (illustrated)
By George MacDonald, illust. Jessie Willcox Smith, pub. 1920

6. The Saga of Eric Brighteyes (illustrated)
By H. Rider Haggard, illust. Lancelot Speed, pub. 1891.

7. The Dragon Ouroboros (illustrated)
By Eric Rücker Eddison, illust. Keith Henderson, pub. 1922

8. The Book of Wonder & The Last Book of Wonder (illustrated)
By Lord Dunsany, illust. S. H. Syme, pub. 1912

9. The Story of King Arthur and his Knights (illustrated)
Written and illustrated by Howard Pyle, pub. 1903

10. Grimms' Fairytales (illustrated)
Translated by Lucy Crane, illust. Walter Crane, pub. 1922

For more about The Professor's Bookshelf series, visit
www.professorsbookshelf.com

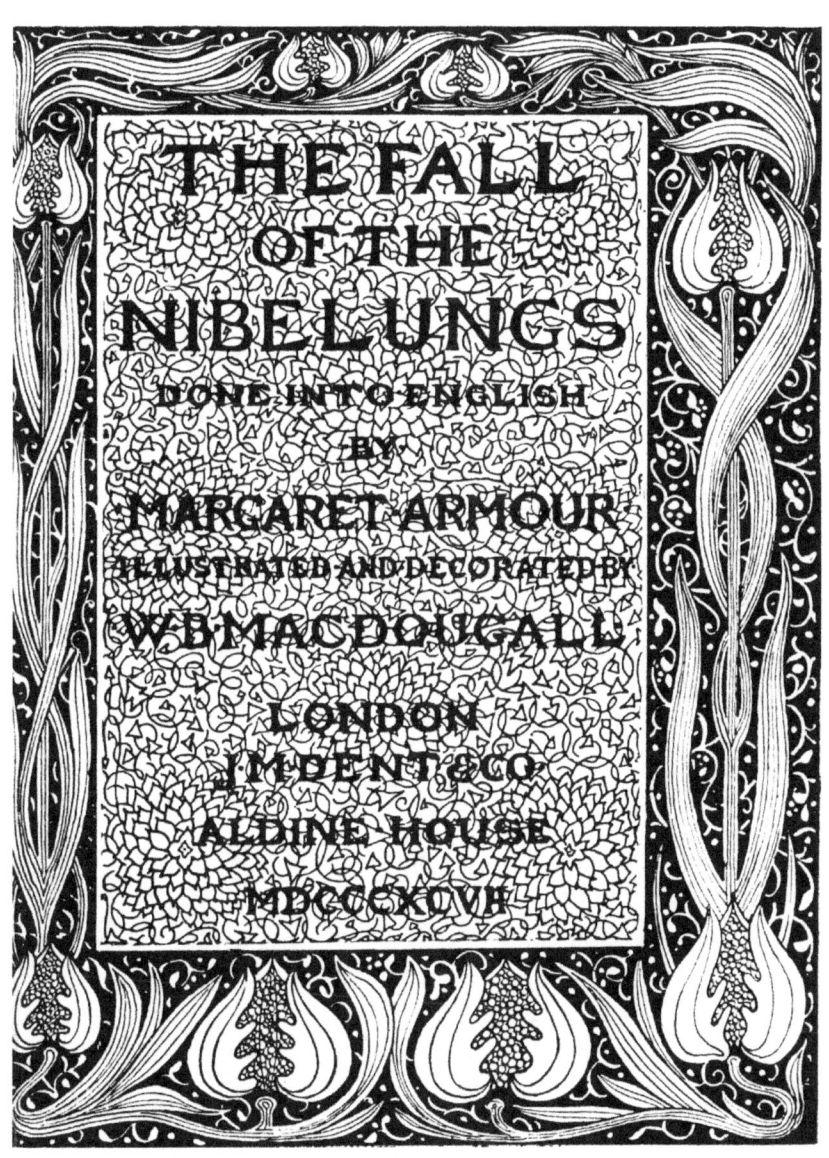

THE FALL
OF THE
NIBELUNGS
DONE INTO ENGLISH
BY
MARGARET ARMOUR
ILLUSTRATED AND DECORATED BY
W B MACDOUGALL
LONDON
J M DENT & CO
ALDINE HOUSE
MDCCCXCVII

Cover of the 1897 edition

INTRODUCTION

The Song of the Nibelungs, a thirteenth century Germanic epic, was a rich source of inspiration for J.R.R. Tolkien. Scholars have noted the influence of its pre-Christian heroic motifs - drawn from historic events and people of the 5th and 6th centuries - on his writing of *The Lord of the Rings* and *The Hobbit*.

Tolkien was five years old when this beautifully illustrated translation by Margaret Armour was published in England under the title 'The Fall of the Nibelungs'. Undoubtedly a copy would have made its way into his hands during his boyhood.

Armour uses an archaic form of English to preserve the high-flown style of the original poem. Here and there throughout *The Lord of the Rings*, Tolkien, too, employs this solemn, dignified and majestic form, which is reminiscent of the language of the King James Bible. A glossary of antiquated terms is provided at the back of this book.

Armour was the wife of W.B. MacDougall, whose illustrations illuminate the text with their delicate beauty. In his turn, MacDougall was a friend of famous art nouveau illustrator Aubrey Beardsley, and his own drawings echo Beardsley's style.

This classic saga, drenched in blood and tragedy, heroism and honour, beauty and nobility, gives us a glimpse into the literature that helped inform Tolkien's imagination, ultimately flowering in his most popular work - *The Lord of the Rings*.

Cecilia Dart-Thornton
Author of The Bitterbynde Trilogy
www.dartthornton.com

for

THE PROFESSOR'S BOOKSHELF

Note: 'The Song of the Nibelungs' should not be confused with Richard Wagner's 'The Ring of the Nibelungs', a derivative but separate work.

The heroes shook the world
With trample of their steeds,
With din of lances hurled.
And song of deathless deeds.

Their hands, I trow, were fashioned
Mighty and strong to move ;
Their hearts were high, and passioned
With god like hate and love.

And so they won their glory,
And, dying, perished not;
So, 'mid the newer story,
The old is unforgot.

Still, in the silent places.
They mingle tears and mirth.
And still the vanished faces
Are young upon the earth.

Still winds the fabled river
Far by the storied strand.
And poets, crowned forever,
Sing through a summer land.

Around the rose of laughter
Is planted still the rue,
And joy brings weeping after.
And love till death is true.

                              M.A

                .

PREFATORY NOTE

Simrock's arrangement of the mediaeval text is the one I have chosen for translation. I have followed Bartsch and Niendorf, however, at the end of the twenty-seventh adventure, and in omitting the twenty-three verses given in parenthesis by Simrock at the beginning of the twenty-eighth adventure.

I hope that the plain prose rendering I have attempted may not be unwelcome to those who like a translation to bring them as near as possible to the original.

M. A.

CONTENTS

BOOK I

BOOK II

LIST OF ILLUSTRATIONS
BOOK I

BOOK II

HERE BEGINNETH THE STORY OF
THE SONG OF THE NIBELUNGS

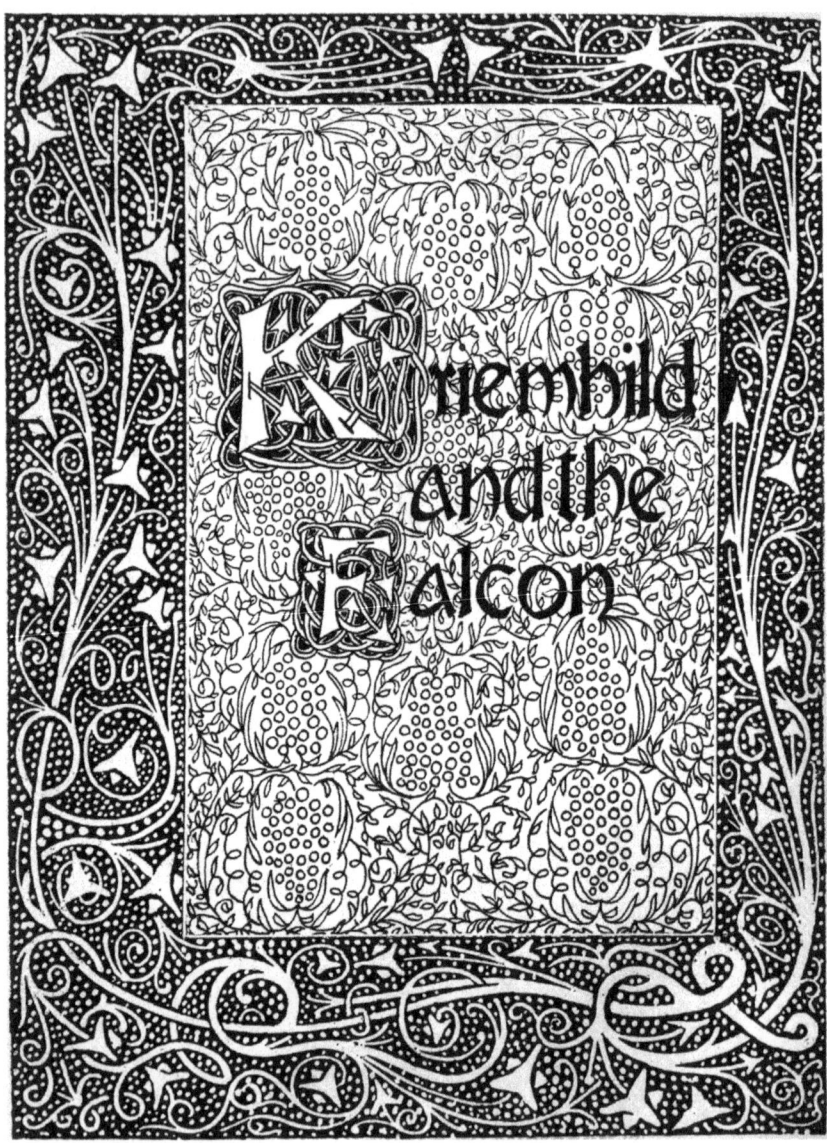

BOOK I
FIRST ADVENTURE
CONCERNING THE NIBELUNGS

I N old tales they tell us many wonders of heroes and of high courage, of glad feasting, of wine and of mourning; and herein ye shall read of the marvellous deeds and of the strife of brave men.

There grew up in Burgundy a noble maiden, in no land was a fairer. Kriemhild was her name. Well favoured was the damsel, and by reason of her died many warriors.

Doughty knights in plenty wooed her, as was meet, for of her body she was exceeding comely, and her virtues were an adornment to all women.

Three kings noble and rich guarded her, Gunther and Gemot, warriors of fame, and Giselher the youth, a chosen knight. The damsel was their sister, and the care of her fell on them. These lords were courteous and of high lineage, bold and very strong, each of them the pick of knights. The name of their country was Burgundy, and they did great deeds, after, in Etzel's land. At Worms, by the Rhine, they dwelled in might with many a proud lord for vassal.

Their mother was a rich queen and hight Uta, and the name of their father was Dankrat, who, when his life was ended, left them his lands. A strong man was he in his time, and one that in his youth won great worship.

These three princes, as I have said, were valiant men, over-lords of the best knights that folk have praised, strong and bold and undismayed in strife. There were Hagen of Trony, and also his brother Dankwart the swift; and Ortwin of Metz; the two Margraves, Gary and Eckewart; Volker of Alzeia, strong of body; Rumolt, the steward, a chosen knight; Sindolt and Hunolt. These last three served at court and pursued honour.

And other knights were there, more than I can name. Dank-wart was the marshal; the nephew of Ortwin of Metz carved at the board; Sindolt was the butler, a worthy warrior: each did his part as a good knight.

The splendour of this court and its might, the high valour and chivalry of its lords, were a tale without end.

Now it so fell that Kriemhild, the pure maid, dreamed a dream that she fondled a wild falcon, and eagles wrested it from her; the which to see grieved her more than any ill that had happened to her heretofore.

This dream she told to Uta, her mother, who interpreted it on this wise. "The falcon that thou sawest is a noble man; yet if God keep him not, he is a lost man to thee."

"What speakest thou to me of a man, mother mine ? Without their love would I still abide, that I may remain fair till my death, nor suffer dole from any man's love."

Said her mother then, "Be not so sure; for wouldst thou ever on this earth have heart's gladness, it cometh from the love of a man. And a fair wife wilt thou be, if God but lead hither to thee a true and trusty knight."

"Say not so, mother mine," answered the maiden, "for on many a woman, and oft hath it been proven, that the meed of love is sorrow. From both I will keep me, that evil betide not."

Long in such wise abode the high, pure maiden, nor thought to love any. Nevertheless, at the last, she wedded a brave man; that was the falcon she dreamed of erstwhile, as her mother foretold it. Yea, bitter was her vengeance on her kinsmen that slew him, and by reason of his death died many a mother's son.

CONCERNING SIEGFRIED

 HERE grew up in the Netherland a rich king's child, whose father hight Siegmund and his mother Sieglind, in a castle high and famous called Xanten, down by the Rhine's side. Goodly was this knight, by my troth, his body without blemish, a strong and valiant man of great worship; abroad, through the whole earth, went his fame.

The hero hight Siegfried, and he rode boldly into many lands. Ha! in Burgundy, I trow, he found warriors to his liking. Before he was a man grown. he had done marvels with his hand, as is said and sung, albeit now there is no time for more word thereof.

Of his best days there were many wonders to tell, how he waxed in goodliness and honour; his, too, was the love of women. As was seemly for such an one, his breeding was well seen to, and of his nature, likewise, he was virtuous. His father's land was famed for his worth, for in all things he was right noble.

When he was of an age to ride to the court, the people saw him gladly, and wedded wives and maids were alike fain that he should tarry there.

By order of Siegmund and Sieglind he was richly clad, and without guards he was suffered not to ride abroad. They that had him in charge were wise men versed in honour, to the end that he might win thereby liegemen and lands.

Now was he grown a stark youth, of stature and strength to bear weapons; he lacked nothing needful thereto, and inclined him already to the wooing of women. Nor did these find the fair youth amiss.

So Siegmund his father declared a hightide, and word thereof came to the kingdoms that were round about. To strangers and to friends alike he gave horses and apparel, and wheresoever they found one of knightly birth, that youth they bade to the hightide, to be dubbed a knight with Siegfried.

Many wonders might one tell of that hightide, and rightly Siegmund and Sieglind won glory from the gifts of their hand, by reason whereof a multitude rode into the land. To four hundred sworded knights and to Siegfried was given rich apparel. Full many a fair damsel ceased not from working with her needle for his sake. Precious stones without stint they set in gold, and embroidered them with silk on the vest of the proud youth. He was little loth thereto. And the king bade them set places for many a hero the mid-summer that Siegfried became a knight.

The rich squires and great knights drew to the minster. Meet is it that the old help the young, even as they in their day were holpen.

The time sped in merriment and sports. First, God to honour, they sang mass. Then the people pressed in hard to behold the youths dubbed knights with such pomp and high observance as we see not the like of nowadays.

Then they ran where they found saddled horses. And the noise of tourney was so great at Siegmund's court that palace and hall echoed therewith, for there was a mighty din of heroes. From old and young came the noise of hurtling and of broken shafts whizzing in the air; and from warring hands flew splintered lances as far as the castle; men and women looked on at the sport. Then the king bade stay the tilting. And they led off the horses. Many shields lay broken, and, strewed on the grass, were jewels from shining bucklers, fallen in the fray.

The guests went in and sat down as they were bidden, and over the choice meats and good wine, drunk to the full, they parted from their weariness.   Friends and strangers were entreated with equal honour.

Albeit they ceased not from tilting all the day, the mummers and the minstrels took no rest, but sang for gold and got it; wherefore they praised the land of Siegmund. The king enfeoffed Siegfried with lands and castles, as in his youth his father had enfeoffed him, and to his sword-fellows he gave with full hand, that it rejoiced them to be come into that country.

The hightide endured seven days. Sieglind, the wealthy queen, did according to old custom. She divided red gold among her guests for love of her son, that she might win their hearts to him.

Among the minstrels none were needy. Horses and raiment were as free as if they that gave had but a day to live. Never company gave readier.

So the hightide ended with glory, and the rich lords were well minded to have Siegfried to their prince. While Siegmund and Sieglind lived, their son, that loved them, desired not to wear the crown, but only, as a brave man, to excel in strength and might. Greatly was he feared in the land; nor durst any chide him, for from the day he bare arms he rested not from strife. Yea, in far countries and for all time, his strong hand won him glory.

HOW SIEGFRIED CAME TO WORMS

ITTLE recked Siegfried of heart's dole till that the news reached him of a fair maid of Burgundy, than whom none could wish a fairer; by reason of her, joy befell him, and sorrow.

Her beauty was rumoured far and wide, and the fame of her virtues, joined thereto, brought many strangers into Gunther's land. Yet, though many wooed her, Kriemhild was firm-minded to wed none.

Thereupon Siegmund's son yearned to her with true love. Weighed with him all other suitors were as wind, for he was meet to be chosen of fair women; and, or long, Kriemhild the high maiden was bold Sir Siegfried's bride.

His kinsmen and his liegemen counselled him to woo a fitting mate, if he meant to love in earnest, whereto Siegfried answered, "It shall be Kriemhild. So measureless fair is the maiden of Burgundy, that the greatest emperor, were he minded to wed, were none too good for her."

The tidings came to Siegmund's ear. His knights told him Siegfried's intent, and it irked him that his son should woo the royal maiden. To Sieglind, the king's wife, they told it also, and she feared for his life, for she knew Gunther and his men. They would have turned him from his quest.

Spake bold Siegfried then, "Dearest father mine, either I will think no more on women at all, or I will woo where my heart's desire is." And for all they could say, he changed not his purpose.

Then said the king, "If thou wilt not yield in this, i'faith, I approve thy choice, and will further thee therein as I best can. Nevertheless, Gunther hath many mighty men, were it none other than Hagen, an arrogant and overweening knight. I fear both thou and I must rue that thou goest after this king's daughter."

"What harm can come thereof?" answered Siegfried. "What I win not for the friendly asking, I will take by the prowess of my hand. I doubt not but I shall strip him of both liegemen and lands."

But Siegmund said, "I am grieved at thy word. If it were heard at the Rhine, thou durst not ride at all into Gunther's country. Both Gunther and Gernot are known to me from aforetime, and by force shall none win the maiden. That have I often heard. But if thou wilt ride thither with warriors, I will summon my friends. They will follow thee nothing loth."

Siegfried answered, "I will not ride with an army of warriors to the Rhine; it would shame me so to win the maiden by force. I would win her with mine own hand. One of twelve I will forth to Gunther's land, and to this shalt thou help me, my father Siegmund."

They gave to his knights cloaks of fur, some grey and some striped.

Sieglind his mother heard it, and sorrowed for her dear son, for fear she might lose him by the hand of Gunther's men. The noble queen wept sore.

Siegfried went where she sat, and spake comfortably to her. "Weep not, mother, for my sake, for I shall be without scathe among foemen. Help me rather to the journey that I make into Burgundy, that I and my fellows may have raiment beseeming proud knights. For this shalt thou have much thanks."

"Since thou wilt not be turned," spake Sieglind, "I will give to thee, my only child, the best apparel that ever knight did on, and to thy companions, for thy journey. Thou shalt receive without stint."

The youth bowed before the queen and said, "Twelve strong we ride forth, no more. I would have raiment for so many; for I would see with mine eyes how it standeth with Kriemhild."

The women sat night and day, nor rested till Siegfried's mantle was ready; for none could dissuade him from his quest. His father let forge for him a coat of mail that might do honour to his land. Bright were the breastplates and the helmet, and the bucklers fair and massy.

Now the time was come to ride forth, and all the folk, men and women, made dole, lest they should return never more. The hero bade load the sumpters with the arms and apparel. The horses were goodly, and their equipment of ruddy gold. None had more cause for pride than Siegfried and his knights. He asked leave to set out for Burgundy, and the king and the queen gave it sorrowing. But he spake comfortably to both of them, and said, "Weep not for my sake; nor fear aught for my life."

The knights were downcast, and the maidens wept. Their hearts told them, I ween, that by reason of this day's doings, many a dear one would lie dead. Needs made they dole, for they were sorrowful.

On the seventh morning after this, the fearless band drew towards Worms on the Rhine. Their garments were woven of ruddy gold, and their riding-gear was to match. Smooth paced the horses, deftly managed by Siegfried's bold warriors. Their shields were new, bright and massy, and their helmets goodly, as Siegfried the hero and his following rode into Gunther's country to the court. Never knights were in seemlier trim.

Their sword-points clanged on their spurs, and in their hands they bare sharp spears; the one that Siegfried carried was broad two spans or more, of the sort that maketh grim wounds. Gold-hued were their bridles, their poitrels of silk; so they rode through the land.

Everywhere the folk marvelled, gazing at them, and Gunther's men ran to meet them; proud warriors, knights and squires, went toward the strangers, as was meet, and welcomed the guests to the court of their king, taking horse and shield from their hands. They would have put the horses in the stalls, but Siegfried spake in haste, "Let our horses stand, for I am minded to depart again speedily. Where I may find Gunther, the great king of Burgundy, let whoso knoweth tell me."

One answered him that knew, "Thou mayest see the king if thou wilt. I saw him amidst of his men in yonder wide hall. Go in to him. Thou shalt find there many brave warriors."

They told the king that a valiant knight, fair equipped and apparelled, that knew none in Burgundy, was come thither. And the king marvelled where those proud knights in shining harness, with their shields new and massy, might hie from. It irked him that none knew it.

Ortwin of Metz, a goodly man of high courage, spake to the king then, "Since we know naught thereof, bid to thee Hagen mine uncle, and show them to him. For he hath knowledge of the mighty men of all lands; and what he knoweth he will tell us."

The king summoned Hagen with his vassals, and he drew nigh with proud step, and asked the king his will.

"Strange knights are come to my court that none knoweth. If thou hast ever seen them afore, tell me thereof truly."

"That will I," spake Hagen, and went to the window, and looked down on the strangers below. The show of them and their equipment pleased him, but he had not seen them afore in Burgundy. And he said, "From wheresoever they be come, they must be princes, or princes' envoys. Their horses are good, and wonderly rich their vesture. From whatso quarter they hie, they be seemly men. But for this I vouch, that, though I never saw Siegfried, yonder knight that goeth so proud is, of a surety, none but he. New adventures he bringeth hither. By this hero's hand fell the brave Nibelungs, Shilbung and Nibelung, the high princes. Wonders hath he wrought by his prowess.

"I have heard tell that on a day when he rode alone, he came to a mountain, and chanced on a company of brave men that guarded the Nibelung's hoard, whereof he knew naught. The Nibelung men had, at that moment, made an end of bringing it forth from a hole in the hill, and oddly enow, they were about to share it. Siegfried saw them and marvelled thereat. He drew so close that they were ware of him, and he of them. Whereupon one said, 'Here cometh Siegfried, the hero of the Netherland!'

"Strange adventure met he amidst of them. Shilbung and Nibelung welcomed him, and with one accord the princely youths asked him to divide the treasure atween them, and begged this so eagerly that he could not say them nay. The tale goeth that he saw there more precious stones than an hundred double waggons had sufficed to carry, and of the red Nibelung gold yet more. This must bold Siegfried divide. In guerdon therefor they gave him the sword of the Nibelungs, and were ill paid by Siegfried for the service. He strove vainly to end the task, whereat they were wroth. And when he could not bear it through, the kings, with their men, fell upon him.

"But with their father's sword, that hight Balmung, he wrested from them both hoard and land. The princes had twelve champions - stark giants, yet little it bested them. Siegfried slew them wrathfully with his hand, and, with Balmung, vanquished seven hundred knights; and many youths there, afraid of the man and his sword, did homage for castles and land. He smote the two kings dead.

"Then he, himself, came in scathe by Albric, that would have avenged the death of his masters then and there, till that he felt Siegfried's exceeding might. When the dwarf could not overcome him, they ran like lions to the mountain, where Siegfried won from Albric the cloud-cloak that hight *Tarnkappe*.

"Then was Siegfried, the terrible man, master of the hoard. They that had dared the combat lay slain; and he bade carry the treasure back whence the Nibelungs had brought it forth; and he made Albric the keeper thereof, after that he had sworn an oath to serve him as his man, and to do all that he commanded him."

"These are his deeds," said Hagen; "bolder knight there never was. Yet more I might tell of him. With his hand he slew a dragon, and bathed himself in its blood, that his skin is as hard as horn, and no weapon can cut him, as hath been proven on him ofttimes.

"Let us welcome the young lord, that we come not in his hate. So fair is he of his body that one may not look unfriendly thereon; with his strength he hath done great deeds."

Then spake the great king, "Belike thou sayest sooth. Knightly he standeth there as for the onset - he and his warriors with him. We will go down to him and greet him."

"Thou mayest do that with honour," answered Hagen; "for he is of high birth, even a great king's son. By Christ, there is somewhat in his bearing that showeth he hath ridden hither on no slight matter."

The king of the land said, "He is right welcome, for I perceive that he is brave and noble, the which shall profit him in Burgundy."

Gunther went out to Siegfried. The king and his men gave the strangers courteous welcome, and the valiant man bowed before them because they greeted him so fair.

"I would know," said the king, "whence noble Siegfried cometh, and what he seeketh at Worms by the Rhine."

The guest answered him, "I will tell thee that readily. Word hath reached me in the land of my father, that, hereby thee, dwell the prowest ever sworn to king. I have heard much of these, and would know them; for this I am come hither. Thy knightliness also I hear praised, and am told that nowhere is a better king. So say the folk throughout the land; and, till I have proven it, I will not depart hence. I also am a king that shall wear a crown, and I would have men say of me that the country and the people are rightly mine. Thereto I pledge both honour and life. If thou art valiant, as they say, I care not whom it liketh or irketh, I will take from thee all thou hast, land and castles, and they shall be mine."

The king and his men marvelled when they heard this strange saying, that he would take their land; when the warriors understood it they were wroth.

"Wherein have I wronged thee," said Gunther the knight, "that I should yield to the might of any man what my father ruled so long with honour? We will show thee to thy hurt that we also are brave knights."

"I will abide by my purpose," said the doughty man. "If thou canst not hold thy land in peace, I will rule it. Also what I have in fee, if thou overcome, shall be thine. With thy country be it even as with mine. To the one of us twain that overcometh shall the whole belong, people and land."

But Hagen and Gernot answered him back straightway. "We desire not," said Gernot, "to win new kingdoms at the cost of dead heroes. Our land is rich, and we are the rightful lords. The folk desire none better."

Grim and angered stood Gunther's kinsmen. Amidst of them was Ortwin of Metz, who said, "This bargain pleaseth me little. Bold Siegfried hath challenged thee wrongfully. Were thou and thy brothers naked, and he with a whole king's army at his back, I would undertake to show the overweening man he did well to abate his pride."

Whereat the knight of the Netherland was wroth and said, "Not such as thou art shall raise a hand against me, for I am a great king; thou art but a king's man. Twelve of thy sort could not withstand me."

Then Ortwin of Metz, the sister's son of Hagen of Trony, cried aloud for his sword. It grieved the king that he had kept silence so long, but Gernot, a warrior bold and keen, came betwixt them. He said to Ortwin, "Calm thyself. Siegfried hath done naught to us, that we should not end this matter peaceably. I counsel that we take him to friend. That were more to our honour."

Then said Hagen the stark man, "It may well irk thy knights that he rideth hither as a foeman. Better had he refrained. My masters had never done the like by him."

Brave Siegfried answered, "If thou like not my words, I will show thee here, in Burgundy, the deeds of my hand."

"That I will hinder," said Gernot, and he forbade to his knights their overweening words, for they irked him. Siegfried also thought on the noble maiden.

"Wherefore should we fight with thee?" said Gernot. "Though every knight lay dead thereby, small were our glory and little thine adventure."

Whereto Siegfried, King Siegmund's son, answered, "Why do Hagen and Ortwin hang back, and their friends, whereof they have enow in Burgundy?"

But these must needs hold their peace, as Gernot commanded them.

"Thou art welcome," said Uta's son; "thou and they comrades that are with thee. We will serve thee gladly, I and my kinsmen."

They let pour for them Gunther's wine, and the host of that land, even Gunther the king, said, "All that is ours, and whatsoever thou mayest with honour desire, is thine to share with us, body and goods."

Then Siegfried was milder of his mood.

What he and his men had with them was seen to; they gave Siegfried's knights good quarters and fair lodging; and they rejoiced to see the stranger in Burgundy. They did him honour many days: more than I can tell. This he won, I trow, by his valour. Few looked on him sourly.

The king and his men busied them with sports, and in each undertaking Siegfried still approved him the best. Whether they threw the stone or shot with the shaft, none came near him by reason of his great strength. Held the doughty warriors tourney before the women, then looked these all with favour on the knight of the Netherland. But, as for him, he thought only on his high love. The fair women of the court demanded who the proud stranger was. "He is so goodly," they said, "and so rich his apparel."

And there answered them folk enow, "It is the king of the Netherland." Whatsoever sport they followed, he was ready. In his heart he bare the beautiful maiden that as yet he had not seen: the which spake in secret kind words also of him. When the youths tilted in the courtyard, Kriemhild, the high princess, looked down at them from her window; nor, at that time, desired she better pastime. Neither had he asked better, had he known that his heart's dear

Kriemhild Gazeth Secretly From Her Window
On Siegfried

one gazed upon him: the fairest thing on earth had he deemed it
to behold her eyes. When he stood there amidst of the heroes in
the tilt-yard, as the custom is, to rest at the tourney, so graceful the
son of Sieglind bare him, that the hearts of many maidens yearned
toward him. And ofttimes would he think, "How shall I attain to
behold the noble lady that I have loved long and dearly? She is still
a stranger. For this reason I am downcast."

When the rich kings rode abroad, it behoved the knights to go
with them, wherefore Siegfried also rode forth, the which irked the
damsel sore; and likewise, for love of her, he was heavy enow of his
cheer.

So in a year (I say sooth) he abode by these princes, nor in all
that time had once seen his dear one, that afterward brought him
so much gladness and dole.

FOURTH ADVENTURE
HOW SIEGFRIED FOUGHT WITH THE SAXONS

OW there were brought into Gunther's land strange tidings by envoys sent from afar by foreign princes that hated him; and when they heard the message they were troubled.

The kings were as I will tell you: Ludger of the Saxons, a high and mighty prince; and Ludgast of Denmark, and many bold warriors with them. These envoys, sent by his foemen, came into Gunther's land, and the strangers were asked their business, and brought before the king.

The king greeted them fair, and said, "I know not who hath sent you hither, and would hear it." So spake the good king, and they greatly feared his wrath.

"If thou wilt have our message, O king, we will tell it plain, and name thee the princes that have sent us. They are Ludgast and Ludger, and will come against thee into they land. Thou are fallen in their displeasure, and we know that they bear thee bitter hate. They come hither with an armed force to Worms by the Rhine - they and their warriors. Wherefore be warned. Inside of twelve days they will ride. If thou hast truly friends, let them appear now; let them help thee to keep thy castles and they country, for, before long, there will be smiting of helmets and shields here. Or wouldst thou treat with them, then declare it straightway, that thy foemen come not night thee to thy hurt, and that goodly knights perish not thereby."

"Tarry a while - ye shall have answer betimes - that I may bethink me," said the good king. "If I have true liegemen, I will not hide it from them, but will take counsel with them on this hard matter."

Heavy enow of his cheer was Gunther. He pondered the message secretly in his heart, and summoned Hagen, and others of his men, and sent to the court in haste for Gernot. His best knights drew round him, and he said, "Without cause, and with a mighty army, foemen come hither against us into our land."

Thereto answered Gernot, a hardy and bold warrior, "We shall hinder that with our swords. They only perish that fate dooms. Let them die. They shall not turn from honour. Our foemen are welcome."

Spake Hagen of Trony then, "Methinketh that were unwise. Ludgast and Ludger are proud men withal, and we can hardly in so few days muster our men." Therefore the bold knight said, "Tell Siegfried."

They bade lodge the envoys in town. Albeit they were his foemen, Gunther, the great king, commanded the folk to entreat them well--rightly he did so--till that he knew the friends that would stand by him. The king was heavy of his cheer, and Siegfried, the good knight, saw that he was downcast, but wist not the reason, and asked King Gunther what ailed him.

"I marvel much," said Siegfried, "that thou takest no part in our sports as heretofore."

And Gunther, the doughty knight, answered him, "Not to every man may I declare the secret heaviness of my heart; only unto true friends shall the heart tell its dole."

Siegfried changed colour, and grew red and white, and he said to the king, "I have denied thee naught, and now I would help thee. If thou seekest friends, I will be one of them, and stand to it truly to my life's end."

"Now God requite thee, Sir Siegfried, for I like thy words; even if thy might availed me nothing, I would rejoice none the less that thou art well-minded toward me; as much and more will I do to thee if I live. I will tell thee the cause of my trouble. Envoys from my foemen have brought a message that with an army they will come against me; such inroad of warriors hath not been aforetime in this country."

"Be not sorrowful for that," answered Siegfried; "be of good cheer, and do now as I say. I will win for thee honour and profit before ever thy foemen reach this land. Had these stark adversaries thirty thousand warriors at their back, and I but one thousand, I would withstand them - trust me for that."

King Gunther answered, "Thou shalt be well paid for this."

"Give me a thousand of thy knights, since of mine own I have but twelve here with me, and I will keep thy land for thee. The hand of Siegfried will serve thee truly. Hagen shall help us in this, and also Ortwin, Dankwart, and Sindolt, thy loving knights, and eke Folker, the bold man, who shall bear the standard: better knight thou wilt not find. Bid the envoys return to their country; tell them they shall see us there soon enow. So shall our castles go scatheless."

The king let summon his kinsmen and his liegemen, and Ludger's messengers went to the court. They were glad to be gone. Gunther, the good king, gave them gifts and an escort, whereat they were well content.

Spake Gunther, "Thou shalt say on this wise to my haughty foemen: They did wisely to turn from their journey, for if my friends fail me not, and they seek me here in my land, they will find work enow."

They brought out rich gifts for the envoys, whereof Gunther had to spare, and these said not "nay." Then they took their leave, and departed rejoicing.

When the messengers were come again to Denmark, and told Ludgast how that the Rhine-men would ride thither, he was wroth at their boldness. They made report to him of the many brave men

Gunther had, and how that they had seen a knight there amidst of them that hight Siegfried, a hero from the Netherland, the which was heavy news for Ludgast.

When they of Denmark heard it, they hastened the more to summon their friends, till that Ludgast had ready for the onset twenty thousand warriors withal.

On like manner Ludger of Saxony summoned his men to the number of forty thousand, ready to march into Burgundy.

The same also did King Gunther to his liegemen, and to his brothers with their vassals, and to Hagen and his knights. These were sorry enow at the news; and by reason thereof many a knight looked on death.

They hasted and made ready for the journey. Brave Folker bare the standard. They purposed to cross the Rhine from Worms. Hagen of Trony led the force. Sindolt and bold Hunolt were there, that they might deserve King Gunther's gold; also Hagen's brother, Dankwart, and Ortwin, fit men and worthy for the undertaking.

"Sit thou at home, O King," spake Siegfried. "Since thy knights are willing to follow me, stay here by the women and be of good cheer; for, by my troth, I will guard for thee both goods and honour. I will see to it, that they that seek thee here at Worms by the Rhine bide where they are; we will pierce deep into their country, till their vaunting is turned to sorrow."

They passed from the Rhine through Hesse against Saxony, where the battle was fought afterward. With plunder and with fire they laid waste to the land, the which both the princes found to their cost.

When they were come to the marches, the warriors hasted forward, and Siegfried began to ask them, "Which of us shall guard the rest from surprise?" More to their hurt the Saxons never took the field.

They answered, "Let bold Dankwart guard the younger knights. He is a good warrior. So shall we come in less scathe by Ludger's men. He and Ortwin shall guard the rear."

"I will myself ride forward," said Siegfried, "and spy out the foe, that I may know rightly who the warriors be."

Fair Sieglind's son did on his armour in haste. He gave his knights in charge to Hagen and bold Gernot when he set out. He rode into Saxony all alone, and won honour by his quest. He perceived a great host encamped on a field, that loomed mightily against him, beyond the strength of one man: forty thousand or more. And the high heart of Siegfried rejoiced.

One of the enemy's knights kept watch warily, and perceived Siegfried, and Siegfried him, and they glared fiercely on each other. I will tell you who he was that kept watch. On his arm he bare a glittering shield of gold. It was King Ludgast that kept ward over his host.

The noble stranger pricked toward him fiercely. Ludgast dressed him also. They put spurs to their horses and smote with all their strength on the shields with their spears, that it was like to go hard with the king. On their horses, pricked forward with the spur, the princes bare down on each other like the wind. Then they wheeled round deftly - these two fierce men - and fell to hacking with their swords.

Sir Siegfried smote, that the field rang therewith; the hero with his mighty blade struck sparks from Ludgast's helmet. Fiercely fought the prince of the Netherland, and Ludgast, likewise, dealt many a grim blow. Each drave with all his might at the other's shield. The combat was spied by thirty of Ludgast's men, but Siegfried, by means of three deep wounds and grisly that he dealt Ludgast through his white harness, overcame the king or these knights came up. His sword drew blood with each stroke, that King Ludgast came in evil plight, and begged for his life, offering his land as the price thereof, and said that his name was Ludgast.

His knights hastened to his rescue, for they had seen the encounter at the ward-post. Siegfried would have led him thence, but thirty of Ludgast's men rode at him. With mighty blows the stark warrior kept his rich captive; and soon his hands did even deadlier deeds. He smote the thirty men dead in his defence, save one that fled and told what happened, the truth whereof was proven by his bloody helmet.

They of Denmark were aghast when they heard their king was taken captive; they told it to his brother, who fell in a great fury by reason of the disaster.

So the mighty Ludgast was taken by Siegfried's prowess, and given in charge to Hagen. When that good knight heard that it was Ludgast he was not sorry.

They bade raise the standard of Burgundy. "Forward!" cried Siegfried, "More shall be done or the day end, if I lose not my life. The Saxon women shall rue it. Hearken now, ye men of the Rhine. I can lead you to Ludger's army. There ye will see helmets hewn by the good hands of heroes. They shall be in evil case or we turn again."

Then Gernot and his men sprang to horse. The banner was unfurled by Folker, the minstrel knight. He rode before the host, and they all made them ready for battle. They numbered not more than a thousand men, and thereto the twelve strangers. The dust rose from their path, and they rode through the land, their shields flashing. The Saxons, also, were come up, bearing well-sharpened swords. So hath the story been told me.

The swords in the heroes' hands dealt grim blows in defence of their castles and their lands. The marshal led the army, and Siegfried was come forward with the twelve men that he had with him from the Netherland. Many a hand was bloody that day in the battle. Sindolt and Hunolt and eke Gernot smote many heroes dead in the fight, that were bold enow till they felt their prowess. For their sake sorrowed women not a few. Folker and Hagen and Ortwin, the fierce warriors, quenched the flash of many helmets with blood. Dankwart, also, did wonders.

The Danes proved their mettle, and loud were heard the hurtling of shields and the clash of sharp swords swung mightily. The Saxons, bold in strife, made havoc enow. Wide were the wounds hewn by the men of Burgundy when they rushed to the encounter. Blood ran down the saddles. So was the honour wooed of these knights bold and swift. Loud rang the keen swords in the hands of the heroes of the Netherland, when they rode with their lord into the fray. They rode with Siegfried like good knights. None from the Rhine kept pace with him. By reason of Siegfried's hand streams of blood ran from bright helmets, till that he lit on Ludgast amidst of his men. Thrice he pierced through the army of the Saxons, and thrice returned. Hagen, by this time, was come up with him, that helped him in his quest. They slew many a brave knight.

When bold Ludger found Siegfried with Balmung, the good sword, swung aloft, wherewith he made a mighty slaughter, he was wroth, and of his mood full grim. With a fierce rush and clash of swords the warriors came together. So exceeding furious was their onset that the host gave way. Terrible was their hate.

The Saxon king knew well that his brother was taken captive, and he was wroth thereat; but he knew it not for Siegfried's work till now. They had blamed Gernot. Now he found out the truth.

Ludger smote so hard that Siegfried's horse reeled under him. But when he was come to, Siegfried was more terrible than afore. Hagen and Gernot, Dankwart and Folker, stood by him.

The dead lay in heaps. Sindolt and Hunolt and Ortwin the knight slew many in the strife. The princes held together in the fray. Bright spears in the hands of heroes flashed above the helmets, that clave the shining bucklers in twain. Many a massy shield was red with blood.

In the fierce encounter many men fell from their horses. Bold Siegfried and King Ludger strove together, and lances whizzed, and sharp spears. Ludger's shield-plate flew off through the strength of Siegfried's hand. Then the hero of the Netherland thought to have gotten the victory over the Saxons that were hard pressed. Ha! what polished bucklers doughty Dankwart brake!

Of a sudden Ludger espied a crown that was painted on Siegfried's shield, and he knew the mighty man, and cried aloud to his friends, "Forbear, my men all. I have seen the son of Siegmund, even bold Siegfried. The Devil hath sent him hither into Saxony."

He bade lower the standard, and sued for peace. They granted this, yet he was compelled by Siegfried to go captive into

Gunther's land. With one accord they ceased from the strife. They threw down their shivered helmets and shields. Blood-red were they all by the hands of the Burgundians. They took captive whom they listed, for they had the power.

Gernot and Hagen gave order to convey the wounded on litters. They led five hundred noble knights as prisoners to the Rhine.

The vanquished warriors rode back to Denmark. Nor had the Saxons fought so as to win them honour, and they were downcast. The dead were mourned by their friends.

They sent the weapons to the Rhine on sumpters. So wondrously had Siegfried done, that all Gunther's men praised him.

Sir Gernot sent word to Worms, and throughout the whole land, to their friends, how it had sped with them; for as bold knights and honourable they had fought. The pages hasted and told it, and the glad news rejoiced the loving ones that had sorrowed. The noble women ceased not from questioning how it had fared with the great king's men.

Kriemhild bade a messenger to her in secret; publicly she durst not, for to one of them she bare dear heart's love.

When the messenger was come to her chamber, Kriemhild, the beautiful maiden, spake him fair. "Now tell me glad tidings; thou shalt have gold therefor; and, sayest thou sooth, I will ever be beholden to thee. How sped my brother Gernot in the battle, and the rest of my friends? Are there many dead? Who did most valiantly? Now tell me."

Whereto the messenger answered truthfully, "We had no coward among us. Yet since thou wilt hear it, noble princess, none rode in the thick of the fight like the knight of the Netherland. Marvellous was the work of Siegfried's hand. All that the knights did in battle - Dankwart and Hagen and the rest - though with honour fought they all, was but as a wind matched with the prowess of Siegfried, the son of Siegmund. Many heroes have they slain, yet of the deeds of Siegfried, done in battle, none shall tell to the end. By reason of him many maidens mourn for their kin. Low lieth the dear one of many a bride. Loud smote he on the helmets, that they ran blood. In all things he is a knight bold and good."

"Ortwin of Metz, also, won worship. Whoso came within range of his sword lieth wounded or dead. Thy brother, too, made fierce havoc in the battle. To his prowess must all testify. The proud Burgundians have so fought that none my question their honour. For many a saddle was emptied by them when the field rang loud with gleaming swords. On such wise fought the knights of the Rhine that their foemen had done better to flee. The brave men of Trony rode fiercely in the strife. Hagen with his hand slew many, whereof Burgundy shall hear. So valiantly fought Sindolt and Hunolt, Gernot's men, and eke Rumolt, that Ludger may well rue that he ever met thy kinsmen by the Rhine. But the mightiest deeds, first and last, were done by Siegfried. He bringeth rich captives into Gunther's land, that his strength hath conquered, by reason whereof King Ludgast and his brother, Ludger of Saxony, suffer dole. For list to the marvel, noble queen: both these princes hath Siegfried's hand taken. Never have so many captives been led into this land, as come hither now through his prowess."

The maiden was glad at the tale.

"Of unwounded men they bring five hundred or more, and eighty red biers (I say sooth) of the wounded, fallen, the most part, by Siegfried's might. They that arrogantly withstood the knights of the Rhine are now Gunther's captives. Our men lead them hither rejoicing."

When she had heard the news aright, her fair cheek reddened, and her lovely face was the colour of the rose, because it had gone well with young and noble Siegfried, and he was come with glory out of peril. She joyed for her kinsmen also, as in duty bound.

And she said, "Thou hast spoken well; for guerdon thereof thou shalt have costly raiment, and ten golden marks, that I will bid them bear to thee." It is good to tell glad tidings to rich women.

He got his envoy's fee of gold and vesture, and the fair maids hasted to the window and looked down the road, where the high-hearted warriors rode home. They drew nigh, whole and wounded, and heard the greeting of friends unashamed. Light of heart Gunther rode to meet them, for now his grim care was turned to joy. He received his own men well and also the strangers. Not to have thanked them that were come to his court, for that they had done valiantly in battle, would have been unseemly in so great a king. And he asked tidings of his friends, and who was slain. None were lost to him save sixty only, and these were mourned as many a hero hath been mourned since.

They that were unhurt brought many battered shields and shivered helmets back to Gunther's land. The warriors sprang down from their horses before the place, and there was a joyful noise of welcome.

Order was given to lodge the knights in the town, and the king commanded that his guests should be courteously entreated, and that the wounded should be seen to and given good chambers. So he approved himself generous to his foes.

He said to Ludger, "Thou are welcome! Much scathe have I suffered through thee; yet, if I prosper henceforth, I will consider myself well paid. God reward my warriors, for well have they served me!"

"Thou has cause to thank them," answered Ludger, "for nobler captives were never won for a king; and gold without stint shall be thine, if thou do well by me and my friends."

Said Gunther, "Ye shall both go free. Yet I must have a pledge that my foemen quit not my land till peace be sealed betwixt us."

And they promised it, and gave their hand thereon. They led them to their quarters to rest, and saw the wounded men laid softly in their beds. They set before them that were whole meat and good wine, and never were men merrier. They are the battered shields away into safe keeping; and the bloody saddles, of which there were enow, they hid, that the women might not grieve thereat. Many a weary knight was there.

The king entreated his guests right royally, and the land was full of friends and of strangers. He bade see to the sore wounded ones whose pride was brought low. To them that were skilled in leech craft they offered a rich fee of unweighed sliver and yellow gold, that they might heal the heroes of their wounds gotten in battle; the king sent also precious gifts to his guests. They that thought to ride home were bidden stay as friends. And the king took counsel how he might reward his liegemen that had done valiantly for his sake.

Sir Gernot said, "Let them go hence for the present, and summon them after six weeks to a hightide. Many will then be whole that now lie sick of their wounds."

Siegfried of the Netherland would have taken leave also, but when King Gunther knew his intent, he besought him lovingly to tarry, the which Siegfried had not done but for Gunther's sister's sake. He was too rich to take money, albeit he well deserved it; the king loved him, and also the king's kinsmen that had seen the deeds wrought by his hand in battle. So, for love of the maiden, he agreed to tarry, that haply he might win to see her, the which, or long, came to pass; for he knew her to his heart's desire, and rode home joyfully afterward to his father's land.

The young knights obeyed the king's command willingly, and practised daily at the tourney. Seats were raised on the stand before Worms for the guests that were coming into Burgundy.

When it was time for them to arrive, fair Kriemhild heard the news, that they were about to hold a hightide with their friends. Then the beautiful women busied them with their kirtles and their headgear that they were to wear.

Uta, the great queen, heard of the proud knights that were coming, and gorgeous robes were taken from their wrapping-cloths. For love of her children she bade them bring forth the garments. Many women and maidens were adorned therewith, and, of the young knights of Burgundy, not a few. To many of the strangers, also, she gave goodly apparel.

HOW SIEGFRIED FIRST SAW KRIEMHILD

vast multitude of them that would attend the hightide drew daily to the Rhine; and unto those that came for love of the king horses were given and goodly raiment, and to each his place, even unto two and thirty princes of the highest and the best. So they tell us.

And the women vied with one another in their attire. Giselher, the youth, and Gernot, and their two squires, rested not from welcoming both friends and strangers. They gave courtly greeting unto the warriors.

The guests brought with them to the Rhine, to the tourney, saddles worked in ruddy gold, and finely-wrought shields, and knightly apparel. And the sick rejoiced, and they that lay on their beds sore wounded forgot that death is an hard thing. When the rumour of the festival was noised abroad, no man took heed more of them that groaned, for each thought only how he might sojourn there as a guest. Joy without measure had all they that were found there, and gladness and rejoicing were in Gunther's land.

On Whitsun morning there drew toward the hightide a goodly company of brave men, fairly clad: five thousand or more, and they made merry far and wide, and strove with one another in friendly combat.

Now Gunther knew well how, truly and from his heart, the hero of the Netherland loved his sister whom he had not yet seen, and whose beauty the people praised before that of all other maidens.

And he said, "Now counsel me, my kinsmen and my lieges, how we may order this hightide, that none may blame us in aught; for only unto such deeds as are good, pertaineth lasting fame."

Then answered Ortwin, the knight, to the king, "If thou wilt win for thyself glory from the hightide, let now the maidens that dwell with honour in our midst appear before us. For what shall pleasure or glad a man more than to behold beautiful damsels and fair women? Bid thy sister come forth and show herself to thy guests." And this word pleased the knights.

"That will I gladly do," said the king; and they that heard him rejoiced. He sent a messenger to Queen Uta, and besought her that she would come to the court with her daughter and her women-folk.

And these took from the presses rich apparel, and what lay therein in wrapping-cloths; they took also brooches, and their silken girdles worked with gold, and attired themselves in haste. Many a noble maiden adorned herself with care, and the youths longed exceedingly to find favour in their eyes, and had not taken a rich king's land in lieu thereof. And they that knew not one another before looked each upon each right gladly.

The rich king commanded an hundred men of his household, his kinsmen and hers, to escort his sister, their swords in their hand. Uta, with an hundred and more of her women, gorgeously attired, came forth from the female apartments, and many noble damsels followed after her daughter. The knights pressed in upon them, thinking thereby to behold the beautiful maidens.

And lo! the fair one appeared, like the dawn from out the dark clouds. And he that had borne her so long in his heart was no more aweary, for the beloved one, his sweet lady, stood before him in her beauty. Bright jewels sparkled on her garments, and bright was the rose-red of her hue, and all they that saw her proclaimed her peerless among maidens.

As the moon excelleth in light the stars shining clear from the clouds, so stood she, fair before the other women, and the hearts of the warriors were uplifted. The chamberlains made way for her through them that pressed in to behold her. And Siegfried joyed, and sorrowed likewise, for he said in his heart, "How should I woo such as thee? Surely it was a vain dream; yet I were liefer dead than a stranger to thee."

Thinking thus he waxed oft white and red; yea, graceful and proud stood the son of Sieglind, goodliest of heroes to behold, as he were drawn on parchment by the skill of a cunning master. And the knights fell back as the escort commanded, and made way for the high-hearted women, and gazed on them with glad eyes. Many a dame of high degree was there.

Said bold Sir Gernot, the Burgundian, then, "Gunther, dear brother, unto the gentle knight, that hath done thee service, show honour now before thy lieges. Of this counsel I shall never shame me. Bid Siegfried go before my sister, that the maiden greet him. Let her, that never greeted knight, go toward him. For this shall advantage us, and we shall win the good warrior for ours."

Then Gunther's kinsmen went to the knight of the Netherland, and said to him, "The king bids thee to the court that his sister may greet thee, for he would do thee honour."

It rejoiced Siegfried that he was to look upon Uta's fair child, and he forgot his sorrow.

She greeted him mild and maidenly, and her colour was kindled when she saw before her the high-minded man, and she said, "Welcome, Sir Siegfried, noble knight and good."

His courage rose at her words, and graceful, as beseemed a knight, he bowed himself before her and thanked her. And love that is mighty constrained them, and they yearned with their eyes in secret. I know not whether, from his great love, the youth pressed her white hand, but two love-desirous hearts, I trow, had else done amiss.

Nevermore, in summer or in May, bore Siegfried in his heart such high joy, as when he went by the side of her whom he coveted for his dear one. And many a knight thought, "Had it been my hap to walk with her, as I have seen him do, or to lie by her side, certes, I had suffered it gladly! Yet never, truly, hath warrior served better to win a queen."

From what land soever the guests came, they were ware only of these two. And she was bidden kiss the hero. He had never had like joy before in this world.

Said the King of Denmark then, "By reason of this high greeting many good men lie low, slain by the hand of Siegfried, the which hath been proven to my cost. God grant he return not to Denmark!"

Then they ordered to make way for fair Kriemhild. Valiant knights in stately array escorted her to the minster, where she was parted from Siegfried. She went thither followed by her maidens; and so rich was her apparel that the other women, for all their striving, were as naught beside her, for to glad the eyes of heroes she was born.

Scarce could Siegfried tarry till they had sung mass, he yearned so to thank her for his gladness, and that she whom he bore in his heart had inclined her desire toward him, even as his was to her, which was meet.

Now when Kriemhild was come forth to the front of the minster, they bade the warrior go to her again, and the damsel began to thank him, that before all others he had done valiantly. And she said, "Now, God requite thee, Sir Siegfried, for they tell me thou hast won praise and honour from all knights."

He looked on the maid right sweetly, and he said, "I will not cease to serve them. Never, while I live, will I lay head on pillow, till I have brought their desire to pass. For love of thee, dear lady, I will do this."

And every day of twelve, in the sight of all the people, the youth walked by the side of the maiden as she went to the court. So they showed their love to the knight.

And there was merriment and gladness and delight in the hall of Gunther, without and within, among the valiant men.

Siegfried Goeth By The Side Of Her
Whom He Coveteth For His Dear One

Ortwin and Hagen did many wonderful deeds, and if any devised a sport, warriors, joyous in strife, welcomed it straightway.

So were the knights proven before the guests, and they of Gunther's land won glory. The wounded also came forth to take part with their comrades, to skirmish with the buckler, and to shoot the shaft, and waxed strong thereby, and increased their might.

Gunther gave order that, for the term of the hightide, they should set before them meats of the daintiest, that he might fail in naught as a king, nor the people blame him.

And he came to his guests, and said, "Receive my gifts ere you go hence, and refuse not the treasure that I would share with you."

The Danes made answer, "Ere we turn again to our land, make thou a lasting peace with us. We have need of such, that have many dear friends dead, slain by thy warriors."

Ludgast and eke the Saxon were healed of their wounds gotten in battle, but many tarried behind, dead.

Then Gunther sought Siegfried and said, "Now counsel me in this. On the morrow our guests ride forth, and they desire of me and mine a lasting covenant. What they offer I will tell thee: as much gold as five hundred horses may carry, they will give me to go free."

And Siegfried answered, "That were ill done. Send them forth without ransom, that they ride no more hither as foemen. And they shall five thee the hand thereon for surety."

And they told it to his enemies; also that none desired their gold. They said it to the war-tired men, by reason of whom the dear ones of their own land sorrowed.

And the king took shields full of treasure, and divided it among them without weighing it, five hundred marks and more. Gernot, the brave knight, counselled him thereto.

And they took their leave, for they were aweary for home. And they passed before Kriemhild and Queen Uta; never were knights dismissed more courteously.

The chambers were void when they left, nevertheless the king abode there still with his lieges and his vassals and knights. And these ceased not to go before Kriemhild.

Then Siegfried, the hero, had also taken leave, for he thought not to attain his desire. But the king heard of it, and Giselher the youth turned him back. "Whither ridest thou, Sir Siegfried? Prithee yield to me in this. Go not from among our knights, and Gunther, and his men. Here are fair maidens enow that thou mayest behold at will."

Said bold Sir Siegfried, "Let stand the horses, bear hence the shields. I would have ridden forth and turned again to my land, but Giselher hath changed my intent."

So he abode among them through love, nor in any land had it been sweeter for him. And Kriemhild, the fair maiden, he saw daily, by reason of whose beauty he tarried.

They passed the time in sports and feats of chivalry. But his heart was weary with love; yea, for love he sorrowed then, and, after, died miserably.

HOW GUNTHER WENT TO ISSLAND TO WOO BRUNHILD

fresh rumour spread beyond the Rhine. It was reported that many maidens dwelt there; and Gunther was minded to woo one of them, whereat his knights and his liegemen were well pleased.

There was a queen high throned across the sea, that had not her like, beyond measure fair and of mickle strength, and her love was for that knight only that could pass her at the spear. She hurled the stone and leapt after it to the mark. Any that desired the noble damsel's love must first win boldly in these three games. If he failed but in one, he lost his head.

And oft had this happened already, when the rumour thereof reached the noble warrior by the Rhine, who fixed his desire upon the maiden, the which, or all was done, cost the life of many heroes.

On a day that the king sat with his men, and they cast to and fro whom their prince might best take to wife for his own comfort and the good of his land, the lord of Rhineland said, "I will hence across the sea to Brunhild, let what will betide. For her sake I will peril my body, for I lose it if I win her not to wife."

"Do so not," said Siegfried. "Cruel is the queen, and he that would woo her playeth too high a stake. Make not this journey."

But King Gunther answered, "Never yet was woman born so stark and bold, that, with this single hand, I could not vanquish her in strife."

But Siegfried said, "Peace! Thou knowest her not. Wert thou four men, thou wert no match for her grim wrath. In good faith I counsel thee to let the matter be. If thou lovest thy life, come not in such straits for her sake."

"Nay, now, I care not how stark she be; I will journey, even as I have said, to Brunhild, and take my chance. For her great beauty I must adventure this. What if God prosper me, and she follow me to the Rhine?"

"Then I counsel thee," said Hagen, "to ask Siegfried to share with thee this hard emprise. It were well, since he knoweth so much of Brunhild."

So the king spake, "Wilt thou help me, most noble Siegfried, to woo the damsel? Grant me this, and if I win the royal maiden for my dear one, I will adventure honour and life for thy sake."

Siegfried, the son of Siegmund, made answer, "Give me thy sister Kriemhild, the high princess, and I will do it. Other meed I ask not."

Said Gunther, "I swear it, Siegfried, on thy hand. If Brunhild come hither, I will give thee my sister to wife; and mayest thou live joyfully with her to thy life's end."

The noble warriors sware an oath; and travail enow they endured, or they led back the fair one to the Rhine; yea, ofttimes they were straightened sore.

I have heard tell of wild dwarfs: how that they dwell in hollow mountains, and wear wonderful cloaks called _Tarnkappes_. And whoso hath this on his body cometh not in scathe by blows or spear-thrusts; nor is he seen of any man so long as he weareth it, but may spy and hearken at his will. His strength also waxeth thereby; so runneth the tale.

Siegfried took the *Tarnkappe* with him that he had wrested from Albric the dwarf. And these high and noble knights made ready for the journey.

When stark Siegfried did on the *Tarnkappe*, he was strong with the strength of twelve men, and with these cunning devices he won the royal maiden; for the cloak of cloud was fashioned on such wise, that who wore it did what him listed, none seeing; and he won Brunhild thereby, that after brought him dole.

"Now tell me, Siegfried, or we depart, how we may cross the sea with honour? Shall we take warriors with us to Brunhild's land? It were easy to summon thirty thousand knights."

But Siegfried answered, "Howsoever great a host we led thither, the cruelty of the queen is such, that every mother's son of them must perish. A better plan is mine, most noble king. Let us down to the Rhine as simple knights, even these friends that I name. Thou and I, and, further, only two. So shall we woo the damsel, let the issue be as it may. I shall be one, and thou shalt be another. Let the third be Hagen, and the fourth Dankwart, the doughty man. A thousand shall not prevail against us."

"Fain would I know," said the king then, "what manner of raiment we should wear before Brunhild. Prithee, counsel me in this matter, Siegfried."

"In the land of Brunhild they wear naught but the beast, wherefore let us appear before the women in goodly apparel, that none may cry shame on us hereafter."

Then said the knight, "I will go, myself, to my dear mother, and beseech her that she let her damsels make ready for us such garments as may bring us honour before the royal maiden."

But Hagen said courteously, "Wherefore beg this service of thy mother? Tell thy sister of thy intent. She is skilled, and will provide thee with goodly raiment."

And Gunther prayed his sister to receive him and Siegfried. The which she did after she had robed her in her best apparel. She was little grieved at the coming of the knights. Her attendants were fitly adorned, and the knights went in. When she saw them, she rose from her seat, and hasted, and received the noble guest and her brother courteously. She said, "Thou are welcome, my brother: thou and they friend. I would know what hath brought you to the court. Tell me, I pray you, noble knights, how it standeth with you."

The king answered, "Lady, I will tell thee. An hard adventure is before us, the which we must bear boldly through. We ride a-wooing into a far and a strange land, and have need of rich apparel."

"Now sit, dear brother," said the king's child, "and tell me plainly who the women are that ye would woo in other kings' lands."

The maiden took both the chosen knights by the hand, and led them to the rich cushion whereon she had sat, and on the which were wrought (for this I know) fair pictures raised with gold. They wearied not, certes, among the women. Of kind glances and soft looks there was no stint. Siegfried bore her in his heart, and loved her as his life, and won her for his wife by noble service.

The great king said, "Dearest sister mine, we need thy help. We go to sojourn in the land of Brunhild, and must have rich apparel to wear before the women."

The princess answered, "If I can aid thee in any wise, believe me, I will do it; sad were Kriemhild if aught were denied thee. Ask of me, nothing doubting, noble knight, and, as a master, command me; all that thou desirest I will readily perform."

"We would have goodly raiment, dear sister, and therein thy white hand shall help us. Let thy maids bestir them, that we be fair equipped, since none shall turn us from this journey."

Said the damsel, "Now mark what I say. We have silk of our own; bid them bring us hither, on the shields, precious stones to work the robes withal, that unashamed ye may wear them before the royal maiden." The princess asked, "Who are they that shall follow thee in rich array to the court?"

And he answered, "We be four. My two liegemen, Dankwart and Hagen, ride with us. And what I tell thee, mark well. For each of four days thou shalt provide us with three changes of good raiment, that we be not scorned in Brunhild's land!"

She promised this to the knights, and they took their leave.

Then Princess Kriemhild summoned from their chambers thirty of her maidens that had great skill in such work.

Silk from Araby, white as snow, and from Zazamanc, green like clover, they embroidered with precious stones. The royal maiden cut them herself. In sooth, they were goodly robes. Linings finely fashioned from fishes' skins, rarely seen then, they covered, as many as they had, with silk, and wrought them with gold. Many a marvel could one tell of these garments. For they had, in plenty, the finest silks from Morocco and Libya that the children of kings ever wore. It was not hard to see that Kriemhild loved the warriors. And because they desired rich apparel, the black-spotted ermine was not spared, the which good knights covet still for hightides.

Precious stones sparkled on gold of Araby. Certes, the women were not idle. Inside of seven weeks the clothes were ready, and also weapons for the knights.

Now when all was done, a stout ship lay waiting on the Rhine to bear them down to the sea. Ill paid were the maidens, after, for their toil.

When they told the knights that the rich vesture they were to wear was ready, and that all they had asked was accomplished, they were eager to quit the Rhine. A messenger was sent to them, that they might try on their new apparel, lest haply it might be too short or too long for any.

But the measure was exact, wherefore they thanked the maidens. All that saw it owned that, in the whole world, none was better. They wore it proudly at the court, and none were praised above them for their attire.

The maidens had sweet thanks, and the doughty warriors took their leave right courteously, and bright eyes were dim and wet with tears.

Kriemhild said, "Dear brother, thou didst better to stay here and woo other women without risk to thy body. It were easy to find, night at hand, a wife of as high lineage."

I ween her heart told her the dole that was to come. And they wept all together, and refused to be comforted, till the gold on their breasts was wet with the tears that rolled down from their eyes.

She spake further, "Sir Siegfried, to thy care and good faith I commend my dear brother, that no evil betide him in Brunhild's land."

The knight gave his hand thereon, and promised it.

He said, "Fear not, lady; if I live, I will bring him back safe to the Rhine. I swear it by mine own body."

And the fair maiden thanked him.

They carried down the shields of ruddy gold to the strand, and stowed their armour in the vessel, and let fetch their horses, for they were eager to be gone. The women made mickle dole. Fair damsels stood at the windows. The fresh wind caught the sail, and lo! the good knights sat on the Rhine.

Then said Gunther, "Who shall be steersman?"

"That will I be," answered Siegfried. "Trust me, ye heroes, and I will pilot you hence, for I know the currents."

So with stout hearts they left Burgundy. Siegfried took hold of the pole and pushed from the strand. Gunther himself took an oar, and they fell away from the shore.

They had rich meats with them, and Rhine wine of the best. Their horses stood easy and quiet; their boat flew light, and misadventure they had none. Their strong sails filled, and they made twenty miles or night fell, for the wind favoured them. But their high emprise brought many women dole. They say that by the twelfth morning the wind had blown them afar to Isenstein in Brunhild's land, the which none had seen before that, save Siegfried.

When King Gunther beheld so many towers and broad marches, he cried out, "Now say, friend Siegfried; knowest thou whose are these castles and these fair lands? By my troth, I have never in my life seen castles so many and so goodly as stand there before us. A mighty man he must be that hath builded them."

Whereto Siegfried made answer, "Yea, I know well. They are all Brunhild's--towers and lands, and the castle of Isenstein. I say sooth;

and many fair women shall ye behold this day. Now I counsel you, O knights, for so it seemeth good to me, that ye be all of one mind and one word; we must stand warily before Brunhild the queen. And when we see the fair one amidst of her folk, be sure that ye tell all the same story: that Gunther is my lord, and I his liegeman. So shall he win to his desire. Yet this I do less for love of thee than for the fair maid, thy sister, that is to me as my soul and mine own body, and for whom I gladly serve, that I may win her to wife."

They promised with one accord, and none gainsayed him through pride, the which stood them in good stead when the king came to stand before Brunhild.

HOW GUNTHER WON BRUNHILD

MEANWHILE the ship was come nigh to the castle, and the king saw many fair maidens that stood above at the windows. It irked him that he knew them not, and he said to Siegfried, his friend, "Knowest thou aught of these maidens that look down at us on the sea? Howso their lord hight, they are, certes, right noble."

Bold Siegfried answered, "Spy secretly among them, and say which thou wouldst have chosen, if thou hadst had the choice." And Gunther said, "I will. I see one standing at yonder window in show-white robe. Goodly is she, and for her fair body's sake, mine eyes choose her. If I had the power, she should be my wife."

"Thine eyes have led thee aright. That is the noble Brunhild, the beautiful lady that thou desirest with thy heart and thy soul." Gunther found no fault in her.

The queen bade her damsels void the windows, nor stand in the gaze of the strangers. They obeyed; but what they did after hath been told us. They adorned them for the warriors, as is the manner of fair women; then they stole to the loopholes and looked curiously at the heroes.

These came only four strong into the land. Bold Siegfried held a horse on the strand, and, by reason thereof, the women that spied through the windows deemed King Gunther of the more worship. He held the good horse, by the bridle; stately it was and sleek, mickle and stark, and King Gunther sat in the saddle, and Siegfried served him; but Gunther forgot this afterward.

Then Siegfried took his own horse from the ship. Seldom before had he held the stirrup for a warrior to mount. And all this the fair women marked through the loopholes.

The heroes were clad alike; both their horses and their apparel were snow-white, and the shields were goodly that shone in their hands. Their saddles were set with precious stones, their poitrels small, and hung with bells of burnished gold. So they rode proudly into Brunhild's courtyard, and came into the land as befitted their might, with new-sharpened spears, and finely-tempered swords, keen and massy, that reached to their spurs. All this Brunhild, the royal maiden, saw.

Dankwart rode with them, and Hagen. These knights, they say, wore clothes of raven-black, and their shields were mickle, broad and goodly. Stones from India shone on their apparel. They left the vessel unguarded on the beach, and rode up to the castle. There they saw eighty and six towers, three great palaces, and a stately hall of costly marble, green like grass, wherein the queen sat with her courtiers.

Brunhild's men unlocked the castle gate and threw it wide, and ran toward them, and welcomed the guests to their queen's land. They bade hold the horses, and take the shields from their hands. And the chamberlain said, "Do off your swords now, and your bright armour."

"Not so," answered Hagen of Trony; "we will bear these ourselves."

But Siegfried told them the custom of the court. "It is the law here that no guest shall bear arms. Wherefore ye did well to give them up."

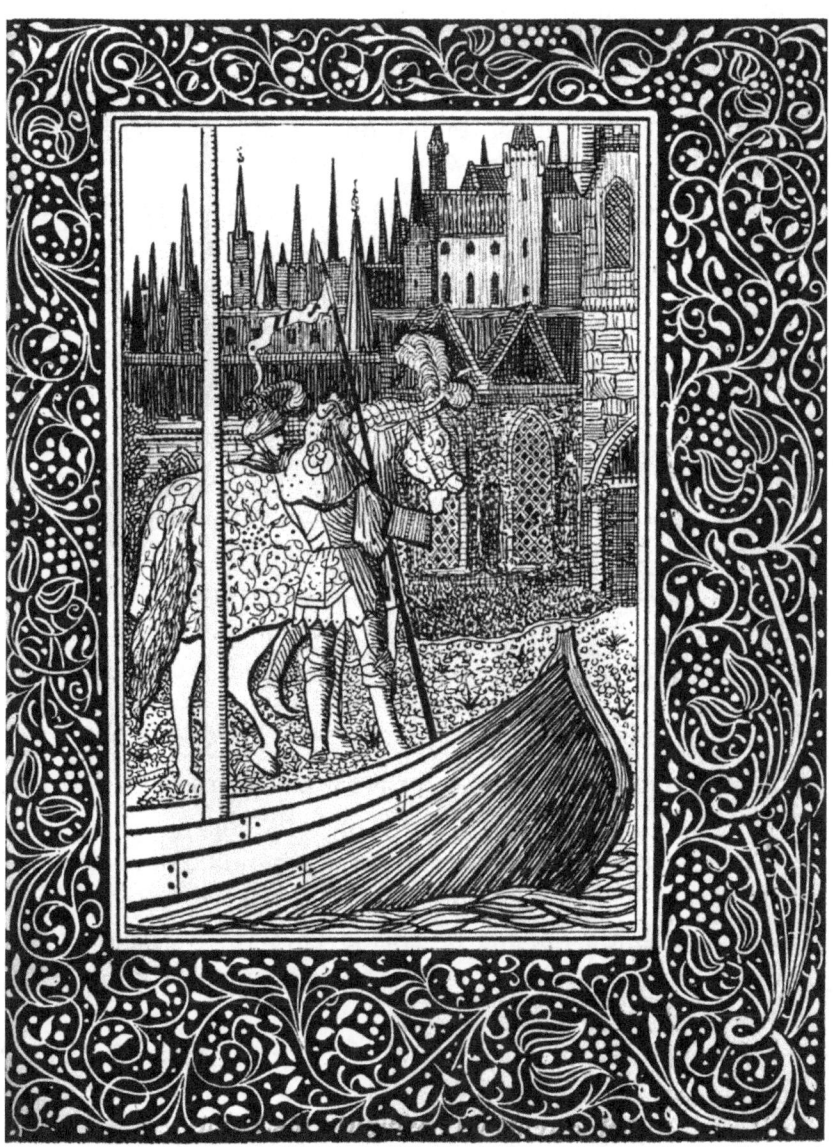

The Heroes Disembark Before The Castle Of Brunhild

Gunther's men obeyed, much loth. They bade pour out the wine for the guests, and see that they were well lodged. Willing knights in princely attire ran to and fro to serve them, spying with many glances at the strangers.

They brought word to Brunhild that unknown warriors in rich apparel were come thither, sailing on the sea, and the beautiful maiden questioned them.

"Tell me," said the queen, "who these strangers be that stand yonder so proudly, and for whose sake they be come."

And one of the courtiers made answer. "In sooth, Lady, albeit I never yet set eyes on them, one among them much resembleth Siegfried, and him I counsel thee to welcome. The second of the company hath so lofty a mien that, if his power be equal thereto, he might well be a great king and a ruler of wide lands, for he standeth right proudly before the others. The third, O Queen, is grim, yet a goodly man withal. His glance is swift and dark; he is fierce-tempered, I ween. The youngest pleaseth me well. Maidenly and modest he standeth, yet it went hard, methinketh, with any that fashioned daintily, if his wrath were once kindled, many a woman might weep, for he is a bold and virtuous knight, and right worshipful."

The queen said, "Bring me my robe. If stark Siegfried be come into my land to woo me, he shall pay for it with his life. I fear him not so greatly that I should yield me to be his wife."

Then Brunhild attired her in haste. An hundred or more of her damsels went with her, richly adorned, whom the guests beheld gladly. Brunhild's knights of Issland gave them escort, to the number of five hundred or thereabout, their swords in their hands, the which irked the bold strangers.

They stood up from their seats; and the queen spake courteously to them when she saw Siegfried. "Thou art welcome, Siegfried, to this land. To what end art thou come? I prithee tell me."

"I thank thee, O Brunhild, fair daughter of a king, that thou greetest me before this worshipful knight. Thou showest Siegfried too much honour, for he is my lord, and the king of the Rhineland.

What boots it to say more? For thy sake we are come hither, for he would woo thee at all hazards. Weigh the matter betimes, for of a surety he will win thee.

'His name is Gunther; he is a great and mighty king, and he desireth naught save thy love. To this end I have followed him, nor had done it, but that he is my master."

She answered, "If he be thy lord, and thou be his man, let him withstand me at the games. If he have the mastery, then I am his wife, but let him fail in one of them, and ye be all dead men."

Then said Hagen of Trony, "Lady, show us the games that thou proposest. It will go hard with Gunther or he yield thee the mastery, for he troweth well to win so fair a maiden."

"He must put the stone, and leap after it, and throw the spear with me. Ye may easily forfeit honour and life; wherefore be not so confident, but bethink you well."

Then bold Siegfried went to the king, and bade him fear naught, but speak freely to the queen. "For," said he, "I will aid thee with cunning devices."

And King Gunther said, "Command me, great queen, and were it more yet, I would risk it for thy sake. I will lose my head, or win thee to wife."

When the queen heard this word, she bade haste to the sports, as was meet, and let them bring her harness, a golden buckler and a goodly shield. She did on a surcoat of silk from Libya, that had never been pierced in combat, cunningly fashioned and embroidered, and shining with precious stones. Her pride greatly angered the knights, and Dankwart and Hagen were downcast, for they feared for their lord, and thought, "Ill-starred was this journey."

Meanwhile, Siegfried, the cunning man, went, when none spied him, to the ship, where he found the *Tarnkappe*, and he did it on swiftly, that none knew. Then he hastened back to the crowd of knights, where the queen gave order for the sports, and, by his magic, he stole in among them, that no man was ware of him.

The ring was marked out in the presence of armed knights to the number of seven hundred. These were the umpires, that should tell truly who won in the sports.

Then came Brunhild. She stood armed, as she had meant to do battle with all the kings of all the world. The silk was covered with gold spangles that showed her white skin. Her attendants brought her, for the strife, a shield of ruddy gold with iron studs, mickle and broad. The maid's thong was an embroidered band, whereon lay stones green like grass, that sparkled among the gold. The knight must, certes, be bold that won such a lady. They say the shield the maiden bore was three spans thick under the folds, rich with steel and gold, that four of her chamberlains scarce could carry it.

When stark Hagen saw them drag the shield forward, the hero of Trony was wroth, and cried, "How now, King Gunther? We be dead men, for thou wooest the Devil's wife!"

Yet more must ye hear of her vesture. Her coat of mail was covered with silk from Azagouc, costly and rich, and the stones thereof sparkled on the queen's body. They brought her the spear, heavy and big and sharp, that she was wont to throw. Stark and huge it was, mickle and broad, and made grim wounds with its edges. And hear, now, the marvel of its heaviness. Three weights and a half of iron were welded for it. Three of Brunhild's lords scarce could carry it.

A woeful man was King Gunther, and he thought, "Lo! now not the Devil in Hell could escape her. Were I in Burgundy with my life, she might wait long enow for my wooing."

He stood dismayed. Then they brought him his armour, and he did it on.

Hagen came nigh to lose his wits for sorrow, and Dankwart, his brother, said, "By my troth, I rue this adventure. Once we hight warriors, and shall we perish in this country by the hand of a woman? Alack! that we ever came hither! Had my brother Hagen but his sword, and I mine, Brunhild's men would abate their pride; I ween they would walk softer. If I had sworn peace with a thousand oaths, that maid should die sooner than that my lord should lose his life."

"It were easy to quit this land," said Hagen, his brother, "if we had our harness for the strife, and our good swords. This dame would be milder, I trow."

The noble maiden heard him plain, and, with smiling mouth, she looked over her shoulder. "Since he deemeth him so bold, bring his harness, and give to the heroes their sharp weapons. It is all one to me whether they be armed or naked. I never feared the might of any man, and doubt not but I shall overcome this king."

When they had brought the weapons, as the maid commanded, bold Dankwart grew red with joy. "Now let them drive what sport they like," he said; "Gunther is safe, since we have our swords."

Brunhild's great strength appeared. They brought her a stone into the circle, heavy and huge, round also, and broad. Twelve strong knights scarce sufficed thereto. And this she threw when she had hurled the spear.

Whereat the Burgundians were sore troubled, and Hagen cried, "Who is this that Gunther wooeth? Would she were the Devil's bride in Hell!"

Then she turned back the sleeves from her white arms, and seized the shield, and brandished the spear above her head, and the contest began.

Gunther was sore dismayed. If Siegfried had not helped him, certes he had lost his life; but Siegfried went up to him secretly, and touched his hand. Gunther fell in fear by reason of his magic, and he thought, "Who touched me?" He looked round and saw no man.

But Siegfried said, "It is I, Siegfried, thy friend. Fear naught from the queen. Give me the shield from thy hands, and let me carry it, and give heed to what I say. Make thou the gestures, and I will do the work." And Gunther was glad when he knew him. "Guard well the secret of my magic, for all our sakes, lest the queen slay thee. See how boldly she challengeth thee."

Thereupon the royal maiden hurled her speak against the mickle and broad shield of Sieglind's child, that sparks flew from it, as before a wind. The stark spear pierced through the shield, and struck fire from the coat of mail below. And the mighty man fell, and had perished but for the *Tarnkappe*.

The blood gushed from Siegfried's mouth. But he sprang up swiftly, and took the spear that she had shot through his buckler, and threw it back again with a great force. He thought, "I will not slay so fair a maiden," and he turned the spear, and hurled it with the haft loud against her harness. From her mail, also, the sparks flew as on the wind, for Siegmund's child threw mightily; and her strength failed before the blow. King Gunther, I ween, had never done it alone.

Brunhild sprang to her feet again, and cried, "I thank thee, Gunther, for that blow." For she thought he had done it with his own strength, nor guessed that a far mightier man had felled her.

Then, greatly wroth, she hasted and lifted the stone on high; she flung it far from her, and leaped after it with loud-ringing armour. The stone landed twenty and four paces off; but the maid sprang further.

Then Siegfried went swiftly where the stone lay. Gunther lifted it, but it was the man they saw not that threw it. Siegfried was mighty, bold and big. He hurled the stone further, and he leaped further; moreover, through his magic, he had strength enow to bear King Gunther with him. The spring was made, the stone lay on the ground, and none was seen there but Gunther, the knight. Fair Brunhild was red with anger.

So Siegfried saved Gunther from death.

Then Brunhild said aloud to her folk, when she saw the hero at the far end of the ring unhurt. "Come hither at once, my kinsmen and my lieges. Ye are subject henceforth to King Gunther."

The bold men laid the weapons from their hands at the feet of great Gunther of Burgundy. For they deemed he had won the game by his own strength.

He greeted them fair, for he was a courteous man, and he took the beautiful maiden by the hand. She gave him power in her kingdom, whereat bold Hagen rejoiced.

She bade the noble knight to the hall, where a multitude was assembled, that showed much observance through fear of his prowess. So, by Siegfried's might, they were delivered from all peril.

But Siegfried was wise, and stowed away his *Tarnkappe* with care; then he went back where the women sat, and said feigningly to Gunther, "Wherefore delayest thou to begin the sports that the queen proposed, let us now behold the issue thereof" - as if the cunning man knew naught of the matter.

The queen answered, "How cometh it to pass, Sir Siegfried, that thou sawest not the game whereat Gunther hath won?"

Said Hagen of Burgundy, "While we were downcast by reason of thee, O Queen, and afterward, when the king of Rhineland had beaten thee at the sports, Siegfried was at the ship, and knoweth naught of what hath passed."

"Right glad am I," said Siegfried, "that thy wooing hath prospered, and that none is thy master. Now must thou follow us, noble Lady, to the Rhine."

But Brunhild answered, "Not yet; I must first summon my friends and my liegemen. Not so lightly can I quit my land. Certes, I will send for my kinsfolk afore I go."

She dispatched envoys over all, and bade her friends and her lieges haste to Isenstein. She gave to each princely apparel.

All day long, late and early, troops of knights rode into Brunhild's castle, till Hagen said, "Alack! What have we done? Some hurt will befall us from Brunhild's men. We know not her real intent. What if she spurn us when her forces are gathered together? Then were we all dead men, and this maiden were born to our woe!"

But stark Siegfried said, "I will see to that, and hinder what thou fearest. I will bring to your help a body of chosen knights that thou knowest not yet. Ask me no further, for I will hence, and God guard you meanwhile. I will return shortly, and bring with me a thousand knights, than whom the world holdeth none better."

"Only tarry not too long," said the king, "for we are right glad of thy help."

He answered, "I will come again in a few days. Tell the queen I left by thy command."

HOW SIEGFRIED JOURNEYED TO THE NIBELUNGS

IEGFRIED hasted thence in his *Tarnkappe* to the haven on the shore, where he found a ship, the which he boarded secretly, and rowed it swiftly, as it had been blown by the wind. None saw the boatman. He made it fly with his great strength. Any that marked it deemed it driven by a tempest, but it was by Siegfried, fair Sieglind's child.

A day and a night brought him to a great country that an hundred days' journey could not compass; this hight the Nibelung land, where he had his vast treasure.

The hero landed alone on a broad meadow, and moored the ship. Then he went to a mountain, whereon a castle stood, and asked for lodging, as he had been a way-weary man. He went up to the door, that stood locked before him. For folk guarded their honour then, even as now. The stranger began to knock at the bolted door, and encountered within a huge giant that kept watch, and that had his weapons ever by him. And this giant said, "Who knocketh so loud on that door?"

Siegfried answered with a feigned voice, "I am a knight. Open to me, else I will rouse some within that had willingly lain soft abed."

The porter was wroth at Siegfried's word. He did on his armour, and put his helmet on his head, and grasped his shield, and swung open the door.

Then he ran grimly at Siegfried, saying, "How durst thou waken so many brave men?" And he smote him hard and swift. The noble stranger made wary fence, but the porter lifted an iron bar and brake his shield-band.

Then the hero came in scathe, and began to fear grim death when the porter smote so hard. Yet his master loved him the more for his daring.

They strove so fiercely that the castle rang, and the din thereof was heard in the hall of the Nibelungs. But Siegfried overcame the porter at last, and bound him. And the news spread through the Nibelung land.

Albric, a bold and savage dwarf, heard their strife from far off through the mountain. He did on his armour straightway, and ran where he found the stranger, that had made an end of binding the giant.

Now Albric was bold and stout, and on his body he had a helmet and coat of mail, and in his hand a heavy scourge of gold. He hasted and fell on Siegfried. The scourge had seven heavy knobs hanging from it, wherewith he smote so heavily to the left upon the shield that he well night brake it.

Then the noble guest came in peril.

He threw away the broken shield and stuck his long sword into the sheath, for he would not slay his chamberlain, but ever spared his own folk; wherein he did honourably. With his strong hands he ran at Albric, and grasped the age-hoary man by the beard, and shook him sore, that he yelled aloud.

Certes, the young hero's handling was dolorous enow to Albric, who cried out, "Spare me. Had I not sworn fealty to a knight already, I would serve thee till I died." This he spake craftily.

Siegfried bound Albric as he had done to the giant, and the dwarf was in evil case through Siegfried's strength, and asked, "What is thy name?"

Siegfried answered, "Siegfried is my name. Methought thou hadst known me."

"Right glad am I to hear it," said Albric the dwarf, "for now I know, by thy prowess, that thou art worthy to be the lord of this land, and I will do all thy behest, if thou spare my life."

Said Siegfried then, "Haste and bring me a thousand Nibelung knights, of the best we have. I would see them here before me. Thou hast naught to fear at my hand."

He loosed the giant and Albric, and Albric ran to the knights, and waked them eagerly, and said, "Rouse ye, O heroes, and go to Siegfried."

They sprang from their beds and were ready on the instant, a thousand good knights and rich attired. They went where Siegfried stood, and he greeted them fair. They lit many tapers, and poured for him the spiced draught. And he thanked them that they had not lingered, and said, "Ye shall follow me hence across the sea;" whereto he found the good knights willing.

Full thirty thousand warriors were come at his bidding, and from these he chose a thousand of the best. And some brought them their helmets, and some their coats of mail, for they had to follow Siegfried into Brunhild's land.

He said then, "Hearken, good knights; ye go to court, and must have rich apparel, for ye shall be seen of fair women. Wherefore array you in your best."

Now a fool might say, "Thou liest. How could so many knights dwell together? Where find the meat, and where the vesture? It were not possible, if Siegfried had thirty lands." But ye have heard that Siegfried was rich, for the kingdom and the hoard of the Nibelungs were his. Wherefore his knights had enow and to spare, for the hoard grew never less for all that he took from it.

They rose up early in the morning (doughty followers had Siegfried won!), and took good horses with them, and sumptuous apparel, and departed proudly for Brunhild's land.

Many beautiful maidens gazed from the windows there, and the queen said, "Do any of you know who they be, that I behold yonder, afar off on the waves? Their sails are rich and whiter than the snow."

The King of Rhineland answered, "They are my men, that I left some little way behind when I journeyed hither. I summoned them, and now, Queen, they are here."

They welcomed the noble guests courteously. Siegfried stood in the prow of the vessel, richly clad, and many warriors beside him.

The queen said, "Tell me, O King, shall I greet the guests, or no?"

He answered, "Go out now before the castle. So shall they see that they are welcome." And the queen did as he counselled her, and greeted Siegfried before any. And they lodged them, and took their arms in charge.

Now so many guests were in the land that they were pressed for room, and the Burgundians were eager to be home.

Then said the queen, "I would thank him that would distribute for me, among mine and the king's guests, the gold and silver that I have in plenty."

Dankwart, bold Giselher's man, answered, "Noble Queen, give me the key, and I will so divide it that, if there be any shame, it shall be mine only."

None could deny that he gave freely. When Hagen's brother held the key, he bestowed costly gifts without stint. Whoso desired a mark received so much that the poorest was rich his life long. Pounds, by the hundred, he gave uncounted, and many an one went forth from the hall richly dight, that never afore had worn so fair vesture.

They told it to the queen, who was wroth, and said, "I would know, King, wherefore thy chamberlain leaveth me naught of my apparel, and spendeth all my gold. I would thank him that stayed his hand. He giveth as he thought I had summoned Death hither. But I trust to live yet a while, and can spend for myself, I trow, what my father left me."

Never had queen so lavished a chamberlain.

But Hagen of Trony made answer, "Know, Lady, that the King of the Rhine hath gold and raiment to give in plenty, nor needeth to bear aught of Brunhild's hence."

"Nay, if thou lovest me," said the queen, "let me fill twenty travelling chests with gold and with silk, that my hand may have somewhat to bestow when we get home to the land of Burgundy."

They filled the chests with precious stones. Her own chamberlain saw to it, for she would not trust Giselher's man. And Gunther and Hagen began to laugh.

Then the queen said, "To whom shall I leave my kingdom? Thy hand and mine must establish that or we depart."

The king answered, "Call forth whom thou wilt, and he shall be regent."

The lady saw her nearest of kin standing night her - her mother's brother - and to him she said, "Take my castles and land in charge, till that King Gunther's own hand holdeth rule here."

She chose from among her knights two thousand men to follow her to the Rhine, and the thousand Nibelung warriors. Then she made ready for the journey, and rode down to the shore. She took with her six and eighty women, and an hundred fair damsels, and they tarried not longer, but set out. They that were left behind wept sore!

Graciously and sweetly the lady quitted her land. She kissed her nearest of kin that stood round. With loving farewells they reached the sea. To the land of her fathers the maiden returned nevermore.

Many hands made music during the voyage, and they had all manner of pastime, and a favouring wind. And so they sailed away; and many a mother's son wept for it.

Brunhild wedded not the king on the voyage, but waited for a hightide that was to be held in the castle of Worms; and thither they speeded merrily with their knights.

NINTH ADVENTURE
HOW SIEGFRIED WAS SENT TO WORMS

HEN they had journeyed full nine days, Hagen of Trony said, "Hearken to my word. We have delayed too long to send the news to Worms on the Rhine. The envoys should have been in Burgundy or now."

King Gunther answered, "Thou sayest sooth. And none were better for this business than thyself, friend Hagen. Ride now into my land, for thou art the fittest to tell of our coming."

"Nay, certes, dear master, I am but a bad envoy. Let me stay here at sea and act the chamberlain. I will look to the women's wardrobe, till we bring them to Burgundy. Bid Siegfried rather carry the message; by reason of his great strength he will bear it through well. If he deny thee, urge him with friendly words, that he do it for thy sister's sake."

So Gunther sent for the knight, who came when they had found him. And the king said, "We are well night home in my land. It is time I sent a messenger to tell my dear sister and my mother that we draw near. Undertake thou the journey, and I will owe thee much thank."

But Siegfried would not do it till that Gunther had begged him and said, "Ride not for my sake only, but for fair Kriemhild's, that the royal maiden requite it, even as I." And when Siegfried heard that, he yielded.

"Command what thou wilt, I will not gainsay it. I will do it for the sake of my beautiful lady. How should I deny aught to her that I bear in my heart? Because of her, I will perform all that thou askest."

"Tell Uta, then, the great queen, that we have prospered in our adventure; and let my brothers hear how that it hath fared well with us. Tell the same news to our friends. And hide nothing from my sister. Greet her from Brunhild and me; greet also the courtiers and all my men. Say to them that I have gotten the desire of my heart. And bid Ortwin, my dear nephew, raise seats by the Rhine.

"Make it known also to the other knights that I will hold a great hightide with Brunhild; and bid my sister, when she heareth I am at hand with my guests, prepare a fair welcome for my bride; for the which I shall ever be beholden to her."

So Siegfried took leave of Brunhild, as was meet, and rode to the Rhine. In the whole world was no better envoy.

With twenty and four knights he rode to Worms. And when it was noised abroad that he was come without the king, Gunther's servants were heavy of their cheer, for they feared that their lord had tarried behind, dead.

The messengers sprang gaily from their horses, and Giselher, the young king, ran to them, and Gernot, his brother, who cried quickly, when he saw not King Gunther with Siegfried, "Thou art welcome, Sir Siegfried. Tell me, now, what thou hast done with my brother the king. If the strength of Brunhild hath reft him from us, a bitter wooing hath it been."

"Fear naught. Thee and his kinsmen my friend greeteth by me, for he hath sent me hither to you with news. Contrive now that I come to the queen and thy sister. For I am charged with the same message to them as to thee, from Gunther and Brunhild: that it standeth well with the twain."

Giselher said, "Go in to them straightway, and it will please my sister. She feareth for my brother; by my troth, she will see thee gladly."

Siegfried answered, "If I can serve her in aught, it shall be done. Where are now the ladies, that I may go to them?"

Giselher, the brave youth, bare the message; he said to his mother and his sister, "Siegfried is come to us, the hero of the Netherland. My brother Gunther hath sent him hither to the Rhine. He bringeth us word how it standeth with the king. Allow him to come to the court, for he bringeth news from Issland."

The noble women were heavy of their cheer. They ran for their robes, and arrayed them, and bade Siegfried to the court; and he went gladly, for he yearned to see them. Kriemhild, the noble maiden, greeted him fair.

"Thou art welcome, Sir Siegfried, valiant knight. Where is my brother Gunther, the noble king? I fear we have lost him by Brunhild's strength. Alack! that ever I was born!"

But the warrior answered, "Give me the guerdon of good news, for, fair women, ye weep without cause. I left him safe and sound - I say sooth - and he hath charged me with a message. He and his wife commend them lovingly to thee, O Queen. Dry thine eyes, for they will be here shortly."

Kriemhild had not heard such good news for many a day. She wiped her bright eyes with her snow-white apron, and began to thank the envoy for his message.

So ended her sorrow and her tears.

She bade Siegfried sit, whereto he was nothing loth, and said sweetly, "I would fain give thee the envoy's guerdon, wert thou not too rich to receive it. Take my good will in lieu thereof."

"Though I had thirty lands," answered Siegfried, "I were proud to take a gift from thy hand."

Kriemhild said, "Be it so." And she bade the chamberlain fetch the envoy's meed. She gave him four and twenty bracelets with precious stones for his fee. The hero would not keep them: he was too rich a prince, but gave them to the maidens that were in the chamber.

Uta, also, greeted him fair, and he said, "I must tell thee further what the king would have thee do when he cometh to the Rhine; for the which, if thou grant it, he will ever be beholden to thee. He would have thee receive his noble guests kindly, and ride out from Worms to the shore to meet them. He begged this of thee with true heart."

The beautiful maiden answered, "I will do it gladly. I will deny him no service. Faithfully and truly will I do it." And she grew red from love.

Never was prince's envoy better entreated. If she had durst kiss him, she had done it readily. On loving wise he took leave of the maiden.

Then did the Burgundians as Siegfried told them. Sindolt, and Hunolt, and Rumolt the knight, hasted and raised seats on the strand before Worms. The king's servants rested not.

And Ortwin and Gary sent messengers out straightway to Gunther's liegemen over all, with news of the hightide. The maidens looked to their apparel. The palace and all the walls were decked out for the guests, and adorned cunningly for the stranger knights.

All the roads were thronged with the kinsmen of the three kings, that had been summoned to welcome Gunther and Brunhild, and many a rich vest was taken from its wrapping-cloth. Then the news spread, that Brunhild's friends had been spied on the way. And great was the press in Burgundy. Bold knights, enow, I ween, were there on both sides! Fair Kriemhild said, "Go now, you of my maidens that will forth with me to the welcome, and seek out your best clothes from the chests, that we may have honour and praise from the guests."

The knights also bade bring out rich saddles, all of red gold, for the women to ride from Worms down to the Rhine. Better riding gear there could not be. Ha! how bright the gold shone on the horses, and the precious stones on the bridles! They brought out gilded side-saddles and goodly trappings for the women. And they were all merry of their cheer.

The horses stood ready in the court for the noble maidens, as I have told you, and the poitrals were of the finest silk that was ever spun. Eighty and six dames in head-coifs, fair, and dight in rich apparel, came to Kriemhild, and thereto, featly adorned, many a beautiful damsel; fifty and four, the fairest in Burgundy, with glittering lace over their yellow hair. All that the king had desired of them they did with good will.

Fair robes of goodly stuffs that matched their white skins they wore before the stranger knights. None but a fool had found any of them amiss. Some had mantles of sable and ermine, and their arms and wrists had bracelets over the silk; none might tell all the goodly show to the end. With girdles cunningly fashioned, rich and long, they bound their gorgeous robes made of silk of Araby. The world held no fairer damsels.

In their tightened bodices they laced them deftly. Certes, they had been grieved if their red cheeks had not outshone their vesture. Never queen had lovelier maidens.

When now the women had done on their apparel, the proud warriors that were to lead them out drew nigh, a mighty force, bearing shields and ashen spears.

TENTH ADVENTURE
HOW BRUNHILD WAS RECEIVED AT WORMS

N the far bank of the Rhine appeared a mighty host--the king with his guests--and they drew nigh to the strand, where damsels, led by the bridle, stood ready with welcome. When they from Issland, and Siegfried's men of the Nibelung, saw that the ships were come, they hasted to the beach and laid hold, for they spied the king's friends that waited on the other side.

It is told of Uta, the rich queen, that she brought her damsels from the castle to ride with her, so that knights and maidens won knowledge of one another. The Margrave Gary held Kriemhild's bridle till they were out from the fortress; then Siegfried hasted to serve her, for the which he was after requited.

Ortwin the bold went by dame Uta's side, and, paired meetly and in sweet fellowship, knights and maidens rode together. Never, in sooth, at such meeting were so many women gathered. The men held tourney in the presence of Kriemhild and the rest, until the ships were landed, and did valiant deeds, that had been ill left undone at such a season.

Then they lifted the rich-attired women from their horses.

Ha! what splintering of lances, what din of shields, what noise and clash of wrought bucklers, when the king and his guests were come over to the fair ones that stood by the haven!

Gunther, with his friends, went down from the ships; he led Brunhild by the hand; garments and precious stones shone bright and sparkled.   And Kriemhild went eagerly toward them, and greeted Brunhild and her following.   They drew back their head-bands with white fingers, and kissed one another through love.

Then Kriemhild, the maid, spake courteously, "Thou art right welcome in this land, to me and to my mother, and to our friends." And they courtsied and embraced.   Never, I ween, was any greeted fairer than the bride, by Uta and her daughter, for they ceased not to kiss her sweet mouth.

When Brunhild's women were all gotten to land, the knights led them before the queen, where welcome was not stinted them, and, where many a red mouth was kissed.   The rich kings' daughters stood long side by side, and the warriors gazed on them.   What these had heard tell they saw with their eyes, that none surpassed those two women in beauty, neither was any blemish found in them.   They that esteem women for the comeliness of the body and what the eye beholdeth, extolled King Gunther's wife, but the wise that look deeper said, "Praised shall Kriemhild be before Brunhild."   And the bright-attired women drew together where the silken canopies were spread, and the goodly tents, in the field before Worms.

The king's kinsmen pressed forward to see them.   They prayed the two queens to go with their women where the shade was, and the Burgundian knights led them thither.

The guests also were now gotten to horse, and there was din of tilting against shields.   The dust swirled up from the plain, as the land had been on fire, and the valour of many knights was proven, while the maidens beheld their prowess.   Siegfried, I ween, rode many a course before the pavilions with his thousand Nibelungs.

The Burgundians Ride Forth To Welcome Brunhild

Then came Hagen of Trony at the king's command, and, on friendly wise, stopped the jousting, lest the dust should irk the fair maidens, and they demurred not, but obeyed gladly.

Gernot said, "Let stand the horses till it groweth cooler, and let us lead the women home. But be ready to ride again when the king giveth the order."

So the tourney ended over all the plain. And the knights went to the women under the high pavilions, and passed the time merrily till it was time to ride home.

At the fall of night, when the sun went down and the air had begun to cool, they tarried not longer, but arose, men and women together, and the knights wooed the fair maidens with their eyes. Then, as was the custom of the land, the good squires spurred forward to the castle gate before the proud knights.

There the king alighted from his horse, and, on knightly wise, the heroes lifted down the women. There, too, the noble queens parted. Uta and her daughter went with their attendants into a wide chamber, and a merry din was heard over all.

The chairs were set, for the king was ready to go to table with his guests, and beautiful Brunhild stood by him, and were her crown in Gunther's land. Certes, she was proud enow.

Many were the seats, they say, and the tables goodly and broad, and laden with food. Little, I trow, was lacking! And many a noble guest sat there with the king. Gunther's chamberlains carried round water in golden ewers. If any tell you of a prince's table better served, believe it not.

Or Gunther took the water, Siegfried, as was meet, minded him of his oath that he had sworn or ever he saw Brunhild in Issland.

He said, "Forget not the vow thou swarest with thy hand, that, if Brunhild came into Burgundy, thou wouldst give me thy sister. Where is thine oath now? Mickle toil was mine on the journey."

The king answered his guest, "Thou hast done well to remind me. I go not back from the oath of my hand. What I can do therein I will do."

They bade Kriemhild to the court before the king. She went up the hall with her maidens, but Giselher sprang down the stair and cried, "Send back these maidens. My sister goeth alone to the king."

They brought Kriemhild before Gunther, where he stood amidst of knights from many lands. And they bade her stand in the middle of the hall.

Brunhild, by this time, was come to the table, and knew naught of what was toward. Then said Dankrat's son to his kinsmen, "Help me now, that my sister take Siegfried to her husband."

And they answered with one accord, "That may she do with honour."

Gunther said, "Dearest sister, I prithee of thy goodness, loose me from mine oath. I promised thee to a knight; and truly thou wilt do my will, if thou take him to husband."

The maiden answered, "Dear brother mine, thou needest not to entreat. Command and I will obey. Him that thou givest me to husband I will gladly wed."

Siegfried grew red for love and joy, and vowed his service to Kriemhild.

And they bade them stand together in a circle, and asked her if she would take the knight.

On maidenly wise she was shamefast at the first, yet so great was Siegfried's good fortune and his grace, that she refused not his hand; and the king of the Netherland, from his side also, plighted his troth to Kriemhild.

When their word was given, Siegfried took his queen in his arms straightway, and kissed her before the warriors.

The circle brake up when this was ended, and Siegfried took the seat of honour with Kriemhild. The vassals served before them, and his Nibelung knights stood nigh.

The king and Brunhild were seated, and Brunhild saw Kriemhild sitting by Siegfried, the which irked her sore; she fell to weeping, and the hot tears ran down her bright cheeks.

Whereupon the host said, "What aileth thee, sweet Lady, that the light of thine eyes is dim? Rejoice shouldst thou rather, for my land and rich castles and true liegemen are all subject to thee."

"I have cause to weep," said the maiden. "I grieve from my heart for thy sister, that she sitteth there by thy vassal. I must ever weep to see her so shamed."

But King Gunther answered, "I prithee, silence! Another time I will tell thee why I gave my sister to Siegfried. May she live happily with the knight."

But she said, "I must grieve for her beauty and her birth. If I knew whither I might flee, I would not suffer thee by me, till that thou hadst told me how Siegfried hath gotten Kriemhild."

Gunther answered them, "Hearken, and I will tell thee. Know that he hath lands and castles even as I, and is a rich king; wherefore I give him my beautiful sister gladly to wife."

Yet, for all the king could say to her, she was downcast.

The knights rose from the table, and the tourney waxed so fierce that the castle rang with the noise. But the king wearied amidst of his guests. He thought, "It were softer alone with my wife." And his heart dwelled on the mickle joy her love must bring him, and he looked at her sweetly.

Then they stopped the tourney, that the king might retire with his wife.

At the foot of the stair that led forth from the hall, Kriemhild and Brunhild came face to face. They were not foes yet. Their attendants followed them, and longer they tarried not. The chamberlains brought candles, and the knights of the two kings parted in two companies, and many followed Siegfried.

Then came the heroes where they were to lie, and each thought to win his wife's favour, whereat their hearts melted.

With Siegfried all went well. He caressed the maiden lovingly, and she was as his life. He had not given her alone for a thousand other women.

Of them I will tell no further. Hear now how it fared with Gunther. Better had been his case with any but Brunhild.

The folk had departed, dames and knights. The door was made fast. He thought to win her love, but it was long yet or she became his wife. He lay down in a white garment and thought, "Now have I my heart's desire."

The king's hand hid the light. He went to Brunhild and embraced her with his arm. He was greatly glad. He would have caressed her sweetly if she had let him. But she was so wroth that he was dismayed. He thought to find joy, but found deep hate.

She said, "Noble knight, let me alone, for it shall not be as thou desirest. Mark well I have naught to do with thee, till that thou has answered me concerning Kriemhild."

Then Gunther began to be angry with her, and fought with her, and tore her raiment. And the royal maiden seized a girdle, a strong embroidered silk cord that she wore round her waist, and did hurt enow to the knight. She bound his hands and his feet, and carried him to a nail, and hung him on the wall. She forbade him to touch her because he disturbed her sleep. He almost perished from her strength.

Then he that should have been master began to pray, "Now loose my bands, most noble queen. I promise never to touch thee, or even to come night thee."

She asked not how he fared while she lay soft. There must he hang the long night through till the day, when the bright morning shone through the window. If he had ever had strength, he had little in his body now.

"Tell me, Sir Gunther," said the beautiful maiden, "doth it not irk thee that thy chamberlains find thee bound by the hand of a woman."

The noble knight answered, "It were the worse for thee. Also little were my honour therein. Of thy charity allow me to lie down. Seeing thou hatest my love, I will no so much as touch thy garment with my hand."

Then she loosed his bands, and let him go, and he laid him down, but so far from her that he ruffled not her beautiful gown. Even that she had gladly forgone.

Thereupon their attendants came and brought them new apparel, as much as they could wear, that had been made ready against the wedding morn. But, amidst of them that rejoiced, the king was heavy of his cheer beneath his crown that day.

According to the good custom of the land, Gunther and Brunhild tarried not longer, but went to the minster to hear mass. Thither also went Siegfried, and there was great press of people.

Crowns and robes were ready for them there; and after they had taken their vows, they stood up, all four, proudly beneath their crowns.

Youths, to the number of six hundred or more, were dubbed knights (I say sooth) in honour of the king. And great joy was in Burgundy, and much splintering of lances by sworded knights.

The beautiful maidens sat at the windows, and underneath them was the flashing of many shields. But the king stood apart from his men, and went about sadly.

He and Siegfried were unlike of their moods. The hero guessed what ailed him, and went to him and asked him, "Tell me how it hath fared with thee."

Then said the host to his guest, "Shame and hurt have I suffered from my wife in my house. When I would have caressed her, she bound me tight, and took me to a nail, and hung me up on the wall. There I dangled in fear the night through till the day, or she loosed me. How soft she lay there! I tell thee this in secret."

And stark Siegfried said, "I grieve for thee. I will tell thee a remedy if thou keep it from her. I will so contrive it that this night she will defy thee no longer." The word was welcome to Gunther after his pain.

"Now see my hands, how they are swollen. She overmastered me, as I had been a child, that the blood spurted all over me from my nails. I thought not to come off with my life."

Said Siegfried, "It will yet be well. Unequal was our fortune last night. Thy sister Kriemhild is dearer to me than mine own body. This day must Brunhild be thy wife. I will come to-night to thy room secretly in my *Tarnkappe*, that none may guess the trick.

"Send the chamberlains to their beds. I will put out the lights in the hands of the pages, and by this sign thou shalt know that I am night. I will win thy wife for thee or perish."

"If only thou winnest her not for thyself. She is my dear wife. Otherwise I rejoice. Do to her what thou wilt. If thou tookest her life, I would bear it. She is a terrible woman."

"I vow to thee on mine honour that I will have naught to do with her. Thy dear sister is more to me than any I have ever seen." And Gunther believed Siegfried's word.

Meanwhile the guests rode at the tourney with fortune good and bad, but, when it was time for the women to go to the hall, they stopped the tilting and the din, and the chamberlains bade the folk void the way.

And now the courtyard was empty of horses and men. A bishop led each queen before the kings to table, and many proud knights followed them to their seats. The king sat beside his wife in good hope, for he minded Siegfried's promise. The one day seemed to him as thirty, for he thought only on Brunhild.

Scarce could he wait till they rose from the table.

Fair Kriemhild and also Brunhild were led to their chambers. Ha! what bold knights went before the queens!

Joyful and without hate Siegfried the knight sat sweetly beside his beautiful wife. With her white hand she caressed his, till, she knew not how, he vanished from before her eyes. When she played with him and saw him no longer, she said to her maidens, "I marvel much where the king is gone. Who took his hands out of mine?" And so the matter dropped.

He had gone where he found the chamberlains with the lights, which he began to put out. By this sign Gunther perceived that it was Siegfried. He knew well what he wanted, and he sent away the women and maidens.

When that was done, the king himself locked the door, and shot two strong bolts before it. He hid the light quickly behind the bed curtain, and the struggle that had to come began between stark Siegfried and the beautiful maiden. King Gunther was both glad and sorry.

Siegfried lay down by the queen, but she said, "Stop, Gunther, lest thou suffer as afore. Thou mayest again receive a hurt at my hand."

Siegfried concealed his voice and spake not. Gunther heard well all that passed, albeit he saw nothing. There was little ease for the twain. Siegfried feigned that he was Gunther, and put his arm round the valiant maiden. She threw him on to a bench, that his head rang loud against a foot-stool.

The bold man sprang up undaunted, but evil befell him. Such defence from a woman I ween the world will never see more. Because he would not let her be, Brunhild rose up.

"It is unseemly of thee," said the brave maiden. "Thou wilt tear my beautiful gown. Thou art churlish and must suffer for it. Thou shalt see!"

She caught the good knight in her arms, and would have bound him as she had done to the king, that she might have peace. Grimly she avenged her torn raiment.

What availed him then his strength and his prowess? She proved to him the mastery of her body, and carried him by force, since there was no other way, and squeezed him hard against a press that stood by the bed.

"Alack!" thought the knight, "if I lose my life by the hand of a woman, all wives evermore will make light of their husbands, that, without this, would not dare."

The king heard it well. He feared for the man. Then Siegfried was ashamed and waxed furious. He grappled fiercely with her, and, in terror of his life, strove to overcome Brunhild. When she squeezed him down, he got up again in spite of her, by dint of his anger and his mickle strength. He came in great scathe. In the chamber there was smiting with many blows.

King Gunther, likewise, stood in peril. He danced to and fro quickly before them. So mightily they strove, it was a wonder they came off with their lives. The trouble of the king was twofold, yet most he feared Siegfried's death. For she had almost killed the knight. Had he dared, he had gone to his help.

The strife endured long atwixt them. Then Siegfried got hold of Brunhild. Albeit she fought valiantly, her defence was grown weak. It seemed long to the king, that stood there, till Siegfried had won. She squeezed his hands till, by her strength, the blood spurted out from his nails. Then he brake the strong will that she had shown at the first.

The king heard it all, but he spake no word. Siegfried pressed her down till she cried aloud, for his might hurt her greatly. She clutched at her side, where she found her girdle, and sought to tie his hands. But he gripped her till the joints of her body cracked. So the strife was ended.

She said, "Noble king, let me live. I will make good to thee what I have done, and strive no more; truly I have found thee to be my master."

Siegfried rose up then and left her, as though he would throw off his clothes. He drew from her hand a gold ring, without that she was ware of it. He took her girdle also, a good silken band. I know not if he did it from pride. He gave them to his wife, and suffered for it after.

The king and the fair maiden were left together, and, for that she was grown weak, she hid her anger, for it availed her nothing. So the abode there till the bright day.

Meanwhile Siegfried went back to his sweet love, that received him kindly. He turned the questions aside that she asked him, and hid from her for long what he had brought with him, till at the last, when they were gotten home to the Netherland, he gave her the jewel; the which brought him and many knights to their graves.

Much merrier was Gunther of his cheer the next morning than afore. Throughout his lands many a noble knight rejoiced, and the guests that he had bidden to the hightide were well feasted and served.

The hightide lasted fourteen days, during the which time the din of the sports, and of the pastimes they practised, ceased not. Mickle was the cost to the king. The king's kinsmen gave, in his honour, to the stranger knights, as their lord willed it, apparel, and ruddy gold and horses, and thereto silver enow; and they that received the gifts took their leave well content.

Also Siegfried of the Netherland and his thousand knights gave all that they had brought with them - goodly horses with saddles. Certes, they lived right royally. Nevertheless, or they had made an end of giving, they deemed it long; for they were weary for their home.

So ended the hightide, and the warriors went their ways.

HOW SIEGFRIED BROUGHT HIS WIFE HOME

HEN the guests were all gone, the son of Siegmund spake to his friends, "We will also go forth to our land." And his wife was glad when she heard the news.

She said to her husband, "When shall we start? Yet be not in too great haste. My brothers shall first divide the land with me." But the word irked Siegfried.

The princes went to him and said, all the three, "Sir Siegfried, we be thy true servants till death. Know this of a surety." And he thanked the knights that they spake him so fair.

"We would also divide with thee," said Giselher the youth, "land and castles, and the rich kingdom that we rule. A full share thereof shalt thou receive with Kriemhild."

But the son of Siegmund made answer, when he had heard their honourable intent. "Blest be your heritage to you evermore, and also the people thereof. The share you would give to my dear wife she may well forego, for when she will wear the crown, she will be, if she live long enow, the richest woman on earth. Command me in aught else, and I will obey."

But Kriemhild said, "Though thou scorn my land, not so lightly shalt thou treat Burgundian warriors. These any king might be proud to take with him, and them, at the least, shall my brothers' hand share with me."

Gunther answered, "Take whom thou wilt. Thou wilt find many ready to ride with thee. Of three thousand knights, choose thou one thousand for thy following."

Then Kriemhild sent for Hagen of Trony and for Ortwin, and asked them if they and their kinsmen would ride with her. But Hagen fell in a fury and cried, "To no man in this world shall Gunther give us. Others can ride with thee. Thou knowest the men of Trony and their way. By the king at the court will we bide, to serve him and follow him as heretofore."

So she let the matter rest, and made ready for the journey; for her followers she won two and thirty maidens and five hundred men, among the which was Eckewart the Margrave. And they took their leave, as was meet: knights and squires, damsels and dames. They parted thence with kisses, and set out from Gunther's land joyfully.

Her kinsmen brought her far on her way, and had night quarters put up where they desired them, in the king's land. And they despatched envoys to King Siegmund, to tell him and Queen Sieglind how that their son drew nigh with fair Kriemhild, Queen Uta's child, from Worms on the Rhine.

They could not have brought them better news.

Siegmund said, "Praised be God that I have lived to see the day when Kriemhild shall wear the crown here. My heritage is increased in worth, and Siegfried himself shall be king."

Queen Sieglind gave the envoys, for fee, red velvet and heavy silver and gold, for she was glad at the news.

Her women began to adorn them in haste, and when Sieglind knew who came with Siegfried, she let seats be builded, where he might be crowned in presence of his kinsmen.

King Siegmund's knights rode out to meet them. Never heroes were better welcomed, I trow, than these, into Siegmund's land.

Sieglind rode forth, herself, to greet fair Kriemhild, with beautiful women and bold knights, a day's journey or they spied the guests. And strangers and friends were pressed alike for room, till that they came to a great castle that hight Xanten, where Siegfried and his wife were crowned afterward.

Siegmund and Sieglind kissed Kriemhild, and Siegfried also, many times with smiling mouth for their sorrow was ended; and Kriemhild's attendants got a gracious welcome.

They brought the guests into Siegmund's palace, and lifted the fair damsels from the horses. There were knights enow eager to serve them.

Howso rich had been the hightide by the Rhine, here the knights received costlier apparel than ever before in their lives. Many marvels might be told of their splendour. So they sat in honour and had plenty. The courtiers wore robes of red gold embroidered with precious stones and silk, that Sieglind, the noble queen, gave them.

Then Siegmund spake in presence of his kinsmen, "Be it known to you all that Siegfried shall henceforth wear my crown." They of the Netherland heard the news gladly. So he made over to Siegfried his crown and his rule and his land, that he became lord and king. And to him that he acquitted, and to him that he condemned, it was done according to his judgment. The husband of Kriemhild was a man greatly feared.

Thus, in high honour (and this is sooth that I say) he lived and reigned, a crowned king, till the tenth year, when a son was born, whereby the king's liegemen saw their desire accomplished. They hasted and christened him, and called him Gunther, after his uncle; that was no shame, for, took he after his kinsmen, he must grow to be a bold man. They reared him well, as was meet.

And in these days Sieglind died, and many wept because death had taken her. Then Uta's child held supreme rule, as befitted so rich a queen.

Now at the same time, they tell us, in Gunther's land of Burgundy, the beautiful Brunhild had borne a son, that, for love of the hero, they named Siegfried. With all care they trained him. Gunther let him be reared by his liegemen at the court in all virtues that might serve him if he grew to be a man. Soon, alack, by an evil fate, he was to lose all his kin!

The fame of Siegfried's court ceased not to be noised abroad, and with what worship his knights abode there; great was the fame also of Gunther's chosen warriors in Burgundy.

The Nibelungs held their land in fee from Siegfried, and none of his kinsmen were so rich as he. For he was overlord to the knights of Shilbung, and owned the treasure of the two brothers. Wherefore his heart was the more uplifted.

The biggest hoard that ever hero won was his; that he had got by means of his strong hand before a mountain, and for the which he smote many heroes to death.

He had honour to the full; yet, if he had possessed nothing at all, none that saw him had denied him to be the prowest champion that ever rode a horse. With good cause the folk feared him.

TWELFTH ADVENTURE
HOW GUNTHER INVITED SIEGFRIED TO THE HIGHTIDE

OW there passed not a day but Gunther's wife thought, "Surely Kriemhild beareth her too proudly. Siegfried, her husband, is our vassal. Little service hath he done for his land."

She pondered it secretly in her heart; for it irked her that they were strangers, and she had fain known wherefore Siegfried's country yielded no tribute. She prayed the king that she might behold Kriemhild again, and told him her secret thought.

But her word pleased him not. "How could we bid them hither?" said the great king. "It cannot be. They dwell too far off. I durst not do it."

But Brunhild answered proudly, "However mighty a king's vassal may be, he must do what his lord commandeth."

But Gunther laughed, for he took it not as homage when he saw Siegfried.

She said further, "Dear lord, for my love, help me thereto, that Siegfried and thy sister visit us, and that we see them here. Truly nothing could rejoice me more. Thy sister's courtesy, her gentle breeding - with what delight my heart dwelleth thereon, and how we sat together the day I became thy wife! That she chose Siegfried to her husband did her honour."

She begged the king for it so long that he said, "Certes! no guests would I gladlier welcome, and willingly I grant it thee. I will bid them hither by my envoys."

The queen answered then, "Send not thither without my knowledge, and inform me, without fail, when my dear friends shall come. And tell me, also, whom thou wilt charge with the embassy."

"That will I," said the king. "I will despatch thirty of my knights."

He bade them to his presence, and sent greeting by them to Siegfried's country. Brunhild clad them in rich apparel, and the king spake, "Ye knights shall keep back naught wherewith I charge you, but shall say to stark Siegfried, and to my sister, that no man in this world is better minded to them than I be. Bid them both hither to the Rhine. If they come, I and my wife will cease not to be beholden to them. Or midsummer is here, he and his knights will find among us many to do them worship. Greet King Siegmund also from me, and say that I and my friends are his true servants; and entreat my sister that, without fail, she ride hither to her friends. No hightide were fitter for her."

Brunhild and Uta, and their women, commended them to the fair women and the bold men at Siegfried's court.

So the envoys made haste to do the king's bidding. They stood ready for the road; horses and harness were there, and they took their leave. They pushed forward with the escort the king gave them. Inside of twelve days they reached the land and the castle of the Nibelungs, and found Siegfried on the march of Norway. Horses and men were weary with the long road.

They brought word to both Siegfried and Kriemhild that knights were come, clad after the manner of the Burgundians.

And Kriemhild sprang from the couch where she lay resting, and bade a maiden run to the window, who saw Gary standing in the courtyard, and his knights that were sent with him. They brought welcome news to her anxious heart.

She cried to the king, "Seest thou, standing there in the courtyard, them that be come with stark Gary, that my brother Gunther hath sent down the Rhine?"

And Siegfried answered, "They are welcome."

All the folk ran when they saw the envoys and greeted them with kind words. Siegfried was right glad at their coming.

Lodging was given to them, and their horses were seen to, whereupon they went straightway where Siegfried sat by Kriemhild. Both were joyful to behold them. The king and his wife rose quickly to receive Gary and Gunther's knights of Burgundy. And they bade Gary sit down.

"Nay, let us way-weary guests stand while we tell thee Gunther's message. After, we will sit. Gunther and Brunhild, with whom it is well, and Queen Uta, your mother, and Giselher, the youth, and eke Gernot, and your nearest kinsmen, send greeting from Burgundy."

"Now God reward them," said Siegfried; "I hold them for good and true, as a man should trust his friends. The like doth their sister. Say on, whether they be of good cheer. Hath any done my wife's brethren a hurt since we parted? Tell me, for I will stand by them till their foemen rue my help."

Margrave Gary, the good knight, answered, "It is well with them, and they are of good cheer. They bid thee to a hightide, and were right glad if thou camest. They bid my Lady also. So soon as the winter shall be ended, before midsummer, they would see you."

But Siegfried said, "That can hardly be."

Whereupon Gary the Burgundian answered, "Your mother Uta, Gernot, and Giselher, pray that ye deny them not. Every day I hear them lament that ye dwell so far. Brunhild my mistress, and her maidens, rejoice in the hope to see you."

The message seemed good to Kriemhild. Gary was her kinsman; and the king bade him sit, and tarried not longer to let pour the wine for the guests.

Thither came Siegmund also, when he saw the messengers, and he spake to them on friendly wise. "Ye be welcome, ye knights, Gunther's men; since Siegfried won Kriemhild to wife, ye should have been seen here oftener, if you would have proved your love."

They answered that, if he willed it, they would come gladly, for that joy had taken from them their mickle weariness.

Then they bade the envoys sit, and set meats before them, whereof Siegfried gave order they should have enow. Nine days they were kept at the court, till at last they murmured, saying that if they tarried longer, they durst not return again to their land.

Meanwhile Siegfried had let summon his friends. He asked them their mind about his journey. "Gunther my brother-in-law, and his kinsmen, have bidden me to a hightide at the Rhine, and Kriemhild also, that she ride with me. And I were fain to go if his country lay not so far off. Now counsel me, dear friends, for the best. Had I to harry thirty lands for their sake, my hand were at their service."

His knights made answer, "If thou wouldst ride to this hightide, we counsel thee on this wise: take with thee a thousand knights to the Rhine, that thou mayest have honour among the Burgundians."

Then said King Siegmund of the Netherland, "Wherefore has thou not told me thou wouldest to the hightide? If thou hast naught against it, I will ride with thee, and will take an hundred knights with me to add to thy train."

"Wilt thou do so, dear father mine?" said bold Siegfried. "Right welcome art thou. Inside of twelve days we will forth."

To them that desired it horses and apparel were given.

Since the king was minded to make the journey, he sent away the swift envoys, and charged them with a message to his wife's brethren at the Rhine, that he would come right gladly to their hightide.

Siegfried and Kriemhild (so runneth the tale) gave so much to the envoys that their horses scarce sufficed to carry it, for Siegfried was a rich king. So, well content, they drave their sumpters before them.

Then Siegfried and Siegmund equipped their folk, and Eckewart, the Margrave, bade bring forth the best women's vesture that was in Siegfried's whole land. They made ready saddles and shields, and to the knights and the gentlewomen that were to ride with them, they gave freely, that they lacked naught. Siegfried led many valiant knights to his kinsmen.

The envoys hasted on their way, and when bold Gary was come into Burgundy, they greeted him fair. The riders sprang from their horses Gunther's hall. And young and old, as their wont is, pressed round them and asked for news. But the good knight answered, "Ye shall have it when I have told it to the king." And he passed on with his comrades to Gunther.

The king sprang from his seat for joy, and Brunhild thanked them that they were so soon back again. To the envoys spake Gunther then, "How fareth it with Siegfried, that hath ever done well by me?"

And Gary answered, "He and thy sister waxed red for joy. Kinder greeting sent man never to his friends than Siegfried and his father Siegmund send to thee."

Then said the queen to the Margrave, "Tell me, I prithee; cometh Kriemhild with them? And hath her body lost nothing of its fairness?"

Whereto Gary answered, "They will both come, and, with them, many knights."

Then Uta bade the envoys to her presence, and showed by her questions what most she desired to know - how it fared with Kriemhild. He told her how he had found her, and that she would come thither shortly.

They declared also the envoy's fee that Siegfried had given them: the apparel and the gold. All the knights of the three kings saw it, and praised Siegfried.

"It is easy for him to give," quoth Hagen. "He could not spend it if he lived for ever, for the hoard of the Nibelungs is in his hand. Would it came our way!"

All the court, both knights and ladies, were glad at their coming. The servants of the three kings were not idle, and started to raise the high-seats. Hunolt and Sindolt had work enow, for they were the sewer and the butler, and they arranged the chairs; to Ortwin, for that he helped them, Gunther gave thanks.

As for Rumult, the chief cook, I ween he knew how to order his underlings. Ha! what meats they made ready against the feast, in their huge cauldrons and pots and pans.

The women too busied them, and saw to their robes, whereon they embroidered gold and bright shining stones, that, when they wore them, they might be well esteemed.

THIRTEENTH ADVENTURE
HOW THEY RODE TO THE HIGHTIDE

LEAVE we all this work now, to tell how Kriemhild and her maidens journeyed from the Nibelung land to the Rhine.

Never sumpters bare such rich apparel. They sent many travelling chests on before them, and Siegfried and the queen rode with their friends and dreamed on joy--that was to end in deep sorrow. As needs was, they left their son at home. Also for him was the journey woeful: his father and his mother he saw nevermore. Siegmund, the king, rode with them, that had, certes, not been there, had he known what was to betide them. Never sorrow was worse than his for dear ones.

They sent forward messengers betimes, and a proud host of Uta's kin, and Gunther's knights, came forth to meet them. Gunther busied him to show his guests worship. He went to Brunhild and said, "How did Kriemhild welcome thee when thou camest first to this land? I would have thee welcome her even so."

She answered, "I will do it gladly, for I have cause to love her."

The king spake further, "They come to-morrow early. If thou wilt receive them, lose no time, lest they surprise us here in the castle, for never have I welcomed dearer guests."

So she gave orders to her women to seek out goodly robes, the best that they had, and to wear them; the which, I trow, they did gladly.

Gunther's men also hasted to meet them; all that he had he led forth; and the queen rode in royal state. Mickle joy was at that greeting. With high honour they welcomed them, yea, with even more, the folk said, than Kriemhild had showed Brunhild aforetime; and the hearts of them that saw it were uplifted. Then Siegfried came up with his men, and the heroes coursed to and fro on the plain, that none had ease for the dust and the press.

When the king saw Siegfried and Siegmund, on what loving wise he spake! "Ye are welcome to me and to all my men. Right joyful have ye made us by this journey."

"Now God reward thee," answered Siegmund, the worshipful man. "Since my son Siegfried won thee to his kinsman, my desire hath ever been to behold thee."

Whereupon Gunther said, "That it hath come to pass doth rejoice me."

Siegfried was received with the honour that was his due; and none wished him ill. From Gernot and Giselher, also, dear guests had never better welcome.

Then the two queens drew nigh to each other.

The saddles were emptied, and the women alighted on the grass with the help of the heroes, that were not slow, I trow, with their service!

The queens met, and the knights rejoiced at so fair a greeting, and ceased not to wait upon the fair women. Hero now to hero held out the hand of welcome; the women courtseyed and kissed, and Gunther's and Siegfried's men looked on well content.

They tarried not longer, but rode to the town, where the host bade it be shown plain that the guests were welcome to Burgundy. There, too, there was tilting before the maidens. Hagen of Trony and Ortwin approved them mighty, for none durst gainsay their command; and they showed the dear guests much honour.

The clash of shields, and the din of piercing and smiting, rose before the castle gate. Long time stood the host there with his guest or they were all gone in, for in pastime the hours flew by. Then they rode merrily to the great reception hall. Gorgeous foot-cloths, rich and cunningly fashioned, hung down from the saddles of the beautiful women.

Gunther's serving-men hasted forward, and led them to their chambers. All this time Brunhild kept not her eyes from Kriemhild, that was, certes, fair enow, and of brighter hue than the gold she wore.

Over all the town of Worms was heard the mirth of the company. King Gunther bade Dankwart, his marshal, see to them well, who gave them goodly quarters. Without and within they feasted; never were strangers fairer entreated; all that they desired stood ready for them, for so rich was the king, that to none was aught denied. They were served well and without hate.

Then the king went to table with his guests. Siegfried they let sit where he had sat aforetime, and many a proud warrior strode after him to the feast. Twelve hundred knights were in the circle at the table; whereat Brunhild thought, "Never afore was vassal so rich." Nevertheless she was well minded to him, nor contrived aught to his hurt.

Many a rich cloak was wetted where the king sat that night, with the wine that the butlers ceased not to pour; for they toiled sore to serve all.

As hath still been the custom at hightides, the women and the damsels were led to their beds betimes; and to each guest, from whencesoever he came, the host gave honour and gifts enow.

When the night was ended, and the morning shone, precious stones sparkled on the rich apparel that the hands of the women drew forth from the travelling chests. Many a rich robe was sought out.

Or it was well day, knights and squires gathered before the hall, and the din of tourney arose again before the early mass that they sang for the king. Gunther thanked the young heroes. Then the trumpets were blown lustily, and the noise of drums and flutes were so loud that Worms, the wide town, rang therewith.

Everywhere the bold heroes sprang to horse, and tourney was held in the land. Many young hearts were there that beat high, and, under their shields, many a doughty knight. In the windows sat stately dames and beautiful maidens, featly adorned, and gazed down at the joisting of the warriors, till that the king himself began to tilt with his kinsmen. So they passed the time, nor thought it long.

Then the bells rang from the dome, whereat they led up the horses, and the women rode forth, with many stark knights following the queens. They alighted before the minster, on the grass. Still was Brunhild well minded to her guests, and, with their crowns on, they went into the great church. But soon jealousy made an end of their love.

When the mass was sung they rode home in state, and went merrily to table. Nor was there an end of joy at the hightide till the eleventh day.

Then the queen thought, "I can hide it no longer. I must contrive by some means that Kriemhild tell me why her husband, that is our vassal, hath so long paid us no tribute. I cannot lose this riddle."

So she waited for the hour when the Devil tempted her, and she turned the joy of the hightide to dole. For it pressed on her heart, and must needs come to light. By reason thereof many lands were filled with mourning.

HOW THE QUEENS QUARRELLED

NE day, before vespers, there arose in the court of the castle a mighty din of knights that tilted for pastime, and the folk ran to see them.

The queens sat together there, thinking each on a doughty warrior. Then said fair Kriemhild, "I have a husband of such might that all these lands might well be his."

But Brunhild answered, "How so? If there lived none other save thou and he, our kingdom might haply be his, but while Gunther is alive it could never be."

But Kriemhild said, "See him there. How he surpasseth the other knights, as the bright moon the stars! My heart is uplifted with cause."

Whereupon Brunhild answered, "Howso valiant thy husband, comely and fair, thy brother Gunther excelleth him, for know that he is the first among kings."

But Kriemhild said, "My praise was not idle; for worshipful is my husband in many things. Trow it, Brunhild. He is, at the least, thy husband's equal."

"Mistake me not in thine anger, Kriemhild. Neither is my word idle; for they both said, when I saw them first, and the king vanquished me in the sports, and on knightly wise won my love, that Siegfried was his man. Wherefore I hold him for a vassal, since I heard him say it."

Then Kriemhild cried, "Evil were my lot if that were true. How had my brothers given me to a vassal to wife? Prithee, of thy courtesy, cease from such discourse."

"That will I not," answered Brunhild. "Thereby should I lose many knights that, with him, owe us homage."

Whereat fair Kriemhild waxed very wroth. "Lose them thou must, for any service he will do thee. He is nobler even than Gunther, my noble brother. Wherefore, spare me thy foolish words. I wonder, since he is thy vassal, and thou art so much mightier than we, that for so long time he hath failed to pay tribute. Of a truth thine arrogancy irketh me."

"Thou vauntest thyself too high," cried the queen; "I would see now whether thy body be holden in like honour with mine."

Both the women were angry.

Kriemhild answered, "That shalt thou see straightway. Since thou hast called Siegfried thy vassal, the knights of both kings shall see this day whether I dare enter the minster before thee, the queen. For I would have thee know that I am noble and free, and that my husband is of more worship than thine. Nor will I be chidden by thee. To-day thou shalt see thy vassals go at court before the Burgundian knights, and me more honoured than any queen that ever wore a crown."

Fierce was the wrath of the women.

"If thou art no vassal," said Brunhild, "thou and thy women shall walk separate from my train when we go to the minster."

And Kriemhild answered, "Be it so."

"Now adorn ye, my maidens," said Siegfried's wife, "that I be not shamed. If ye have rich apparel, show it this day. She shall take back what her mouth hath spoken."

She needed not to bid twice; they sought out their richest vesture, and dames and damsels were soon arrayed.

The Two Queens Quarrel

Then the wife of the royal host went forth with her attendants. Fair to heart's desire were clad Kriemhild and the forty and three maidens that she had brought with her to the Rhine. Bright shone the stuffs, woven in Araby, whereof their robes were fashioned. And they came to the minster, where Siegfried's knights waited for them.

The folk marvelled much to see the queens apart, and going not together as afore. Many a warrior was to rue it.

Gunther's wife stood before the minster, and the knights dallied in converse with the women, till that Kriemhild came up with her meiny. All that noble maidens had ever worn was but as a wind to what these had on.

So rich was Kriemhild that thirty king's wives together had not been as gorgeous as she was. None could deny, though they had wished it, that the apparel Kriemhild's maidens wore that day was the richest they had ever seen. Kriemhild did this on purpose to anger Brunhild.

So they met before the minster. And Brunhild, with deadly spite, cried out to Kriemhild to stand still. "Before the queen shall no vassal go."

Out then spake Kriemhild, for she was wroth. "Better hadst thou held thy peace. Thou hast shamed thine own body. How should the leman of a vassal become a king's wife?"

"Whom namest thou leman?" cried the queen.

"Even thee," answered Kriemhild. "For it was Siegfried my husband, and not my brother, that won thee first. Where were thy senses? It was surely ill done to favor a vassal so. Reproaches from thee are much amiss."

"Verily," cried Brunhild, "Gunther shall hear of it."

"What is that to me? Thine arrogancy hath deceived thee. Thou hast called me thy vassal. Know now of a truth it hath irked me, and I am thine enemy evermore."

Then Brunhild began to weep, and Kriemhild tarried not longer, but went with her attendants into the minster before the king's wife. There was deadly hate, and bright eyes grew wet and dim.

Whether they prayed or sang, the service seemed too long to Brunhild, for her heart and her mind were troubled, the which many a bold and good man paid for afterward.

Brunhild stopped before the minster with her women, for she thought, "Kriemhild, the foul-mouthed woman, shall tell me further whereof she so loud accuseth me. If he hath boasted of this thing, he shall answer for it with his life."

Then Kriemhild with her knights came forth, and Brunhild began, "Stop! thou hast called me a wanton and shalt prove it, for know that thy words irk me sore."

Said Kriemhild, "Let me pass. With this gold that I have on my hand I can prove it. Siegfried brought it when he came from thee."

It was a heavy day for Brunhild. She said, "That gold so precious was stolen from me, and hath been hidden these many years. Now I know who hath taken it."

Both the women were furious.

"I am no thief," cried Kriemhild. "Hadst thou prized thine honour thou hadst held thy peace, for, with this girdle round my waist, I can prove my word, and that Siegfried was verily thy leman." She wore a girdle of silk of Nineveh, goodly enow, and worked with precious stones.

When Brunhild saw it she started to weep. And soon Gunther knew it, and all his men, for the queen cried, "Bring hither the King of Rhineland; I would tell him how his sister hath mocked me, and sayeth openly that I be Siegfried's leman."

The king came with his warriors, and, when he saw that his dear one wept, he spake kindly, "What aileth thee, dear wife?"

She answered, "Shamed must I stand, for thy sister would part me from mine honour? I make my plaint to thee. She proclaimeth aloud that Siegfried hath had me to his leman."

Gunther answered, "Evilly hath she done."

"She weareth here a girdle I have long lost, and my red gold. Woe is me that ever I was born! If thou clearest me not from this shame, I will never love thee more."

Said Gunther, "Bid him hither, that he confess whether he hath boasted of this, or no."

They summoned Siegfried, who, when he saw their anger and knew not the cause, spake quickly, "Why weep these women? Tell me straight; and wherefore am I summoned?"

Whereto Gunther answered, "Right vexed am I. Brunhild, my wife, telleth me here that thou hast boasted thou wert her leman. Kriemhild declareth this. Hast thou done it, O knight?"

Siegfried answered, "Not I. If she hath said so, I will rest not till she repent it. I swear with a high oath, in the presence of all thy knights, that I said not this thing."

The king of the Rhine made answer, "So be it. If thou swear the oath here, I will acquit thee of the falsehood."

Then the Burgundians stood round in a ring, and Siegfried swore it with his hand; whereupon the great king said, "Verily, I hold thee guiltless, nor lay to thy charge the word my sister imputeth to thee."

Said Siegfried further, "If she rejoiceth to have troubled thy fair wife, I am grieved beyond measure." The knights glanced at each other.

"Women must be taught to bridle their tongues. Forbid proud speech to thy wife: I will do the like to mine. Such bitterness and pride are a shame."

Angry words have divided many men. Brunhild made such dole, that Gunther's men had pity on her. And Hagen of Trony went to her and asked what ailed her, for he found her weeping. She told him the tale, and he sware straightway that Kriemhild's husband should pay for it, or never would Hagen be glad again.

While they talked together, Ortwin and Gernot came up, and the warriors counselled Siegfried's death. But when Giselher, Uta's fair child, drew nigh and heard them, he spake out with true heart, "Alack, good knights, what would ye do? How hath Siegfried deserved such hate that he should lose his life? A woman is lightly angered."

"Shall we rear bastards?" cried Hagen. "That were small honour to good knights. I will avenge on him the boast that he hath made, or I will die."

But the king himself said, "Good, and not evil, hath he done to us. Let him live. Wherefore should I hate the knight? He hath ever been true to me."

But Ortwin of Metz said, "His great strength shall not avail him. Allow, O Lord, that I challenge him to his death."

So, without cause, they banded against him. Yet none had urged it further, had not Hagen tempted Gunther every day, saying, that if Siegfried lived not, many kings' lands were subject to him.

Whereat the warrior began to grieve.

Meanwhile they let the matter lie, and returned to the tourney. Ha! what stark spears they brake before Kriemhild, atween the minster and the palace; but Gunther's men were wroth.

Then said the king, "Give over this deadly hate. For our weal and honour he was born. Thereto the man is so wonderly stark and grim, that, if he were ware of this, none durst stand against him."

"Not so," said Hagen. "Assure thee on that score. For I will contrive secretly that he pay for Brunhild's weeping. Hagen is his foe evermore."

But Gunther said, "How meanest thou?"

And Hagen answered, "On this wise. Men that none here knoweth shall ride as envoys into this land and declare war. Whereupon thou wilt say before thy guests that thou must to battle with thy liegemen. When thou hast done this, he will promise to help thee. Then he shall die, after I have learnt a certain thing from his wife."

Evilly the king followed Hagen, and they plotted black treason against the chosen knight, without any suspecting it. So, through the quarrel of two women, died many warriors.

HOW SIEGFRIED WAS BETRAYED

O

N the fourth morning, thirty and two men were seen riding to the court. They brought word to Gunther that war was declared against him. The women were woeful when they heard this lie.

The envoys won leave to go into the king, and they said they were Ludger's men, that Siegfried's hand had overcome in battle and brought captive into Gunther's land.

The king greeted them, and bade them sit, but one of them said, "Let us stand, till that we have declared the message wherewith we are charged to thee. Know that thou hast to thy foemen many a mother's son. Ludger and Ludgast, whom thou hast aforetime evilly entreated, ride hither to make war against thee in this land."

The king fell in a rage, as if he had known naught thereof. Then they gave the false messengers good lodging. How could Siegfried or any other guess their treason, whereby, or all was done, they themselves perished?

The king went whispering up and down with his friends. Hagen of Trony gave him no peace. Many of the knights were fain to let it drop, but Hagen would not be turned from it.

On a day that Siegfried found them whispering, he asked them, "Wherefore are the king and his men so sorrowful? If any hath done aught to their hurt, I will stand by them to avenge it."

Gunther answered, "I grieve not without cause. Ludgast and Ludger ride hither to war against me in my land."

Then said the bold knight, "Siegfried's arm will withstand them on such wise, that ye shall all come off with honour. I will do to these warriors even as I did aforetime. Waste will be their lands and their castles, or I be done. I pledge my head thereto. Thou and thy men shall tarry here at home, and I will ride forth with my knights that I have with me. I serve thee gladly, and will prove it. Doubt not that thy foemen shall suffer scathe at my hand."

"These be good words," answered the king, as he were truly glad, and craftily the false man bowed low.

Then said Siegfried further, "Have no fear."

The knights of Burgundy made ready for war, they and their squires, and dissembled before Siegfried and his men. Siegfried bade them of the Netherland lose no time, and they sought out their harness.

Then spake stark Siegfried, "Tarry here at home, Siegmund, my father. If God prosper us, we shall return or long to the Rhine. Meanwhile, be thou of good cheer here by the king."

They made as if to depart, and bound on the standard. Many of Gunther's knights knew nothing of how the matter stood, and a mighty host gathered round Siegfried. They bound their helmets and their coats of mail on to the horses and stood ready. Then went Hagen of Trony to Kriemhild, to take his leave of her, for they would away.

"Well for me," said Kriemhild, "that ever I won to husband a man that standeth so true by his friends, as doth Siegfried by my kinsmen. Right proud am I. Bethink thee now, Hagen, dear friend, how that in all things I am at thy service, and have ever willed thee well. Requite me through my husband, that I love, and avenge not on him what I did to Brunhild.

Already it repenteth me sore. My body hath smarted for it, that ever I troubled her with my words. Siegfried, the good knight, hath seen to that."

Whereto Hagen answered, "Ye will shortly be at one again. But Kriemhild, prithee tell me wherein I can serve thee with Siegfried, thy husband, and I will do it, for I love none better."

"I should fear naught for his life in battle, but that he is fool-hardy, and of too proud a courage. Save for that, he were safe enow."

Then said Hagen, "Lady, if thou fearest hurt for him in battle, tell me now by what device I may hinder it, and I will guard him afoot and on horse."

She answered, "Thou art my cousin, and I thine. To thy faith I commend my dear husband, and thou mayst watch and keep him."

Then she told him what she had better have left unsaid.

"My husband is stark and bold. When that he slew the dragon on the mountain, he bathed him in its blood; wherefore no weapon can pierce him. Nevertheless, when he rideth in battle, and spears fly from the hands of heroes, I tremble lest I lose him. Alack! for Siegfried's sake how oft have I been heavy of my cheer! And now, dear cousin, I will trust thee with the secret, and tell thee, that thou mayst prove thy faith, where my husband may be wounded. For that I know thee honourable, I do this. When the hot blood flowed from the wound of the dragon, and Siegfried bathed therein, there fell atween his shoulders the broad leaf of a lime tree. There one might stab him, and thence is my care and dole."

Then answered Hagen of Trony, "Sew, with thine own hand, a small sign upon his outer garment, that I may know where to defend him when we stand in battle."

She did it to profit the knight, and worked his doom thereby. She said, "I will sew secretly, with fine silk, a little cross upon his garment, and there, O knight, shalt thou guard to me my husband when ye ride in the thick of the strife, and he withstandeth his foemen in the fierce onset."

"That will I do, dear lady," answered Hagen.

Kriemhild thought to serve Siegfried; so was the hero betrayed.

Then Hagen took his leave and went forth glad; and his king bade him say what he had learned.

"If thou wouldst turn from the journey, let us go hunting instead; for I have learned the secret, and have him in my hand. Wilt thou contrive this?"

"That will I," said the king.

And the king's men rejoiced.

Never more, I ween, will knight do so foully as did Hagen, when he bade his faith with the queen.

The next morning Siegfried, with his thousand knights, rode merrily forth; for he thought to avenge his friends. And Hagen rode nigh him, and spied at his vesture. When he saw the mark, he sent forward two of his men secretly, to ride back to them with another message: that Ludger bade tell the king his land might remain at peace.

Loth was Siegfried to turn his rein or had he done battle for his friends. Gunther's vassals scare held him back. Then he rode to the king, that thanked him.

"Now, God reward thee, Siegfried, my kinsman, that thou didst grant my prayer so readily. Even so will I do by thee, and that justly. I hold thee trustiest of all my friends. Seeing we be quit of this war, let us ride a hunting to the Odenwald after the bear and the boar, as I have often done."

Hagen, the false man, had counselled this.

"Let it be told to my guests straightway that I will ride early. Whoso would hunt with me, let him be ready betimes. But if any would tarry behind for pastime with the women, he shall do it, and please me thereby."

Siegfried answered on courtly wise, "I will hunt with thee gladly, and will ride to the forest, if thou lend me a huntsman and some brachs."

"Will one suffice?" asked Gunther. "I will lend thee four that know the forest well, and the tracks of the game, that thou come not home empty-handed."

Then Siegfried rode to his wife.

Meanwhile Hagen had told the king how he would trap the hero. Let all men evermore avoid such foul treason. When the false man had contrived his death, they told all the others.

Giselher and Gernot were not hunting with the rest. I know not for what grudge they warned him not.

But they paid dear for it.

HOW SIEGFRIED WAS SLAIN

UNTHER and Hagen, the fierce warriors, went hunting with false intent in the forest, to chase the boar, the bear, and the wild bull, with their sharp spears. What fitter sport for brave men?

Siegfried rode with them in kingly pomp. They took with them good store of meats. By a cool stream he lost his life, as Brunhild, King Gunther's wife, had devised it.

But or he set out, and when the hunting-gear was laid ready on the sumpters that they were to take across the Rhine, he went to Kriemhild, that was right doleful of her cheer. He kissed his lady on the mouth.

"God grant I may see thee safe and well again, and thou me. Bide here merry among thy kinsfolk, for I must forth."

Then she thought on the secret she had betrayed to Hagen, but durst not tell him. The queen wept sore that ever she was born, and made measureless dole.

She said, "Go not hunting. Last night I dreamed an evil dream: how that two wild boars chased thee over the heath; and the flowers were red with blood. Have pity on my tears, for I fear some treachery. There be haply some offended, that pursue us with deadly hate. Go not, dear lord; in good faith I counsel it."

But he answered, "Dear love, I go but for a few days. I know not any that beareth me hate. Thy kinsmen will me well, nor have I deserved otherwise at their hand."

"Nay, Siegfried, I fear some mischance. Last night I dreamed an evil dream: how that two mountains fell on thee, and I saw thee no more. If thou goest, thou wilt grieve me bitterly."

But he caught his dear one in his arms and kissed her close; then he took leave of her and rode off.

She never saw him alive again.

They rode thence into a deep forest to seek sport. The king had many bold knights with him, and rich meats, that they had need of for the journey. Sumpters passed laden before them over the Rhine, carrying bread and wine, and flesh and fish, and meats of all sorts, as was fitting for a rich king.

The bold huntsmen encamped before the green wood where they were to hunt, on a broad meadow. Siegfried also was there, which was told to the king. And they set a watch round the camp.

Then said stark Siegfried, "Who will into the forest and lead us to the game?"

"If we part or we begin the chase in the wood," said Hagen, "we shall know which is the best sportsman. Let us divide the huntsmen and the hounds; then let each ride alone as him listeth, and he who hunteth the best shall be praised." So they started without more ado.

But Siegfried said, "One hound that hath been well trained for the chase will suffice for me. There will be sport enow!"

Then an old huntsman took a limehound, and brought the company where there was game in plenty. They hunted down all the beasts they started, as good sportsmen should.

Whatsoever the limehound started, the hero of the Netherland slew with his hand. His horse ran so swift that naught escaped him; he won greater praise than any in the chase. In all things he was right manly. The first that he smote to the death was a half-bred boar. Soon after, he encountered a grim lion, that the limehound started. This he shot with his bow and a sharp arrow;

the lion made only three springs or he fell. Loud was the praise of his comrades. Then he killed, one after the other, a buffalo, an elk, four stark ureoxen, and a grim shelk. His horse carried him so swiftly that nothing outran him. Deer and hind escaped him not.

The limehound tracked a wild boar next that began to flee. But Siegfried rode up and barred the path, whereat the monster ran at the knight. He slew him with his sword. Not so lightly had another done it.

They leashed their limehound then, and told the Burgundians how Siegfried had prospered. Whereupon his huntsman said, "Prithee, leave something alive; thou emptiest to us both mountain and forest." And Siegfried laughed.

The noise of the chase was all round them; hill and wood rang with shouting and the baying of dog, for the huntsmen had loosed twenty and four hounds. Many a beast perished that day, for each thought to win the prize of the chase. But when stark Siegfried rode to the tryst-fire, they saw that could not be.

The hunt was almost over. The sportsmen brought skins and game enow with them to the camp. No lack of meat for cooking was there, I ween.

Then the king bade tell the knights that he would dine. And they blew a blast on a horn, that told the king was at the tryst-fire.

Said one of Siegfried's huntsmen, "I heard the blast of a horn bidding us back to the camp. I will answer it." And they kept blowing to assemble the company.

Siegfried bade quit the wood. His horse bare him smoothly, and the others pricked fast behind. The noise roused a grim bear, whereat the knight cried tot hem that came after him, "Now for sport! Slip the dog, for I see a bear that shall with us to the tryst-fire. He cannot escape us, if he ran ever so fast."

They slipped the limehound; off rushed the bear. Siegfried thought to run him down, but he came to a ravine, and could not get to him; then the bear deemed him safe. But the proud knight sprang from his horse, and pursued him. The beast had no shelter. It could not escape from him, and was caught by his hand, and, or it could wound him, he had bound it, that it could neither scratch nor bite. Then he tied it to his saddle, and, when he had mounted up himself, he brought it to the tryst-fire for pastime.

How right proudly he rode to the camping ground! His boar-spear was mickle, stark and broad. His sword hung down to the spur, and his hunting-horn was of ruddy gold. Of better hunting-gear I never heard tell. His coat was black samite, and his hat was goodly sable. His quiver was richly laced, and covered with a panther's hide for the sake of the sweet smell. He bare, also, a bow that none could draw but himself, unless with a windlass. His cloak was a lynx-skin, pied from head to foot, and embroidered over with gold on both sides. Also Balmung had he done on, whereof the edges were so sharp that it clave every helmet it touched. I ween the huntsman was berry of his cheer. Yet, to tell you the whole, I must say how his rich quiver was filled with good arrows, gilt on the shaft, and broad a hand's breadth or more. Swift and sure was the death of him that he smote therewith.

So the knight rode proudly from the forest, and Gunther's men saw him coming, and ran and held his horse.

When he had alighted, he loosed the band from the paws and from the mouth of the bear that he had bound to his saddle.

So soon as they saw the bear, the dogs began to bark. The animal tried to win back to the wood, and all the folk fell in great fear. Affrighted by the noise, it ran through the kitchen. Nimbly started the scullions from their place by the fire. Pots were upset and the brands strewed over all. Alack! the good meats that tumbled into the ashes!

Then up sprang the princes and their men. The bear began to growl, and the king gave order to slip the hounds that were on leash. I'faith, it had been a merry day if it had ended so.

Hastily, with their bows and spears, the warriors, swift of foot, chased the bear, but there were so many dogs that none durst shoot among them, and the forest rang with the din. Then the bear fled before the dogs, and none could keep pace with him save Kriemhild's husband, that ran up to him and pierced him dead with his sword, and carried the carcase back with him to the fire. They that saw it said he was a mighty man.

Then they bade the sportsmen to the table, and they sat down, a goodly company enow, on a fair meadow. Ha! what dishes, meet for heroes, were set before them. But the cup-bearers were tardy, that should have brought the wine.

Save for that, knights were never better served. If there had not been false-hearted men among them, they had been without reproach. The doomed man had no suspicion that might have warned him, for his own heart was pure of all deceit. Many that his death profited not at all had to pay for it bitterly.

Then said Sir Siegfried, "I marvel, since they bring us so much from the kitchen, that they bring not the wine. If good hunters be entreated so, I will hunt no more. Certes, I have deserved better at your hands."

Whereto the king at the table answered falsely, "What lacketh to-day we will make good another time. The blame is Hagen's, that would have us perish of thirst."

Then said Hagen of Trony, "Dear master, Methought we were to hunt to-day at Spessart, and I sent the wine thither. For the present we must go thirsty; another time I will take better care."

But Siegfried cried, "Small thank to him. Seven sumpters with meat and spiced wines should he have sent here at the least, or, if that might not be, we should have gone nigher to the Rhine."

Hagen of Trony answered, "I know of a cool spring close at hand. Be not wroth with me, but take my counsel, and go thither."

The which was done, to the hurt of many warriors. Siegfried was sore athirst and bade push back the table, that he might go to the spring at the foot of the mountain. Falsely had the knights contrived it. The wild beasts that Siegfried's hand had slain they let pile on a waggon and take home, and they that saw it praised him.

Foully did Hagen break faith with Siegfried. He said, when they were starting for the broad lime tree, "I hear from all sides that none can keep pace with Kriemhild's husband when he runneth. Let us see now."

Bold Siegfried of the Netherland answered, "Thou mayst easily prove it, if thou wilt run with me to the brook for a wager. The praise shall be to him that winneth there first."

"Let us see then," said Hagen the knight.

And stark Siegfried answered, "If I lose, I will lay me at thy feet in the grass."

A glad man was King Gunther when he heard that!

Said Siegfried further, "Nay, I will undertake more. I will carry on me all that I wear - spear, shield, and hunting gear."

Whereupon he girded on his sword and his quiver in haste.

Then the others did off their clothes, till they stood in their white shirts, and they ran through the clover like two wild panthers; but bold Siegfried was seen there the first. Before all men he won the prize in everything.

He loosed his sword straightway, and laid down his quiver. His good spear he leaned against the lime tree; then the noble guest stood and waited, for his courtesy was great. He laid down his shield by the stream. Albeit he was sore athirst, he drank not till that the king had finished, who gave him evil thanks.

The stream was cool, pure, and good. Gunther bent down to the water, and rose again when he had drunk. Siegfried had gladly done the like, but he suffered for his courtesy. Hagen carried his bow and his sword out of his reach, and sprang back and gripped the spear. Then he spied for the secret mark on his vesture; and while Siegfried drank from the stream, Hagen stabbed him where the cross was, that his heart's blood spurted out on the traitor's clothes.

Never since hath knight done so wickedly. He left the spear sticking deep in his heart, and fled in grimmer haste than ever he had done from any man on this earth afore.

When Siegfried felt the deep wound, he sprang up maddened from the water, for the long boar spear stuck out from his heart. He thought to find bow or sword; if he had, Hagen had got his due. But the sore-wounded man saw no sword, and had nothing save his shield. He picked it up from the water's edge and ran at Hagen. King Gunther's man could not escape him.

For all that he was wounded to the death, he smote so mightily that the shield well-nigh brake, and the precious stones flew out. The noble guest had fain taken vengeance.

Hagen fell beneath his stroke. The meadow rang loud with the noise of the blow. If he had had his sword to hand, Hagen had been a dead man.

But the anguish of his wound constrained him. His colour was wan; he could not stand upright; and the strength of his body failed him, for he bare death's mark on his white cheek. Fair women enow made dole for him.

Then Kriemhild's husband fell among the flowers. The blood flowed fast from his wound, and in his great anguish he began to upbraid them that had falsely contrived his death.

"False cowards!" cried the dying knight. "What availeth all my service to you, since ye have slain me? I was true to you, and pay the price for it. Ye have done ill by your friends. Cursed by this deed are your sons yet unborn. Ye have avenged your spite on my body all too bitterly. For your crime ye shall be shunned by good knights."

All the warriors ran where he lay stabbed. To many among them it was a woeful day. They that were true mourned for him, the which the hero had well deserved of all men.

The King of Burgundy, also, wept for his death, but the dying man said, "He needeth not to weep for the evil, by whom the evil cometh. Better had he left it undone, for mickle is his blame."

Then said grim Hagen, "I know not what ye rue. All is ended for us - care and trouble. Few are they now that will withstand us. Glad am I that, through me, his might is fallen."

"Lightly mayst thou boast now," said Siegfried; "if I had known thy murderous hate, it had been an easy thing to guard my body from thee. My bitterest dole is for Kriemhild, my wife. God pity me that ever I had a son. For all men will reproach him that he hath murderers to his kinsmen. I would grieve for that, had I the time."

He said to the king, "Never in this world was so foul a murder as thou hast done on me. In thy sore need I saved thy life and thine honour. Dear have I paid for that I did well by thee." With a groan the wounded man said further, "Yet if thou canst show truth to any on this earth, O King, show it to my dear wife, that I commend to thee. Let it advantage her to be thy sister. By all princely honour stand by her. Long must my father and my knights wait for my coming. Never hath woman won such woe through a dear one."

He writhed in his bitter anguish, and spake painfully, "Ye shall rue this foul deed in the days to come. Know this of a truth, that in slaying me ye have slain yourselves."

The flowers were all wet with blood. He strove with death, but not for long, for the weapon of death cut too deep. And the bold knight and good spake no more.

When the warriors saw that the hero was dead, the laid him on a shield of ruddy gold, and took counsel how they should conceal that Hagen had done it. Many of them said, "Evil hath befallen us. Ye shall all hide it, and hold to one tale--when Kriemhild's husband was riding alone in the forest, robbers slew him."

But Hagen of Trony said, "I will take him back to Burgundy. If she that hath troubled Brunhild know it, I care not. It concerneth me little if she weep."

Of that very brook where Siegfried was slain ye shall hear the truth from me. In the Odenwald is a village that hight Odenheim, and there the stream runneth still; beyond doubt it is the same.

Siegfried Is Stabbed By Hagen

SEVENTEENTH ADVENTURE
ḢOW ṢIEGFRIED WAṢ MOURNED AND BURIED

THEY tarried there that night, and then crossed the Rhine. Heroes never went to so woeful a hunt. For one thing that they slew, many women wept, and many a good knight's body paid for it. Of overweening pride ye shall hear now, and grim vengeance.

Hagen bade them bear dead Siegfried of the Nibelung land before the chamber where Kriemhild was, and charged them to lay him secretly outside the door, that she might find him there when she went forth to mass or it was day, the which she was wont to do.

The minster bell was rung as the custom was. Fair Kriemhild waked her maidens, and bade them bring her a light and her vesture.

Then a chamberlain came and found Siegfried. He saw him red with blood, and his garment all wet, but he knew not yet that he was his king. He carried the light into the room in his hand, and from him Kriemhild heard evil tidings.

When she would have gone with her women to the minster, the chamberlain said, "Lady, stop! A murdered knight lieth on the threshold."

"Woe is me!" cried Kriemhild. "What meanest thou by such news?"

Or she knew for certain that it was her husband, she began to think on Hagen's question, how he might guard him. From that moment her dole began; for, with his death, she took leave of all joy. She sank on the floor speechless; they saw the miserable woman lying there. Kriemhild's woe was great beyond measure, and after her swoon she cried out, that all the chamber rang.

Then said her attendants, "What if it be a stranger?"

But the blood burst from her mouth by reason of her heart's anguish, and she said, "Nay, it is Siegfried, my dear husband. Brunhild hath counselled it, and Hagen hath done it."

The lady bade them show her where the hero lay. She lifted his beautiful head with her white hands. Albeit he was red with blood, she knew him straightway. Pitifully the hero of the Netherland lay there.

The gentle, good queen wailed in anguish, "Woe is me for this wrong! Thy shield is unpierced by swords. Thou liest murdered. If I knew who had done this deed, I would not rest until he was dead."

All her attendants wailed and cried with their dear mistress, for they were woe for their noble master that they had lost. Foully had Hagen avenged Brunhild's anger.

The sorrowful one said, "Go and wake Siegfried's men quickly; and tell Siegmund also my dole, that he may help me to mourn for brave Siegfried."

Then a messenger ran in haste where Siegfried's heroes of the Nibelung land lay, and took from them their joy with heavy tidings. They believed it not, till they heard the wailing.

The messenger also came quickly where the king was. Siegmund slept not. I ween his heart told him what had happened, and that he would see his dear son never more.

"Arouse thee, Sir Siegmund! Kriemhild, my lady, hath sent me. For a wrong hath been done her, that lieth heavier on her heart than any other hath done. Thou shalt help her to mourn, for it is thy sorrow also."

Up rose Sir Siegmund then, and said, "What is fair Kriemhild's grief, whereof thou tallest me?"

The messenger answered, weeping, "She mourneth with cause. Bold Siegfried of the Netherland is slain."

But Siegmund said, "Jest not with these evil tidings of my son, and say to none that he is slain; for never to my life's end could I mourn him enow."

"If thou believest not what I tell thee, hearken thyself to Kriemhild, how she maketh dole for Siegfried's death with all her maidens."

Then Siegmund feared and was sore affrighted. With an hundred of his men he sprang out of his bed; they grasped their long swords and keen, with their hands, and ran sorrowfully where they heard the sound of weeping.

They thought not on their vesture till they were there, for they had lost their wits through grief. Mickle woe was buried in their hearts.

Then came Siegmund to Queen Kriemhild, and said, "Woe is me for our journey hither! Who, among such good friends, hath murderously robbed me of my child, and thee of thy husband?"

"If I knew that," answered the noble woman, "I were ever his foe with heart and soul. Trust me, I would so contrive his hurt that all his friends, by reason of me, would yet weep for sorrow."

Siegmund took the prince in his arms; the grief of his friends was so great that, with their loud wailing and their weeping, palace and hall and the town of Worms rang again.

None could comfort Siegfried's wife. They took the clothes off his beautiful body, and washed his wounds and laid him on a bier, and all his folk were heavy with great grief.

Then spake his knights of the Netherland, "Our hands are ready for vengeance. He that hath done it is in this house."

Siegfried's men armed them in haste; the valiant knights assembled to the number of eleven hundred. These had Siegmund, the mighty king, for his following; and, as his honour bade him, he had gladly avenged the death of his son. They knew not whom they should fall on, if it were not Gunther and his men, with whom Siegfried had gone hunting.

But when Kriemhild saw them armed, she was greatly grieved. For all her dole and her pain, she so feared the death of the Nibelungs at the hand of her brother's men that she forbade their vengeance, and warned them in love, as friend doth with dear friend.

The sorrowful queen said, "My lord, Siegmund, what wouldst thou do? Surely thou knowest not how many bold knights Gunther has. If ye come to grips with them, ye must certainly perish."

They stood eager for strife with their shields dressed, but the queen begged and commanded them to forbear; that they would not, grieved her sore.

She said, "My lord Siegmund, let be, till more fitting season, and I will help thee to avenge my husband. Verily, I will show him that took him from me that he hath done it to his hurt. Here by the Rhine there are so many overweening men that I would have thee, for the present, forbear from battle; for thy one man they have at least the thirty. God do to them as they have done to us. Tarry here, brave knights, and mourn with me till it is day, and help me to lay my dear husband in his coffin."

The warriors answered, "Dear lady, be it so."

None might tell to the end the wailing that arose there from knights and women. It was so loud that they in the town heard it, and the noble burghers hasted thither, and mourned with the guests, for they were right sorrowful. They knew no fault in Siegfried for which he had lost his life, and the good burgesses' wives wept with the women of the court.

They bade the smiths go and make a coffin of silver and of gold, mickle and stark, and brace it strongly with good steel. Right heavy of their cheer were all the folk.

The night was ended. They told them it was day, and the queen gave order to bear the dead knight, her dear husband, to the minster; and all the friends he had there followed weeping.

When they came to the minster, how many a bell rang out! On all sides they sang requiems. Thither came King Gunther with his men, and also grim Hagen, that had better stayed away.

Gunther said, "Dear sister, woe is me for this grief of thine, and that this great misadventure hath befallen us. We must ever mourn Siegfried's death."

"Ye do wrongly," said the wailing queen. "If it grieved thee, it had never happened. I was clean forgotten by thee when thou didst part me from my dear husband. Would to God thou hadst done it to me instead!"

But they held to their lie, and Kriemhild went on. "Let him that is guiltless prove it. Let him go up to the bier before all the folk, and soon we shall know the truth."

It is a great marvel, and ofttimes seen even now, how that, when the murderer standeth by the dead, the wounds bleed again. And so it fell then, and Hagen's guilt was plain to all.

The wounds burst open and bled as they had done afore; and they that had wept already wept now much more. King Gunther said, "Hear the truth. He was slain by robbers. Hagen did it not."

"These robbers," she answered, "I know well. God grant that his kinsmen's hands may avenge it. By you, Gunther and Hagen, was it done."

Siegfried's knights had fain fallen on them, but Kriemhild said, "Help me to bear my woe."

Gernot her brother, and Giselher the youth, both came and found Siegfried dead; they mourned for him truly, and their eyes were blind with tears. They wept for Kriemhild's husband from their hearts.

It was time to sing mass, and men and women flocked from all quarters. Even they that missed him little mourned with all the rest.

Gernot and Giselher said, "Comfort thee, sister, for the dead, for so it must needs be now. We will make it good to thee while we live." But comfort her could none.

His coffin was ready by the middle of the day, and they lifted the dead man from the bier whereupon he lay, but the queen would not let them bury him yet. All his folk must first toil sore.

They wound him in a rich cloth. Not one, I ween, was there that wept not. Uta, the noble queen and all her women wailed bitterly for Siegfried.

When the folk heard they sang the requiem, and that Siegfried was in his chest, they crowded thither, and brought offerings for his soul. Amidst of his enemies, he had good friends enow.

Then poor Kriemhild said to her chamberlain, "For my sake, stint not thy labour. For Siegfried's soul, divide his wealth among them that were well minded to him, and are true to me."

The smallest child, if he understood all, must go with its offering or he was buried. They sang at the least an hundred masses a day. And great was the press among Siegfried's friends.

When they had done singing, the folk rose and departed; but Kriemhild said, "Leave me not alone to watch the valiant knight. With his body lieth all my joy. Three days and three nights will I keep him here, till that I have had my fill of my dear husband. What if God let death take me too? So the sorrow of poor Kriemhild were ended."

The townsfolk went home; and priests, and monks, and all them that had served Siegfried, she bade tarry. Heavy were their nights and toilsome their days. Many a man neither ate nor drank, but they that desired it were bidden take their fill. Siegmund saw to that.

No easy time had the Nibelungs. They say that all that could sing got no rest. What offerings were brought! The poorest was rich enow, for they that had naught were bidden bring an offering from the gold of Siegfried's own hoard. When he lived no more, they gave many thousand marks for his soul. Kriemhild bestowed lands and revenues over all, on cloisters and holy men. Silver and clothes in plenty they gave to the poor. She showed plain the love she bare Siegfried.

On the third morning, when mass was due, the great church-yard by the minster was full of weeping countryfolk; for they served him in death as dear friends should.

They say that, in these four days, thirty thousand marks, or more, were given to the poor for his soul's sake, when his beauty and life were brought to nothing.

God had been served; the song was done. The folk were shaken with weeping. They bade carry him from the minster to the grave, and naught was heard but crying and mourning.

With loud wail the people followed after. None was joyful, neither woman nor man. They sang and read or they buried him. Ah, what good priests were at his funeral!

Or Siegfried's wife came to the grave, her faithful body was wrung with such grief that they ceased not from sprinkling her with water. None could measure her sorrow. It was a wonder that she lived.

Her weeping women helped her.

Then said the queen, "Ye men of Siegfried, as ye love me, do me this grace. Give me, in my sorrow, this little joy: to see his dear head once more." She begged this so long, and with such bitter weeping, that they brake open the rich chest.

Then they bought the queen where he was. She lifted his lovely head with her white hand, and kissed him. Her bright eyes, for grief, wept blood. It was a pitiful parting.

Then they carried her thence, for she could not walk. And she lay in a swoon, as her fair body would have perished for sorrow.

When the noble knight was buried, they that were come with him from the land of the Nibelungs made measureless dole. Little joy was seen in Siegmund. For three whole days some neither ate nor drank for woe. Longer than that their bodies endured it not. And so they ate and got well of their grief, as many a one doth still.

Kriemhild lay senseless in a swoon all that day and that night, till the next morning; she knew nothing that they said. And in like case lay also King Siegmund. Scarce got the knight his wits again, for his strength was weakened by reason of his great dole.

It was no wonder.

Then his men said, "Sir knight, let us home. We may not tarry longer here."

The Burial Of Siegfried

HOW SIEGMUND RETURNED HOME

RIEMHILD'S father-in-law went to her and said, "Let us hoe to our land. I ween we are unwelcome guests by the Rhine. Kriemhild, dear lady, return to my country with me. That treason has bereft thee here of thy dear husband shall not be avenged on thee. I will stand by thee truly, for love of thy husband and his noble child.

Thou shalt also have all the power that Siegfried, the valiant knight, gave thee. The land and the crown are thine, and all Siegfried's men shall serve thee gladly."

They told the squires they would away. There was hurrying for the horses, for life was a burden to them among their stark foemen. Women and maidens were bidden seek out their clothes.

But when King Siegmund would have set out, Kriemhild's mother began to beg that she would remain among her kinsfolk.

The wretched queen said, "That could hardly be. How could I have ever before mine eyes him that hath brought this woe upon me, miserable woman that I am?"

Giselher the youth said, "Dear sister mine, thy duty is here by thy mother. Thou need'st no service from them that have wounded and darkened thy spirit, for thou shalt live at my sole charge."

But she answered the knight, "It cannot be; I must die of grief but to look on Hagen."

"Nay, I counsel thee, dear sister, to stay by thy brother Giselher; and I will make good to thee thy husband's death."

But the God-forsaken one answered, "Need enow hath Kriemhild of comfort."

While the youth besought her so kindly, Uta and Gernot began to pray her, and her faithful kinsmen also, that she should tarry, for she had few kinsmen among Siegfried's men.

"They are all strangers to thee," said Gernot, "and however strong a friend may be, one day he must die. Consider it, dear sister, and take comfort and stay here by thy kinsfolk. It were better for thee."

So she promised Giselher she would remain there.

The horses were led out for Siegmund's men, for they were ready to ride back to the land of the Nibelungs; and their harness was laid on the sumpters.

Then went Siegmund to Kriemhild, and said to her, "Siegfried's men wait by their horses. Let us away, for it irketh me here by the Burgundians."

Kriemhild answered, "They that are faithful among my kinsfolk counsel me to abide here with them. I have no kinsmen in the Nibelung land."

Siegmund was woeful when he heard this from Kriemhild, and he said, "Let none tell thee that. Before all my kinsmen shalt thou wear the crown, and have dominion as aforetime; no man shall avenge on thee the loss of the hero. Come with us for thy little child's sake. Leave it not an orphan. When thy son is grown to a man he shall comfort thee; and meanwhile many a bold knight and good shall serve thee."

But she answered, "My lord Siegmund, I cannot go. Whatso come of it, I must tarry here with my kinsfolk, who will help me to mourn."

The warriors liked not the news, and they said with one accord, "Then might we bewail our wrong indeed, if thou shouldst abide here by our foemen. Heroes never rode to a sorrier hightide."

"Depart without fear, and in God's keeping. I will see that ye come well escorted to your land. I commend my dear child to your care."

When they saw plain that she would not go, Siegmund's men all fell to weeping.

How right piteously Siegmund parted from Kriemhild! His grief was bitter, and he said, "Woe is me for this hightide! Never yet hath such evil befallen a king and his men at a feast. They shall see us no more in Burgundy."

Siegfried's men said openly, "Nay, we might well ride hither again if we knew who had murdered our master. Among his kinsmen they have stark foes enow."

Siegmund kissed Kriemhild, and spake dolefully when he saw she would tarry, "We fare home joyless to our land. Now, for the first time, I know all my sorrows."

They rode, without an escort, from Worms across the Rhine. Well might the Nibelungs fear nothing from the assault of foemen, with their own strong hand to guard them.

They took leave of none; but Gernot and Giselher went to them lovingly, for they grieved for their loss, and told them so.

Gernot said courteously, "God in Heaven knoweth that I had no blame in Siegfried's death; neither was it told me, that any here bare him malice. With true heart I sorrow for him."

Giselher the youth gave them good escort. He brought the king and his knights home to the Netherland without further mischance.

How it fared with them after, I cannot tell. But Kriemhild was ever heard mourning, and none comforted her save Giselher - he was true and good.

Fair Brunhild sat misproud, and recked little how Kriemhild wept. She was never kind to her again. Also to her, afterward, Kriemhild caused bitter heart's dole.

HOW THE NIBELUNG HOARD CAME TO WORMS

HEN noble Kriemhild was widowed, Count Eckewart stayed by her in Burgundy with his men, as honour bade him, and served his mistress with goodwill till his death.

At Worms, by the minster, they gave her a room, wide and high, rich and spacious, where she sat joyless with her attendants. To church she went often and gladly. Since her dear one was buried, how seldom she failed there! She went thither sorrowfully every day, and prayed to great God for his soul. Faithfully and without stint the knight was mourned.

Uta and her women ceased not to comfort her. But her heart was wounded so deep that she could not be cheered. She sorrowed for Siegfried more than wife ever did for husband. Her great love appeared therein, and she mourned him to the end, while her life endured. Strong and true she took vengeance at the last.

So she remained (I say sooth) till the fourth year after her husband's death, and had spoken no word to Gunther, nor once, in the whole of that time, had looked on Hagen, her foe.

Then said Hagen of Trony, "Couldst thou contrive that thy sister took thee to friend again? So would the Nibelung gold come into this land. Thou mightest win much thereof for thyself, if the queen were appeased."

"We will try it," answered the king. "I will send my brothers thither, that haply they may prevail upon her to do it gladly."

But Hagen said, "I doubt that will never be."

Gunther sent Ortwin and the Margrave Gary to the court. When that was done, they brought Gernot, and Giselher the youth. And on friendly wise they essayed it with Kriemhild.

Bold Gernot of Burgundy said, "Lady, thou mournest Siegfried's death too long. The king will prove to thee that it was not he that slew him. Evermore thou art heard wailing bitterly."

She said, "No one blameth the king. Hagen's hand slew him, and from me he discovered where he should stab. How could I know he hated him? Good care had I taken then not to betray his beautiful body, and had not needed now to weep, wretched woman that I am. I will never be the friend of them that did it."

Then began Giselher, the valiant man, to entreat her.

She said, "Ye give me no peace. I must greet him, but great is your blame therein, for without fault of mine the king hath brought on me bitter heart's dole. With my mouth I may pardon him, but with my heart, never."

"After this it will be better," thought her friends. "What if he so entreat her that she grow glad again?"

"He may yet make it good to her," said Gernot, the warrior.

And the sorrowful woman said, "See, I will do as ye desire; I will greet the king."

When they told him that, the king went with his best friends to her. But Hagen durst not come before her. Well he knew his guilt, and that he had done her a wrong.

Since she had hid her hate to him, Gunther deemed it well to kiss her. If he had not wrought her such woe, he might have gone often and boldly into her presence.

Friends were never reconciled with so many tears, for her wrongs weighed heavy on her heart. She forgave them all, save the one man, for none but Hagen had slain him.

Soon after, they contrived that Kriemhild won the great hoard from the land of the Nibelungs, and brought it to the Rhine. It was her marriage-morning gift, and rightly hers. Giselher and Gernot went for it. Kriemhild sent eighty hundred men to fetch it from where it lay hid, and where Albric with his nearest kinsmen guarded it.

When they saw the men of the Rhine come for the treasure, bold Albric spake to his friends, "We dare not refuse her the treasure, for it is the noble queen's wedding gift. Yet we had never parted with it, if we had not lost with Siegfried the good *Tarnkappe*. At all times it was worn by fair Kriemhild's husband. A woeful thing hath it proved for Siegfried that he took from us the *Tarnkappe*, and won all this land to his service."

Then the chamberlain went and got the keys. Kriemhild's men and some of her kinsmen stood before the mountain. They carried the hoard to the sea, on to the ships, and bare it across the eaves from the mountain to the Rhine.

Now hear the marvels of this treasure. Twelve wagons scarce carried it thence in four days and four nights, albeit each of them made the journey three times. It was all precious stones and gold, and had the whole world been bought therewith, there had not been one coin the less.

Certes, Hagen did not covet it without cause.

The wishing-rod lay among it, the which, if any discovered it, made him master over every man in all the world.

Many of Albric's kinsmen went with Gernot. When Gernot and Giselher the youth got possession of the hoard, there came into their power lands, and castles, also, and many a good warrior, that served them through fear of their might.

When the hoard came into Gunther's land, and the queen got it in her keeping, chambers and towers were filled full therewith. One never heard tell of so marvelous a treasure. But if it had been a thousand times more, but to have Siegfried alive again, Kriemhild had gladly stood bare by his side. Never had hero truer wife.

Now that she had the hoard, it brought into the land many stranger knights; for the lady's hand gave more freely than any had ever seen. She was kind and good; that must one say of her.

To poor and rich she began to give, till Hagen said that if she lived but a while longer, she would win so many knights to her service that it must go hard with the others.

But King Gunther said, "It is her own. It concerneth me not how she useth it. Scarcely did I win her pardon. And now I ask not how she divideth her jewels and her red gold."

But Hagen said to the king, "A wise man would leave such a treasure to no woman. By reason of her largess, a day will come that the bold Burgundians may rue."

Then King Gunther said, "I sware an oath to her that I would do her no more hurt, nor will I do it. She is my sister."

But Hagen said, "Let me be the guilty one."

And so they brake their oath and took from the widow her rich hoard. Hagen got hold of all the keys.

Gernot was wroth when he heard thereof, and Giselher said, "Hagen hath greatly wronged Kriemhild. I should have withstood him. Were he not my kinsman, he should answer for it with his life."

Then Siegfried's wife began to weep anew.

And Gernot said, "Sooner than be troubled with this gold, let us sink it in the Rhine. Then it were no man's."

She went wailing to Giselher, and said, "Dear brother, forsake me not, but be my kind and good steward."

He answered her, "I will, when we win home again. For the present we ride on a journey."

The king and his kinsmen left the land. He took the best he had with him. Only Hagen tarried behind through the hate he bare Kriemhild, and that he might work her ill.

Or the great king came back, Hagen had seized all the treasure and sunk it in the Rhine at Lochheim. He thought to profit thereby, but did not.

Or Hagen hid the treasure, they had sworn a mighty oath that it should remain a secret so long as they lived. Neither could they take it themselves nor give it to another.

The princes returned, and with them many knights. Thereupon Kriemhild, with her women and her maidens, began to bewail her wrong bitterly. She was right woeful.

And the knights made as to slay Hagen, and said with one accord, "He hath done evilly." So he fled from before their anger till they took him in favour again. They let him live, but Kriemhild hated him with deadly hate.

Her heart was heavy with new grief for her husband's murder, and that they had stolen her treasure, and till her last day she ceased not to wail.

After Siegfried's death (I say sooth) she mourned till the thirteenth year, nor could she forget the hero. She was ever true to him, and for this folk have praised her.

Uta founded a rich abbey with her wealth after Dankrat's death, and endowed it with great revenue, the which it draweth still. It is the Abbey of Lorsch, renowned to this day. Kriemhild also gave no little part thereto, for Siegfried's soul, and for the souls of all the dead. She gave gold and precious stones with willing hand. Seldom have we known a truer wife.

After that Kriemhild forgave Gunther, and yet, through his fault, lost her great treasure, her heart's dole was a thousand times worse than afore, and she was fain to be gone. A rich palace was built for Uta fast by the cloister of Lorsch. She left her children and went thither, and there she lieth still, buried in her coffin.

Then said the queen, "Dearest daughter mine, since thou canst not tarry here, dwell with me in my house at Lorsch, and cease from weeping."

But Kriemhild answered, "To whom then should I leave my husband?"

"Leave him here," said Uta.

"God in Heaven forbid!" said the good wife. "That could I never do, dearest mother; he must go with me."

The sorrowful one had his body taken up, and his noble bones were buried again at Lorsch beside the minster with great honour; and there the bold hero lieth in a long coffin.

But when Kriemhild would have journeyed thither with her mother, the which she was fain to do, she was forced to tarry, by reason of news that came from far beyond the Rhine.

BOOK II
TWENTIETH ADVENTURE
HOW KING ETZEL SENT TO BURGUNDY FOR KRIEMHILD

IT was in the days when Queen Helca died, and King Etzel wooed other women, that his friends commended to him a proud widow in the land of Burgundy, that hight Queen Kriemhild.

Seeing fair Helca was dead, they said, "If thou wouldst win a noble wife, the highest and the best that ever a king won, take this woman. Stark Siegfried was her husband."

The great king answered, "How could that be, since I am a heathen, and have not received baptism? The woman is a Christian - she will not consent. It were a wonder, truly, if it came to pass."

But the good knights said, "What if she do it gladly, for thy high name's sake, and thy great possessions? One can ask her at the least; she were a fitting and comely mate for thee."

Then the noble king answered, "Which among ye knoweth the folk by the Rhine, and their land?"

Said good Rudeger of Bechlaren, "From a child I have known the high and noble kings, Gunther and Gernot, good knights both. The third hight Giselher; each of these doeth whatso goeth best with honour and virtue. The like did their fathers."

But Etzel said, "Friend, tell me now, is she meet to wear the crown in my land? If her body be so fair as they say, my best friends shall never rue it."

"She resembleth great Helca, my mistress, for beauty. No king's wife in the world could be fairer. Whom she taketh to friend may well be comforted!"

He said, "Then woo her, Rudeger, in my name and for my sake. And come I ever to wed Kriemhild, I will reward thee as I best can. Thereto, thou wilt have done my will faithfully. From my store I will bid them give thee what thou requirest of horses and apparel, that thou and thy fellows may live merrily. They shall give thee therefrom without stint for thine embassy."

Rudeger, the rich Margrave, answered, "I were much to blame if I took from thy store. I will gladly ride, an envoy to the Rhine, at mine own cost, and with what I have received from thy hand."

Then the rich king said, "When thinkest thou to set out for the fair one? God guard thine honour by the way, and also my wife, if kind fortune help us to her favour."

Said Rudeger, "Or we quit this land, we must let fashion weapons and apparel, that we may win worship when we come before the princes. I will lead to the Rhine five hundred valiant men, that when they see me and mine at Burgundy, they may say that never king sent so many men so far as thou hast sent to us, to the Rhine. And know, great king, if thou art set on this, that she belonged to Siegfried, a right goodly man, the son of Siegmund. Thou hast seen him here. Soothly, much worship might be said of him."

King Etzel answered, "If she was that knight's wife, the noble prince was of so high renown, that I may not scorn his queen. By reason of her great beauty she pleaseth me well."

Then the Margrave said, "I promise thee that we will ride hence in four and twenty days. I will send word to Gotelind, my dear wife, that I, myself, go as envoy to Kriemhild."

So Rudeger sent messengers to Bechlaren to his wife, the highborn Margravine, and told her that he would go wooing for the king.

The Margravine still thought lovingly on good Helca, and when she heard the message, she was one part sorry, and began to weep, lest she might not win such a mistress as afore. When she thought on Helca she was heavy of her cheer.

Rudeger rode out of Hungary in seven days, whereat King Etzel rejoiced. They made ready his equipment at the town of Vienna, and he delayed his journey no longer.

Gotelind awaited him at Bechlaren, and the young Margravine, Rudeger's daughter, saw her father and his men gladly. They got a fair greeting from beautiful women.

Or noble Rudeger rode to Bechlaren from the town of Vienna, the clothes, whereof there were enow, came on the sumpters. So strong they rode, that little was stolen from them by the way.

When they were come into the town of Bechlaren, the host bade lodge his comrades, and give them good quarters. Wealthy Gotelind rejoiced to see her husband, the like did also his dear daughter, the young Margravine, that was as merry as could be at his coming. Right gladly she saw the heroes from Hungary.

The noble maiden said, with laughing mouth, "Ye be very welcome, my father and his men."

And the good knights were not slow to thank her.

Well Gotelind knew the mind of Rudeger. When she lay by him at night, she asked him sweetly whither the king of the Huns had sent him.

He answered, "I will tell thee gladly, my wife Gotelind. I go to woo a wife for my master, now that fair Helca is dead. I go to Kriemhild, on the Rhine, that shall become a great queen here among the Huns."

"God grant it fall so, for much good have we heard of her. Haply she will make up to us for our mistress of aforetime. We might well rejoice to have her wear the crown here."

Said the Margrave, "To them that ride with me to the Rhine, thou shalt give graciously of thy goods, dear wife. When heroes go richly attired, they be of high courage."

She answered, "There is none, if he will take it, but shall have what suiteth him well, or thou and thy men depart."

And the Margrave said, "Thou wilt please me well thereby."

Ha! what rich stuffs they took from their chambers! They hasted and provided the noble warriors with vesture enow from neck to spur. What pleased him the beast, Rudeger chose for himself.

On the seventh morning the host rode from Bechlaren with his knights. They took a goodly store of weapons and raiment through Bavaria, and were seldom fallen upon by robbers on the way.

Within twelve days they came to the Rhine. The news was not slow to spread. They told the king and his men that stranger guests had arrived. Then the king began to ask that, if any knew them, he might declare it. They perceived that their sumpters were heavy laden, and saw that they were rich; and they gave them lodging in the wide city straightway.

When the stranger were arrived, the folk spied at them curiously. They wondered whence they had journeyed to the Rhine.

The king asked Hagen who the knights were, and the hero of Trony answered, "I have not seen them aright. When we meet them, I will tell thee whence they have ridden into this land. They be strangers indeed if I know them not straightway."

The guests had been to their lodging. The envoy and his train were richly arrayed. Their clothes were good, and cunningly fashioned; and they rode to the court.

Then said bold Hagen, "So far as I know, for it is long since I saw the knights, they ride like the men of Rudeger, a bold warrior from the land of the Huns."

"How could I believe," said the king, "that he of Bechlaren should come into this land?" King Gunther had scarcely made an end of speaking, when bold Hagen saw the good Rudeger.

He and all his friends ran to him. Five hundred knights sprang from their horses. The Huns were well received; never were envoys so richly clad.

Then cried Hagen of Trony, "Welcome, in God's name, is this knight, the prince of Bechlaren, and all his men."

Worshipful greeting got the Huns. The nearest of kin to the king pressed forward, and Ortwin of Metz said to Rudeger, "We have not, for long, seen guests so gladly. I speak the truth."

They thanked the heroes for their welcome. Then they went with the warriors into the hall, where they found the king amidst of many bold men.

Gunther rose from his seat out of courtesy. On what friendly wise he went toward the envoys! He and Gernot hasted to meet the guests and his men, as beseemed them, and Gunther took Rudeger by the hand. He led him to the highseat where he sat himself, and bade his men set before the strangers goodly meats, and the best wine that was to be found in all the land round about the Rhine; the which was done gladly.

Giselher and Gary, Dankwart and Folker, came in, for they had heard of the worthy guests. They rejoiced to see them, and welcomed, in the presence of the king, the noble knights and good.

Then said Hagen of Trony to his master, "Thy knights are greatly beholden for what the Margrave hath done for our sake. The husband of fair Gotelind should be well requited."

King Gunther said, "I pray thee tell me, for I would know, how it standeth with Etzel and Helca in the land of the Huns."

The Margrave answered, "I will tell thee gladly."

Then he rose from his seat with all his men, and said to the king, "Give me leave to deliver the message that King Etzel hath sent me with, here to Burgundy."

Gunther answered, "I will hear the message wherewith thou art charged, without taking counsel with my friends. Speak it before me and my men, for with all honour shall thy suit be heard."

Then said the faithful envoy, "My great lord commendeth his true service to thee at the Rhine, and to all the friends thou hast. This he doth with true heart. The noble king biddeth thee mourn for his loss. His people are joyless, for my mistress, great Helca, my lord's wife, is dead; whereby many high-born maidens, children of great princes, that she hath reared, are orphaned. By reason thereof the land is full of sorrow, for these, alack! have none now to care for them. The king also ceaseth not to make dole."

"Now God requite him," said Gunther, "that he commendeth his service so fair to me and to my men. I have hearkened gladly to his greeting. My kinsmen and my liegemen will repay him."

Then said Gernot of Burgundy, "The world may well rue beautiful Helca's death, for the sake of her many virtues."

Hagen and many another knight said the same.

But Rudeger, the noble envoy, went on: "If thou allow it, O king, I will tell thee further what my dear master hath charged me with. Dolefully hath he lived since Helca's death. And it hath been told him that Kriemhild is without a husband, for that Siegfried is dead. If that be so, and thou grant it, she shall wear the crown before Etzel's knights. This hath my lord bidden me say."

Then the great king spoke courteously, "If she be willing, she followeth my desire therein. In three days I will let thee know. If she say not nay to Etzel, wherefore should I?"

Meanwhile they gave the guests good lodging. On such wise were the entreated that Rudeger was fain to confess he had friends among Gunther's men. Hagen served him gladly, the which Rudeger had done to Hagen aforetime.

So Rudeger tarried there till the third day. The king did prudently, and called a counsel, to ask his friends whether it seemed good to them that Kriemhild should take King Etzel to husband.

And they all counselled it save Hagen, that said to Gunther, the bold knight, "If thou be wise, thou wilt see to it that she do it not, even if she desire it."

"Why should I hinder it?" said Gunther. "If any good fall to the queen, I may well grant it. She is my sister. If it be to her honour, we ourselves should seek the alliance."

But Hagen answered, "Say not so. Didst thou know Etzel as I do, thou wouldst see that thou, first of all, must suffer if she wedded him as thou consellest."

"How so?" answered Gunther. "Were she his wife, I need not come so nigh him that I must feel his hate."

But Hagen said, "I will never approve it."

They summoned Gernot and Giselher, and asked whether it seemed good to them that Kriemhild should take the great king. And none save Hagen was against it.

Then said Giselher, the knight of Burgundy, "Do fairly by her for once, friend Hagen. Make good to her the hurt thou hast done her. Let her prosper without grudging it. Thou hast caused her much sorrow, and well might she hate thee. Never was woman bereft by any man of more joy."

"Trow me, I know that well. And were she to take Etzel, and to live long enow, she would do us all the hurt she could. She will have many valiant men to serve her."

But bold Gernot answered Hagen, "Belike we shall never come into Etzel's land till they both be dead. Let us do truly by her, and it will be to our honour."

Said Hagen, "None need tell me that. If Kriemhild wear Helca's crown, she will do us all the hurt she can. Let the thing alone; it were better for you knights."

Then Giselher, fair Uta's son, spake angrily, "We will not all do basely. If aught good befall her, we shall be glad. For all thou canst say, Hagen, I will serve her truly."

When Hagen heard that, he was wroth. Gernot and Giselher, the proud knights and good, and Gunther, the great king, agreed in the end, that they would allow it gladly, if Kriemhild were so minded.

Then Prince Gary said, "I will tell the lady, that she may incline her heart to King Etzel, for many a knight is his vassal. He may make good to her the wrong she hath suffered."

The good knight went to Kriemhild. She welcomed him kindly, and he said without ado, "Greet me gladly, and give me the envoy's meed, for good fortune parteth thee from all thy dole. One of the best men that ever ruled a king's land with honour, or wore a crown, hath sent hither to sue for thy love. Noble knights are come wooing for him; thy brother bade tell thee this."

But the sorrowful one said, "God forbid that thou and all my friends should mock my misery. What could I be to a man that hath known the heart's love of a good wife?"

She would none of it. But Gernot, her brother, and Giselher the youth, came to her, and lovingly they bade her be comforted, for, if she took the king, it were truly to her profit.

But none could prevail on the lady to wed with any man. Then the knights prayed her, saying, "Receive the envoys, at the least, if thou wilt not yield."

"That I will do," said the queen; "I am fain to see Rudeger, by reason of his many virtues. Were it not he, but another envoy, I had remained a stranger to him." She said, "Send him hither to my chamber to-morrow early, and I will tell him my mind on this matter."

Then her bitter weeping began afresh.

Rudeger desired nothing better than to see the queen. He knew himself so skilful in speech that, could it be at all, he must prevail with her.

Early the next morning when they were singing the mass, the noble envoys came. The press was great, and the valiant men that were bound for the court with Rudeger were richly arrayed.

Poor Kriemhild, the sad-hearted one, waited for Rudeger, the noble envoy. He found her in the clothes that she wore every day, albeit her attendants were in rich raiment enow. She went to the door to meet him, and received Etzel's man kindly.

With twelve knights only he came before her. They were well entreated, for never were better envoys. They bade the warrior and his men sit down. The two Margraves, Eckewart and Gary stood before her, but all were sad of their countenance by reason of the sorrowful queen; many fair women sat round her, and Kriemhild did nothing but weep; that her robe on the bosom was wet with hot tears.

The Margrave saw this, and rose from his seat and spake courteously, "Most noble king's daughter, grant to me and my friends that are with me, to stand before thee and tell thee the message we bring hither."

"Thou hast permission," said the queen; "say what thou wilt, and I will hear it gladly, for thou art a good envoy."

The others perceived her unwilling mind, but Prince Rudeger of Bechlaren said, "Etzel, a great king, commendeth his true love to thee, here in this land. He hath sent many good knights to sue for thy love. Love without sorrow he offereth thee, and the like firm affection that he showed erstwhile to Queen Helca, that lay upon his heart. Thou shalt wear the crown, even as my mistress did aforetime."

Then said the queen, "Margrave Rudeger, none that knew my bitter woe would counsel me to wed another man, for I lost one of the best that ever woman had."

"What comforteth more in grief," said the bold man, "than true love? He that chooseth to his heart's desire findeth that naught healeth sorrow like love. If thou consent to wed my noble master, twelve royal crowns shall be thine; thereto, my lord will give thee thirty princes' lands that his strong hand hath overcome. And thou shalt be mistress of many worshipful men, that were subject to my lady Helca, and of many beautiful maidens, the kin of kings, that she ruled over. My master bade me say that, if thou wilt wear the crown with him, he will give thee all the high power that Helca had. Mightily shalt thou wield it over Etzel's men."

But the queen answered, "How could I incline my heart again to be a hero's wife? Death hath wrought me such a woe through one, that I must stand joyless till my life's end."

The Huns answered, "Great queen, thy life by Etzel will be so glad that thou wilt know nothing save delight, if thou consent. For the king hath many a peerless knight. Helca's maidens, and thine together, shall be thy attendants, by reason whereof many warriors shall rejoice. Be counselled, O queen, for thy good."

She said courteously, "Let the matter stand till to-morrow morning. Come to me then; and I will answer you concerning your business."

To the which the bold knights agreed.

When they were all gone to their lodging, the lady sent for Giselher and her mother. To both she said that weeping beseemed her better than aught else.

But her brother Giselher said, "Sister, something telleth me, and I trow it, that King Etzel will end all thy dole. It seemeth good to me that thou take him to husband, whatso any other may counsel. He may give thee again all that thou hast lost. From the Rhone to the Rhine, from the Elbe to the sea, no king is so mighty as he is. Thou mayest well rejoice that he chooseth thee for his queen."

She answered, "Dear brother, wherefore counsel me thus? Mourning and weeping suit me better. How could I appear before the knights at court? Had my body ever beauty, it hath lost it."

Then said queen Uta to her dear daughter, "Dear child, do what thy brother saith. Be counselled by thy friends, and good will betide thee. Too long have I seen thee mourning bitterly."

Then she asked mighty God to guide her. Albeit she might have gold and silver and apparel to give, as aforetime, when her husband lived, never again could she have the happy hours.

She thought to herself, "Shall I give myself to a heathen? I am a Christian woman. I should be shamed before the world. Though he gave me the riches of the whole earth, it could never be."

At that point she left it; and all night long, till the day, the woman lay on her bed full of thoughts. Her bright eyes were never dry till she went to mass in the morning.

The kings also came at the hour of mass, and took their sister by the hand. They counselled her to wed the king of the Huns. But the lady was no merrier of her cheer.

Then they bade Etzel's men come before her, that were fain to be gone with her answer, whether it was a "yea" or a "nay." So Rudeger came to the court. His comrades urged him to learn the princes' mind without delay. This seemed good to them all, for it was a far way back to their land.

They brought Rudeger to Kriemhild. And the knight asked the queen gently to let him hear the message she sent to Etzel. He won nothing from her but denial, for never could she love another man.

Then said the Margrave, "That were ill done. Wherefore ruin so fair a body? Still mayest thou with honour become a good man's wife."

Yet all their entreaty availed not, till that Rudeger said secretly to the queen that he would make good to her any hurt that might befall her. At that, her grief abated somewhat.

He said to the queen, "Weep no more. If thou hadst none among the Huns save me, my faithful kinsmen, and my men, sore must he pay for it that did thee wrong."

Much milder was the lady's mood, and she said, "Swear me an oath that, should any do aught against me, thou wilt be the first to avenge it."

The Margrave answered, "I will swear it."

So Rudeger swore with all his men always to serve her truly, and to deny her nothing in Etzel's land that her honour called for, and he confirmed it with his hand.

Then thought the faithful woman, "Since I, a forlorn woman, can win so many friends, I will let the folk say what they please. Haply I may yet avenge my dear husband's death. Etzel hath so many knights that, were they mine to command, I could do what I would. Thereto, he is so wealthy that I shall have wherewith to bestow gifts. Cruel Hagen hath taken my treasure from me."

She said to Rudeger, "Had I not heard he was a heathen, I would go gladly at his bidding, and take him to husband."

The Margrave answered, "Say no more of that, Lady. He is not quite a heathen, be assured, for my dear master hath been christened; albeit he hath turned again. Haply he will think better of it shouldst thou wed him. He hath so many Christian knights that no ill could betide thee. And thou mightst easily win back the good prince, heart and soul, to God."

Her brothers said, "Promise it, sister, and give over grieving."

They begged it so long that at the last the sorrowful woman promised, before the warriors, to become Etzel's wife.

She said, "Poor queen that I am, I will follow you! I will go to the Huns, if I find friends to lead me thither."

Fair Kriemhild gave her hand on it before the knights.

Then said the Margrave, "Thou hast two knights for thy liegemen, and I have more. Thou canst fare across the Rhine with honour. I will not leave thee longer here among the Burgundians. I have five hundred men and also my kinsmen. These shall serve thee here, and at home likewise, and do thy bidding. I will do it also, and will never shame me when thou mindest me on my word. Bid them fetch thee forth thy horse-gear, for thou wilt never rue Rudeger's counsel, and tell it to the maidens that thou takest with thee. Many a chosen knight will meet us on the road."

They had still the trappings that they rode with in Siegfried's time, so that she could take many maidens with her in fitting pomp when she departed. Ha! what goodly saddles they brought out for the fair women! All the rich clothes they had ever worn were made ready for the journey, for they had heard much of the king. They opened the chests that had stood shut, and busied them for five days and a half, and took from the presses the store of things that lay therein. Kriemhild unlocked her chambers, that she might make Rudeger's men rich. She had still some gold from the Nibelung hoard, that she purposed to divide with her hand among the Huns. An hundred mules scarce carried it.

Hagen heard the news, and said, "Since Kriemhild will never forgive me, Siegfried's gold shall stay here. Wherefore should I let my foemen get so much wealth. Well I know what Kriemhild will do with this treasure. If she took it hence, she would divide it, certes, to my hurt. Tell her that Hagen will keep it."

When she heard this, her anger was grim. They told it to the three knights, that would gladly have put it right; when they could not, noble Rudeger said joyfully, "Great Queen, why weep for thy gold? King Etzel's love is not small. When his eyes behold thee, he will give thee more than thou canst ever spend. Take my word for it, lady."

But the queen said, "Most noble Rudeger, never had a king's daughter more wealth than Hagen hath taken from me."

Then came her brother Gernot to her chamber, and, with his kingly might, stuck a key into the door, that they got Kriemhild's gold out--thirty marks or more. He bade the guests take it, the which pleased Gunther.

Rudeger Urgeth Etzel's Suit

But Gotelind's husband of Bechlaren said, "Had my mistress all that was ever brought from the Nibelung land, neither mine nor the queen's hand would touch it. Bid them keep it, for I will none of it. I brought with me so much from my home that we can lightly dispense with it, and yet live merrily by the way."

But her maidens had filled twelve chests of the best gold that could be; they took that with them, and many women's trinkets for the journey. But even in this thing she feared grim Hagen's might. She had still a thousand gold marks for masses, and this she gave for the soul for her dear husband; the which Rudeger thought well done.

Then said the weeping queen, "Where are now the friends that will leave their home for my sake? Let them ride with me into the land of the Huns, and take of my treasure to buy them horses and apparel."

The Margrave Gary spoke at once, "From the day I was first given to thee for thine attendant, I have served thee faithfully," said the knight, "and will do the same to my life's end. I will take with me also five hundred men; these, with true heart, I make over to thee. Only death shall part us."

Kriemhild thanked the knight for his word and for his good offer.

Then they brought round the horses, for they were ready to start. There was bitter weeping of friends. Great Uta and many a fair maiden showed their grief for the loss of Kriemhild.

She took with her an hundred high-born maidens, arrayed as beseemed them. The tears ran down from bright eyes. But at Etzel's court they had joyful days again.

Then Giselher and Gernot came with their followers, as courtesy bade them, and escorted their dear sister. Brave Gary came, and Ortwin. Rumolt the cook had also to go. They prepared the night-quarters for the women on the way. Folker was the marshal, and saw to their lodging.

After the kisses there was loud weeping, or they came from the castle to the plain. Many rode and followed on foot unbidden, but Gunther went only a little way from the town.

Or they left the Rhine, they had sent forward swift messengers to the land of the Huns, that told the king how Rudeger had won the noble queen for his wife.

They envoys sped fast; needs must they haste, for honour's sake and the guerdon of good news. When they and their horses got home, King Etzel had never heard such welcome tidings. The king bade give the envoys so much for their message that they could live merrily ever after, till their death.

For love had chased away the king's trouble and his dole.

HOW KRIEMHILD JOURNEYED TO THE HUNS

ET the envoys ride, and list rather while we tell you how the queen journeyed through the land, and where Giselher and Gernot parted from her. They had served her well as honour bade them. They rode as far as the Danube at Bergen; then they took their leave, that they might return to the Rhine. Among friends so good, this could not be done without weeping.

Bold Giselher said to his sister, "If thou hast need of me at any time, sister, or standest in any peril, let me know it, and I will ride to thy succour into Etzel's land."

She kissed all her kinsmen on the mouth, and on friendly wise the bold Burgundians took leave of Rudeger's men. With the queen went many fair maidens, an hundred and four, richly clad in gay and costly stuffs; and they that followed Kriemhild bare broad shields enow. Then Folker, the goodly knight, turned back also.

When they were come over the Danube into Bavaria, the news was noised abroad that unknown guests were advancing. Where a cloister still standeth, and the Inn floweth into the Danube, a bishop dwelled in the town of Passau. The houses were emptied of the folk, and also the prince's palace, and they hasted to meet the strangers in Bavaria, where Bishop Pilgerin found fair Kriemhild.

The knights of the country were not sorry when they saw so many beautiful maidens following her, and they wooed the heroes' daughters with their eyes. Good lodging was given to the strangers, and they rested at Pledelingen. The folk rode from all quarters toward them, and they got freely all they needed. Both there and elsewhere they took it, nor lost honour thereby.

The bishop rode with his niece to Passau. When the burghers of the town got word that Kriemhild, the child of their prince's sister, came thither, she was received with great worship by the merchants. The bishop thought she would tarry there, but Eckewart said, "It cannot be, for we must down into Rudeger's land. Many knights await us that know of our coming."

Fair Gotelind also had heard the news. She and her high-born child made them ready in haste, for Rudeger had bidden her cheer the queen by riding to meet her with all his men, as far as the Enns. This was no sooner done than the roads were thronged with folk riding and running afoot to meet the guests.

The queen was now come to Efferding. There many a Bavarian robber had gladly plundered them on the road, as their custom is, and had easily done them a hurt. But noble Rudeger had guarded against this; he had with him a thousand knights or more. Rudeger's wife, Gotelind, too, was come thither, and with her many bold warriors.

When they had crossed the Traun at Enns, they found booths and tents pitched for them on the plain where they were to sleep. Rudeger took all the charges on himself.

Gotelind set out from her quarters, and many horses with jingling bridles took the road. It was a fair welcome, and done for Rudeger's sake. The knights, from both sides, pricked gallantly to the greeting, and showed their horsemanship in the presence of the maidens, that saw it gladly enow. When Rudeger's men rode up to the strangers, many a splinter flew into the air from the hands of the heroes, that tilted on knightly wise.

They rode to win praise from the women. When the tourney was ended, the men greeted each other, and fair Gotelind was led up to Kriemhild. There was little rest for any skilled to wait upon women.

The Margrave rode to meet his wife, that was not sorry to see him come back safe from the Rhine. In her joy she forgot her long dole. When she had welcomed him, he bade her alight on the grass with her attendants. The knights hasted to serve them.

When Kriemhild saw the Margravine standing with her train, she went no further, but stayed her horse and bade them lift her quickly from the saddle. The bishop led his sister's child, he and Eckewart, to Gotelind, and all that stood in the way fell back.

Then the stranger kissed the Margravine on the mouth, and Rudeger's wife said sweetly, "Well for me, dear lady, that I have seen with mine eyes thy fair body here in this land! Naught so welcome hath, for long, befallen me."

"God reward thee, noble Gotelind," answered Kriemhild. "If I be spared alive to live with Botlung's child, it may indeed be well for thee that thou hast seen me."

Neither of them knew that which was to be.

The maidens, attended by the knights, advanced and greeted each other courteously; then they sat down on the clover, and many that had been strangers became acquainted. They bade pour out the wine for the women; and, seeing it was already noon, they rested there no longer, but rode till they came to broad pavilions, where they were well served. They stayed there the night through, till the early morning.

The folk of Bechlaren had not failed to make them ready for the many worshipful guests, and Rudeger had so ordered it that these wanted for little. The windows in the walls were thrown wide, the Castle of Bechlaren stood open, and the welcome guests rode in. The noble host bade provide good lodging for them all. Rudeger's daughter advanced with her attendants and received the queen right sweetly, and her mother, the Margravine, was there also. Many a maiden was lovingly greeted. They took hands and went together into a wide and goodly hall, below which flowed the Danube. There they sat merrily, and the breeze blew upon them.

What they did further, I cannot say. Kriemhild's knights were heard mourning that they must away so soon; it irked them sore. Ha! what good warriors rode with them from Bechlaren.

Rudeger did them right loving service. The queen gave Gotelind's daughter twelve red armlets, and, thereto, goodly raiment of the best that she had brought with her into Etzel's land.

Albeit she was bereft of the Nibelung gold, she won to her all that saw her with the small store that remained to her. Goodly were the gifts she bestowed on the followers of the host. In return, the lady Gotelind did the guests from the Rhine such honour that it had been hard to find any among them without jewels or rich apparel from her hand.

When they had eaten, and it was time to be gone, the hostess commended her true service to Etzel's wife, who, from her side, embraced the fair Margravine lovingly. And the maiden said to the queen, "Well I know, if it seem good to thee, that my father would gladly send me into the land of the Huns to be with thee." Kriemhild found her true indeed!

The horses stood ready before Bechlaren; the noble queen had taken leave of Rudeger's wife and daughter, and, with many a sweet farewell, the maidens parted; seldom did they meet again.

The folk of Medilick brought out in their hands rich golden vessels, and offered them, full of wine, to the guests on the road, and bade them welcome. The host of the place hight Astolt, that showed them the way into Austria, by Mautern down below on the Danube; and here, again, the great queen was paid much worship.

At that point the bishop parted lovingly from his niece, after that he had prayed earnestly that she might prosper, and win herself honour even as Helca had done. Ha! what fame was hers after, among the Huns!

So the strangers fared on to the Traisem, diligently waited on by Rudeger's men, till that the Huns were seen riding across the land. Mickle worship was done there to the queen.

Fast by the Traisem the King of the Huns had a goodly castle and a famous, called Traisenmauer. There Helca had dwelled and ruled more mildly than any hath done since, save Kriemhild, who likewise gave freely of her goods. Well might she live happily after her mourning, and win praise from Etzel's men, the which the heroes soon gave her to the full.

So famed was Etzel's rule that the boldest knights ever heard of among Christians or heathens drew ceaselessly to his court; and all these were come with him. One saw there what one never sees now - Christian and heathen together. Howso divers their beliefs were, the king gave with such free hand that all had plenty.

HOW SHE WAS RECEIVED AMONG THE HUNS

HE tarried at Traisenmauer till the fourth day, during which time the dust on the road was never still, but rose like flame from all sides. And King Etzel's men rode thither through Austria.

When it was told to the king how proudly Kriemhild advanced through the land, his old sorrow vanished clean from his mind, and he set out to meet the fair one. In front of him on the way rode many a bold knight - a vast host of Christians and heathens of many divers tongues. When they spied the queen, they came on in stately array.

Russians and Greeks were there. Polacks and Wallachians spurred along, deftly managing their good horses, displaying themselves each according to the custom of his own land. From Kiow came many a knight. Savage Petschenegers were there also, that shot with their bows at the birds that flew by, and drew their arrowheads strongly to the utmost stretch of the bow.

In Austria, by the Danube, is a town that hight Tulna. There Kriemhild learned many a strange custom that she had not seen afore, and was welcomed by not a few that, after, suffered dole through her.

The men of King Etzel's household rode before him, merry and rich-attired, fair accoutred and courtly: full four and twenty princes, great and noble. To behold their queen was all they sought. Duke Ramung of Wallachia spurred up to her with seven hundred men. Then came Prince Gibek with a gallant host. Hornbog, the swift, pricked forward from the king's side to his mistress with echoing shouts, after the fashion of his country. Etzel's kinsmen, likewise, spurred hotly toward her. Next came bold Hawart of Denmark, and swift Iring, free from guile; and Irnfried of Thuringia, a brave man. These, with the twelve hundred men that made up their host, received Kriemhild with all worship. Then came Sir Bloedel, King Etzel's brother, from the land of the Huns; with great pomp, he drew nigh to the queen. The next was King Etzel, with Sir Dietrich and all his knights, among the which were many good warriors faithful and true; whereat the heart of Queen Kriemhild was uplifted.

Then Sir Rudeger said to the queen, "Lady, the king would welcome thee here. Kiss them that I bid thee kiss. It is not meet that all Etzel's men be greeted on like manner."

So they lifted the queen down from her palfrey. Etzel, the great monarch, tarried no longer, but sprang from his horse with many a bold knight, and hasted joyfully toward Kriemhild. Two mighty princes, they tell us, walked by the queen and carried her train when King Etzel went toward her, and she received him sweetly with kisses. She pushed back her head-band, and her bright skin shone from out the gold, till many a man vowed that queen Helca could not have been fairer. Bloedel, the king's brother, stood close at hand, whom Rudeger, the wealthy Margrave, bade her kiss; also King Gibek, and Dietrich likewise. Twelve knights were kissed by her, and many others were kindly greeted.

All the time that Etzel stood by Kriemhild, the youths did as the custom is still. Christian knights and heathen jousted, each after his own fashion. Dietrich's men, as beseemed good warriors, hurled the whizzing shafts high above the shields, with undaunted hand. Bucklers enow were pierced before the German guests.

Mickle din was there of splintered lances. All the knights of the land were gathered together, and the king's guests also, among the which were many noble men.

Then the great king went with the queen into a stately pavilion. The field round about was full of tents, that they might rest after their labour. Thither the heroes led the beautiful maidens after the queen, who sat down therein on a rich couch. The Margrave had so ordered it, that they found it all goodly and fair.

High beat the heart of Etzel.

What they said to each other I know not. Kriemhild's white hand lay in the king's. They sat lovingly together, but Rudeger allowed not the king to caress his bride in secret. They bade stay the tourney.

The din of the fray ended with honour, and Etzel's men went to their tents, where they had spacious lodging. That evening, and through the night, they rested in comfort, till the morning light began to shine. Then they got to horse again. Ha! what sports they drave for the glory of the king! Etzel exhorted his Huns to do as honour bade.

Then they rode from Tulna to the town of Vienna. There they found many women featly adorned, that received Etzel's wife with much worship. All that they needed was there in plenty, and the heroes rejoiced against the festival.

Lodging was given them, and the king's hightide began merrily. There was not room for all in the town, and Rudeger bade them that were not guests take up their quarters in the country round about. All this time, I trow, the king was not far from Kriemhild.

Sir Dietrich, and many another knight beside, slacked not in their endeavour to cheer the hearts of the strangers. Rudeger and his friends had good pastime.

The festival fell on a Whitsuntide, when King Etzel wedded Kriemhild in the town of Vienna. She had not, certes, had so many men to serve her in her first husband's time.

With her gifts she made herself known to many that had never seen her afore, among the which were some that said to the guests,

"We deemed that Kriemhild possessed naught. Yet here she doeth wonders with her wealth."

The hightide lasted seventeen days. Of no king, I ween, is it told, that he held a longer marriage feast; at the least we wot of none. All the guests wore new apparel.

At home, in the Netherland, Kriemhild had never sat before so many knights; yea, I trow, that albeit Siegfried had great possessions, he had never at command so many noble warriors as stood before Etzel. Nor had nay king ever given at his own wedding such store of rich mantles, long and wide, nor such goodly vesture, whereof he had enow and to spare. For Kriemhild's sake he did it all.

Friends and strangers were of one mind. They grudged not their dearest possession. Whatso any asked for was readily given, till that many a knight, through his charity, was left bare and without clothes.

When the queen thought how once she had sat by the Rhine with her noble husband, her eyes grew wet. But she hid it, that none knew. Great honour was now hers after her mickle dole.

Howso freely the others gave, it was but a wind compared with Dietrich. What Botlung's son had given him was no wall spent. The open hand of Rudeger also did great wonders. Prince Bloedel, too, of Hungary, bade empty many a travelling chest, and scatter freely both silver and gold.

Right merrily lived the warriors of the king. Werbel and Schwemmel, the court minstrels, won, each, at the hightide, when Kriemhild wore the crown beside Etzel, a thousand marks or more.

On the eighteenth morning they rode away from Vienna. Many a shield was pierced in knightly encounter by the spears which the heroes bare in their hands. So Etzel returned to the land of the Huns rejoicing.

They stayed the night at ancient Haimburg. None could number the host, nor tell how many strong they rode through the land. Ha! what beautiful women they found waiting them in their home!

At Misenburg, the wealthy city, they went aboard ships. The water was covered with horses and men, as if the dry land had begun to float. There the way-weary women had ease and comfort. The good ships were lashed together, that wave and water might not hurt them, and fair awnings were stretched above, as they had been still on the plain.

When word thereof came to Etzel's castle, both women and men rejoiced. Etzel's household, that Helca had aforetime ruled, passed many a happy day with Kriemhild. Noble maidens stood waiting, that since Helca's death had suffered heart's dole. Kriemhild found there seven kings' daughters that were for an adornment to Etzel's whole land. The charge of the damsels was with Herrat, Helca's sister's daughter, famed for virtue, and the betrothed of Dietrich, a noble king's child, the daughter of Nentwine; the which afterward had much worship. Glad of her cheer was she at the coming of the guests, and many a goodly thing was made ready.

What tongue might tell how merrily King Etzel dwelled there? Never under any queen fared the Huns better.

When the king rode up with his wife from the strand, Kriemhild was told the name of them that led forward the maidens, that she might greet them the more fitly.

Ha! how mightily she ruled in Helca's stead! She had true servants in plenty. The queen gave gold and vesture, silver and precious stones. All that she had brought with her from over the Rhine to the Huns, she divided among them. All the king's kinsmen and liegemen vowed their service to her, and were subject to her, so that Helca herself had never ruled so mightily as Kriemhild, that they had all to serve till her death.

So famous was the court and the country, that each found there, at all times, the pastime he desired; so kind was the king and so good the queen.

TWENTY-THIRD ADVENTURE
HOW KRIEMHILD THOUGHT OF REVENGING HER WRONG

S O, in high honour (I say sooth), they dwelled together till the seventh year. Meanwhile Kriemhild had borne a son. Nothing could have rejoiced Etzel more. She set her heart on it that he should receive Christian baptism. He was named Ortlieb, and glad was all Etzel's land.

For many a day Kriemhild ruled virtuously, even as Helca aforetime. Herrat, the foreign maiden, that still mourned bitterly for Helca in secret, taught her the customs of the country. Strangers and friends alike praised her, and owned that never queen had ruled a king's land better or more mildly. For this she was famed among the Huns till the thirteenth year.

When now she saw that none withstood her (the which a king's knights will sometimes do to their prince's wife), and that twelve kings stood ever before her, she thought on the grievous wrongs that had befallen her in her home. She remembered also the honour that was hers among the Nibelungs, and that Hagen's hand had robbed her of it by Siegfried's death, and she pondered how she might work him woe.

"It were easily done, could I but bring him hither."

She dreamed that she walked hand in hand with Giselher her brother, and oft, in sweet sleep, she kissed him. Evil came of it after.

It was the wicked Devil, I ween, that counselled Kriemhild to part from Gunther in friendship, and to be reconciled to him with a kiss in the land of Burgundy. She began to wet her vesture anew with hot tears. Late and early it lay on her heart, how that, through no fault of hers, she had been forced to wed a heathen. Hagen and Gunther had done this wrong to her.

Never a day passed but she longed to be revenged. She thought, "Now I am so rich and powerful that I could do mine enemies a mischief. Were it Hagen of Trony, I were nothing loth. My heart still yearneth for my beloved. Could I but win to them that worked me wore, well would the death of my dear one be avenged. It is hard to wait," said the sorrowful woman.

All her knights, the king's men, loved her, as was meet. Her chamberlain was Eckewart, that thereby won many friends. None durst withstand Kriemhild's will.

Every day she thought to herself, "I will ask the king." She deemed that, of his goodness, he would send for her friends and bring them into the land of the Huns. None guessed her evil intent.

One night, when she lay by the king, and he held her in his arms, as was his wont, for she was to him as his life, the royal woman thought on her foes, and said to him, "My dearest lord, I would fain beg a boon of thee. I would have thee show, if I have deserved it at thy hand, that my kinsmen have found favour in thy sight."

The great king answered with true heart, "That will I readily prove to thee. All that profiteth and doth honour to the knights rejoiceth me, for through no woman's love have I won better friends."

Then said the queen, "Thou knowest well that I have noble kinsmen. It irketh me that they visit me so seldom. The folk here deem me kinless."

Whereto King Etzel answered, "My dearest wife, if it be not too far, I will invite across the Rhine whomsoever thou wouldst gladly see, and bid them hither to my land."

The woman was well content when she discovered his mind on the matter, and said, "If thou wouldst truly please me, my lord, thou wilt dispatch envoys to Worms beyond the Rhine. I will inform my friends of my desire by these; so, many good knights will come hither into our land."

He answered, "Thy wish shall be obeyed. Thy kinsmen, noble Uta's sons, will not be so welcome to thee as to me. It irketh me sore that they have been strangers so long. If it seem good to thee, dearest wife, I will send my minstrels as envoys to thy friends in Burgundy."

He bade summon the good fiddlers straightway, that hasted to where he sat by the queen, and he told them both to go as envoys to Burgundy. He let fashion rich clothes for them; for four and twenty knights they made apparel, and the king gave them the message wherewith they were to invite Gunther and his men. And Kriemhild began to speak to them in secret.

Then said the great king, "I will tell ye what ye shall do. I send to my friends love and every good wish, and pray them to ride hither to my land. I know few other guests so dear. And if Kriemhild's kinsmen be minded to do my will, bid them fail not to come, for love of me, to my hightide, for my heart yearneth toward the brethren of my wife."

Whereto Schwemmel, the proud minstrel, answered, "When shall thy hightide fall, that we may tell thy friends yonder?"

King Etzel said, "Next midsummer."

"Thy command shall be obeyed," answered Werbel.

The queen bade summon the envoys secretly to her chamber, and spake with them. Little good came thereof.

She said to the two envoys, "Ye shall deserve great reward if ye do my bidding well, and deliver the message wherewith I charge you, at home, in my land. I will make you rich in goods, and give you sumptuous apparel. See that ye say not to any of my friends at

Worms, by the Rhine, that ye have ever seen me sad of my cheer, and commend my service to the heroes bold and good. Beg them to grant the king's prayer and end all my sorrow.

"The Huns deem me without kin. Were I a knight, I would go to them myself. Say to Gernot, my noble brother, that none is better minded to him in the world than I. Bid him bring here our best friends, that we win honour. And tell Giselher to remember that never, through his fault, did ill betide me; for which reason mine eyes are fain to behold him. Evermore I would serve him. Tell my mother, also, what worship is mine. And if Hagen of Trony tarry behind, who shall lead them through the land? From a child up he hath known the roads hither to the Huns."

The envoys guessed not why she could not leave Hagen of Trony at the Rhine. They knew it afterward to their cost, for, through him, many a knight was brought face to face with grim death.

Letters and greetings were given to them. They rode forth rich in goods, that they might live merrily by the way. They took leave of Etzel and his fair wife. Their bodies were adorned with goodly vesture.

HOW WERBEL AND SCHWEMMEL
BROUGHT THE MESSAGE

HEN Etzel sent his fiddlers to the Rhine, the news flew from land to land. By means of swift messengers, he invited guests to his hightide. There many met their death.

The envoys rode from the country of the Huns to the Burgundians, even to the three noble kings and their men, to bid them to Etzel's court, and hasted on the way.

They came to Bechlaren, where they were well seen to, and nothing lacked to their entertainment. Rudeger and Gotelind, and the Margrave's child also, sent their greeting by them to the Rhine.

Not without gifts went Etzel's men forth, that they might fare the better on the road. Rudeger commended him to Uta and her sons; never Margrave was so true to them as he.

To Brunhild, likewise, they commended their true service and their steadfast faith and love. When the envoys had heard the message, they set out again, and the Margravine prayed God in Heaven to guard them.

Or they left Bavaria, swift Werbel sought out the bishop: what greeting he sent to his friends by the Rhine I know not. But he gave his red gold to the envoys out of love, and let them ride on.

Bishop Pilgerin said, "Right gladly would I see my sister's sons here. Seldom, alack! can I win to them at the Rhine."

I cannot tell by what road they fared through the land; but none took from them their silver and fine clothes, for all feared the wrath of their master: the great king was mighty and of high lineage.

Within twelve days Werbel and Schwemmel reached Worms on the Rhine. And the king sand their men were told the news, that foreign envoys were come. Thereupon Gunther, the prince of the Rhine, began to question his folk, and said, "Who will tell us whence these strangers are come riding into the land?"

And none knew, till that Hagen of Trony saw the envoys, and said to Gunther, "We shall have news, I promise thee, for I have seen Etzel's fiddlers here. Thy sister hath sent them. Let us welcome them right heartily for their master's sake."

They rode straight to the palace. Never goodlier show made the minstrels of a king. Gunther's courtiers hasted to meet them, and gave them lodging, and bade see to their gear. Their travelling clothes were rich and well fashioned. With all honour they might have gone before the king therein. Yet the scorned to wear them at the court, and asked whether any desired them. There was no lack of needy folk, that took them gladly, and to these they were sent. Then the guests clad them in rich apparel, as beseemed the envoys of a king.

Etzel's men got leave to go before Gunther. They that saw them rejoiced. Hagen sprang from his seat and ran to them, and received them lovingly, for which the youths thanked him. He asked for news of Etzel and his men, whereto the fiddlers made answer, "The land was never more prosperous, nor the people more joyful; know that of a surety."

He led them before the king, through the hall full of folk, and the guests were well received, as envoys should ever be in foreign kings' lands. Werbel found many a knight by Gunther.

The gracious prince greeted them, and said, "Ye are both welcome, Etzel's minstrels, ye and your followers. Wherefore hath the mighty Etzel sent you into Burgundy?"

They bowed before him, and Werbel answered, "My dear master, and Kriemhild thy sister, commend their service to thee. With true intent they have sent us hither to you, O knights."

Then said the noble prince, "I rejoice at the tidings. How fareth it with Etzel, and Kriemhild my sister?"

Whereto the fiddler answered, "Never was king of any land better or happier, nor his kinsmen nor vassals; know that for certain. Right glad were they when we set forth on this journey."

"Thank him and my sister for their greeting. I rejoice that it is well with the king and his folk, for I asked, much fearing."

The two young kings were also come in, and had heard the news for the first time. Giselher, the youth, was glad to see the envoys, for love of his sister, and said to them kindly, "Ye be heartily welcome. If ye came oftener to the Rhine, ye would find friends worth the seeing. Small ill should betide you here."

"I trow it well," answered Schwemmel. "Word of mine cannot tell thee how right lovingly Etzel commendeth him to thee, and eke thy sister, that is holden in high esteem. The king's wife biddeth thee remember thy love and faith, and that thou wert ever true to her in heart and soul. And, first of all, we are sent to the king, to invite you to ride into Etzel's land, and Sir Gernot with you. Mighty Etzel commanded me to say to you all that, even if ye desire not to see your sister, he would fain learn what wrong he hath done you, that ye are such strangers to him and his court. Had ye never known the queen, he deserveth no less of you than that ye come to see him. If ye consent to this, ye shall please him well."

And Gunther answered, "A sennight from now I will let thee know what I and my friends have determined on. Go meanwhile to thy lodging and rest."

But Werbel said, "Might we not, ere we seek repose, win audience of great Uta?"

Whereto the noble Giselher answered courteously, "None shall hinder you, for in this ye shall have done my mother's will. For the sake of my sister, Queen Kriemhild, she will see you gladly. Right welcome shall ye be."

Giselher brought them before the lady, who rejoiced to see envoys from the land of the Huns. Kindly and lovingly she greeted them, and the courtly messengers and good delivered their tidings.

"My mistress commendeth to thee," said Schwemmel, "her service and her true love. Could she but have sight of thee oftener, naught on earth were dearer to her."

But the queen answered, "That cannot be. The noble king's wife dwelleth, alack! too far from me. Blessed evermore be she and Etzel. Fail not to send me word of your departure, when ye are about to return home. It is long since envoys were so welcome as ye are." And the youths promised that they would do it.

The Huns went to their lodging. Meanwhile, the great king had sent for his friends, and noble Gunther asked his men how the message pleased them. And many of them began to say that he might well ride into Etzel's land. The best among them counselled him thereto--all save Hagen. Him it irked exceedingly.

He said to the king apart, "Ye strike at your own life. Surely you know what we have done. Evermore we stand in danger from Kriemhild. I smote her husband dead with my hand. How dare we ride into Etzel's land?"

But the king answered, "My sister forgot her anger. With a loving kiss she forgave us for all we had done to her or she rode away. Hath she aught against any, it is against thee alone, Hagen."

"Be not deceived," said Hagen, "by the words of the Hunnish envoys. If thou goest to see Kriemhild, thou mayst lose thine honour and thy life. The wife of King Etzel hath a long memory."

Then Gernot spake out before the assembly, "Because thou fearest death with reason among the Huns, it were ill done on our part to keep away from our sister."

And Sir Giselher said to the knight, "Since thou knowest thyself guilty, friend Hagen, stay thou at home, and guard thyself well, and let them that dare, journey with us to the Huns."

Then the knight of Trony fell into a passion. "None that ye take with you will be readier to ride to the court than I. And well I will prove it, since ye will not be turned."

But knight Rumolt, the cook, said, "Strangers and friends ye can entertain at home, at your pleasure. For here is abundance. Hagen, I trow, hath never held you back afore. If ye will not follow him in this, be counselled by Rumolt (for your true and loving servant am I) and tarry here as I would have ye do, and leave King Etzel yonder by Kriemhild. Where in the wide world could ye be better? Here ye are safe from your enemies. Ye can adorn your bodies with goodly vesture, drink the best wine, and woo fair women. Thereto, ye are given meats, the best on earth that ever king ate. The land is prosperous. Ye may give up Etzel's hightide with honour, and live merrily at home with your friends. Even had ye nothing else to feat on here, I could always give you your fill of one dish - cutlets fried in oil. This is Rumolt's advice, my masters, since there is danger among the Huns. Never again, I trow, will Kriemhild be your friend, nor have you and Hagen deserved otherwise. Stay here, ye knights, else ye may rue it. Ye shall find in the end that my counsel is not bad: wherefore heed my words. Rich are your lands. Here you can redeem your pledges better than among the Huns. Who knoweth how things stand there. Abide where ye are. That is Rumolt's counsel."

"We will not stay here," said Gernot. "Since my sister and great Etzel have bidden us so lovingly, why should we refuse? He that will not with us may tarry at home."

"By my troth," said Rumolt, "I, for one, will never cross the Rhine for Etzel's hightide. Why should I hazard what I have? I will live while I may."

"I am of thy mind for that," said knight Ortwin. "I will help thee to order things at home."

And there were many that would not go, and said, "God guard you among the Huns."

The king was wroth when he saw they desired to take their ease at home. "We will go none the less. The prudent are safe in the midst of danger."

Hagen answered, "Be not wroth at my word. Whatever betide, I counsel thee in good faith to rid strongly armed to the Huns. Since thou wilt not be turned, summon the best men thou canst find, or knowest of, among thy vassals, and from among the I will choose a thousand good knights, that thou come not in scathe by Kriemhild's anger."

"I will do this," said the king straightway. And he bade messengers ride abroad through the country. Three thousand or more heroes they brought back with them.

They thought not to meet so grim a doom. Merrily they rode into Gunter's land. To all them that were to journey to the Huns horses and apparel were given. The king found many willing. Hagen of Trony bade Dankwart, his brother, lead eighty of their knights to the Rhine. They came in proud array, bringing harness and vesture with them. Bold Folker, a noble minstrel, arrived with thirty of his men for the journey. He told Gunther that these would also visit the Huns.

I will tell you who Folker was. He was a noble knight, and many good warriors in Burgundy were his vassals. He was called a minstrel because he played on the viol.

Hagen chose a thousand that he knew well, and the prowess of whose hand he had seen in grim battle, and in warlike deeds. None could deny their valour.

It irked Kriemhild's envoys to be delayed, for they greatly feared their master, and every day they desired to be gone. But Hagen kept them for his crafty ends. He said to his lord, "We must beware of letting them go or we be ready to follow them, in a sennight. We shall be safer so, if they mean us harm. Kriemhild will not have the time to contrive our hurt. Or, if she be minded thereto, it may go ill with her, since we lead with us to the Huns so many chosen men."

Shields and saddles and all the vesture they were to take with them, to Etzel's land, were now ready, and Kriemhild's envoys were bidden to Gunther's presence.

When they appeared, Gernot said, "The king will obey Etzel's wish. We go gladly to his hightide to see our sister. She may count on us."

Gunther asked, "Can ye tell us when the hightide falleth, or when we must set forth?"

And Schwemmel answered, "Next midsummer, without fail."

The king gave them leave, for the first time, to visit Brunhild, but Folker, to please her, said them nay.

"Queen Brunhild is not well enow for you to see her," said the good knight. "Wait till morning, and ye shall win audience of her." They had fain beheld her, but could not.

Then the rich prince, that he might show favour to the envoys, bade bring thither of his own bounty gold upon broad shields. He had plenty thereof. His friends also gave them rich gifts. Giselher and Gernot,

Gary and Ortwin, let it be seen that they could give freely. They offered such costly things to the envoys that these durst not take them, for fear of their master.

Then said Werbel to the king, "Keep your gifts, O king, in your own land. We may not carry them with us. My lord forbade us to take aught. Thereto, we have small need."

But the prince of the Rhine was angry because they refused so great a king's gift. So, at the last, they were constrained to take his gold and vesture, and carry them home into Etzel's land.

They desired to see Uta or they departed. Giselher, the youth, brought the minstrels before his mother, and the lady bade them say that she rejoiced to hear how that Kriemhild was had in worship. For the sake of Kriemhild, that she loved, and of King Etzel, the queen gave the envoys girdles and gold. Well might they receive this, for with true heart it was offered.

The envoys had now taken leave of both men and women, and rode merrily forth to Swabia. Gernot sent his warriors with them thus far, that none might do them a hurt.

When their escorts parted from them, Etzel's might kept them safe by the way, that none robbed them of horses or vesture. Then they spurred swiftly to the land of the Huns. Them that they knew for friends, they told that the Burgundians from the Rhine would pass there shortly. They brought the tidings also to Bishop Pilgerin.

When they rode down by Bechlaren, they failed not to send word to Rudeger and Dame Gotelind, the Margrave's wife, that was merry of her cheer because she was to see the guests so soon.

The minstrels were seen spurring through the land. They found Etzel in his town of Gran. They gave the king, that grew red for joy, the greetings that had been sent him.

When the queen heard for certain that her brothers would come, she was well content, and requited the minstrels with goodly gifts, which did her honour.

She said, "Now tell me, both of you, Werbel and Schwemmel, which of my friends, of the best that we have bidden, come to the hightide. What said Hagen when he heard the news?"

"He came to the council one morning early. He had little good to say of the hightide. It was named by grim Hagen the death-ride. Thy brothers, the three kings, come in merry mood. Who further are with them I cannot say. Folker, the bold minstrel, is one."

"I had made shift to do without Folker," said the king's wife. "Hagen I esteem; he is a good knight. I am right glad that wee shall see him here."

Then Kriemhild went to the king, and spake to him right sweetly, "How doth the news please thee, dearest lord? All my heart's desire shall now be satisfied."

"Thy will is my pleasure," answered the king. "I were less glad had it been mine own kinsmen. Through love of thy dear brethren all my cares have vanished."

Etzel's officers bade fit up the palace and hall everywhere with seats for the welcome guests. They took much joy from the king.

HOW THE KINGS JOURNEYED TO THE HUNS

UT of their doings there we shall tell no further. High-hearted heroes never rode so proudly into any king's land. All that they wanted they had, both of weapons and apparel. They say that the Prince of the Rhine equipped a thousand and three score of knights, and nine thousand squires for the hightide. They that tarried at home were soon to weep for them.

Whilst they carried their harness across the court at Worms, an old bishop from Spires said to fair Uta, "Our friends will ride to the hightide. God help them there."

Then noble Uta said to her children, "Stay here, good heroes. Last night I dreamed an evil dream, that all the birds in this land were dead." "He that goeth by dreams," said Hagen, "careth little for his honour. I would have my noble master take leave without delay, and ride forward merrily into Etzel's land. There kings need heroes' hands to serve them, and we must see Kriemhild's hightide."

Hagen counselled them now to the journey, but he rued it later. He had withstood them, but that Gernot had mocked him. He minded him on Siegfried, Kriemhild's husband, and said, "It is for that, that Hagen durst not go."

But Hagen said, "I hold not back from fear. If ye will have it so, heroes, go forward. I am ready to ride with you to Etzel's land."

Soon many a helmet and shield were pierced by him.

The ships lay waiting for the kings and their men. They carried their vesture down to them, and were busy till eventide. Merry of cheer they quitted their homes. On the camping ground across the Rhine they pitched tents and put up booths. The king's fair wife entreated him to stay, for much she loved him. Flutes and trumpets rang out early in the morning, and gave the signal to be gone. Many a true lover was torn from his loved one's arms by King Etzel's wife.

King Uta's sons had a liegeman bold and true. When he saw they would forth, he spake to the king secretly, "Much I grieve that thou goest to this hightide." Rumolt was his name, a chosen knight. He said, "To whom wilt thou leave thy folk and thy land? Alack! that none can turn you knights from your purpose! Kriemhild's message never pleased me."

"I leave my land and child in thy charge. I will have it so. Comfort them that thou seest weeping. Etzel's wife will do us no hurt!"

The king held a council with his chief men or he started. He left not land and castles defenceless. Many a chosen knight stayed behind to guard them.

The horses stood ready for the kings and their followers. With sweet kisses parted many whose hearts still beat high. Noble women soon wept for them. Wailing was there, with tears enow.

The queen bare her child in her arms to the king. "How canst thou leave us both desolate? Stay for our sake," said the sorrowful woman.

"Weep not for me, but be of good cheer here at home. We shall return shortly, safe and sound."

So they waited no longer, but lovingly took leave of their friends. When the bold knights were gotten to horse, many women stood sorrowing. Their hearts told them it was a long parting. None is merry of his cheer when bitter woe is at hand.

The swift Burgundians rode off, and there was hurrying in the land. On either side the mountains both men and women wept. But, for all the folk could do, they pressed forward merrily. A thousand of the Nibelung knights in habergeons went with them, that had left fair women at home, the which they never saw more. The wounds of Siegfried gaped in Kriemhild's heart.

The Christian faith was still weak in those days. Nevertheless they had a chaplain with them to say mass. He returned alive, escaped from much peril. The rest tarried dead among the Huns.

Gunther's men shaped their course toward the Main, up through East Frankland. Hagen led them, that knew the way well. Their Marshal was Dankwart, the knight of Burgundy.

As they rode from East Frankland to Schwanfeld, the princes and their kinsmen, knights of worship, were known by their stately mien.

On the twelfth morning the king reached the Danube. Hagen of Trony rode in front of the rest. He was the helper and comforter of the Nibelungs. The bold knight alighted there on the bank, and tied his horse to a tree. The river was swoln, there was no boat, and the knights were troubled how to win across. The water was too wide. Many a bold knight sprang to the ground.

"Mischief might easily befall thee here, King of Rhineland," said Hagen; "thou canst see for thyself that the river is swoln, and the current very strong. I fear me we shall lose here to-day not a few good knights."

"Wherefore daunt me, Hagen?" said the proud king. "Of thy charity fright us no more. Look out a ford for us, that we bring both horses and baggage safe across."

"I am no so weary of life," said Hagen, "that I desire to drown in these broad waves. Many a man in Etzel's land shall first fall by my hand. That is more to my mind. Stay by the water side, ye proud knights and good, and I will seek the ferrymen by the river, that will bring us safe into Gelfrat's land."

Thereupon stark Hagen took his good shield. He was well armed. He bare his buckler. He laced on his shining helmet. He wore a broad weapon above his harness, that cut grimly with both its edges.

Then he sought the ferrymen up and down. He heard the splash of water and began to listen. It came from mermaidens that bathed their bodies in a clear brook to cool them.

Hagen spied them, and stole up secretly. When they were ware of him, they fled. Well pleased were they to escape him. The hero took their garments, but did them no further annoy.

Then one of the mermaids (she hight Hadburg) said, "We will tell thee, noble Hagen, if thou give us our clothes again, how ye shall all fare on this journey among the Huns."

They swayed like birds in the water before him. He deemed them wise and worthy of belief, so that he trusted the more what they told him.

They informed him concerning all that he asked them. Hadburg said, "Ye may ride safely into Etzel's land; I pledge my faith thereon, that never yet heroes journeyed to any court to win more worship. I say sooth."

Hagen's heart was uplifted at her word; he gave them back their clothes and stayed no longer. When they had put on their wonderful raiment, they told him the truth about the journey.

The other mermaid, that hight Sieglind, said, "Be warned, Hagen, son of Aldrian. My aunt hath lied to thee because of her clothes. If ye go to the Huns, ye are ill-advised. Turn while there is time, for ye bold knights have been bidden that ye may die in Etzel's land. Who rideth thither hath death at his hand."

But Hagen said, "Your deceit is vain. How should we all tarry there, dead, through the hate of one woman?"

Then they began to foretell it plainer, and Hadburg said also, "Ye are doomed. Not one of you shall escape, save the king's chaplain: this we know for a truth. He, only, shall return alive into Gunther's land."

Hagen And The Mermaids

Grimly wroth spake bold Hagen then. "It were a pleasant thing to tell my masters that we must all perish among the Huns! Show us a way across the water, thou wisest of womankind."

She answered, "Since thou wilt not be turned from the journey, up yonder by the river standeth an inn. Within it is a boatman; there is none beside."

He betook him thither to ask further. But the mermaidens cried after the wrothful knight, "Stay, Sir Hagen. Thou art too hasty. Hearken first concerning the way. The lord of this march hight Elsy. The name of his brother is Gelfrat, a prince in Bavaria. It might go hard with thee if thou wentest through his march. Look well to thyself, and proceed warily with the boatman. He is so grim of his mod that he will kill thee, if thou speak him not fair. If thou wouldst have him ferry thee across, give him hire. He guardeth this land, and is Gelfrat's friend. If he come not straightway, cry across the river to him that thou art Amelrich; he was a good knight, that a feud drove from this land. The boatman will come when he heareth that name."

Proud Hagen thanked the women for their warning and their counsel, and said no more. He went up the river's bank, till he came to an inn that stood on the far side. He began to shout across the water, "Boatman, row me over, and I will give thee, for thy meed, an armlet of red gold. I must across."

The boatman was so rich that he needed not to serve for hire, and seldom took reward from any. His men also were overweening, and Hagen was left standing on the bank of the river.

Thereupon he shouted so loud that all the shore rang with it. He was a stark man. "Row across for Amelrich. I am Elsy's liegeman, that, for a feud, fled the country." He swung the armlet aloft on his sword - it was of red gold, bright and shining - that they might ferry him over to Gelfrat's march.

At this the haughty boatman himself took the oar, for he was greedy and covetous of gain, the which bringeth oft to a bad end. He thought to win Hagen's red gold, but won, in lieu thereof, a grim death by his sword.

He rowed over to the shore with mighty strokes. When he found not him that had been named, he fell into a fury; he saw Hagen, and spake wrothfully to the hero, "Thy name may be Amelrich, but, or I err greatly, thy face is none of his. By one father and one mother he was my brother. Since thou hast deceived me, thou canst stay where thou art."

"Nay, for the love of God," said Hagen. "I am a stranger knight that have the charge of other warriors. Take thy fee and row me over, for I am a friend."

But the boatman answered, "I will not. My dear masters have foemen, wherefore I must bring no stranger across. If thou lovest thy life, step out on to the shore again."

"Nay now," said Hagen, "I am sore bested. Take, as a keepsake, this goodly gold, and ferry us over with our thousand horses and our many men."

But the grim boatman answered, "Never!" He seized an oar, mickle and broad, and smote Hagen (soon he rued it), that he staggered and fell on his knees. Seldom had he of Trony encountered so grim a ferryman.

Further, to anger the bold stranger, he brake a boat-pole over his head, for he was a strong man. But he did it to his own hurt.

Grimly wroth, Hagen drew a weapon from the sheath, and cut off his head, and threw it on the ground. The Burgundians were soon ware of the tidings.

In the same moment that he slew the ferryman, the boat was caught by the current, which irked him no little, for he was weary or he could bring her head round, albeit Gunther's man rowed stoutly. With swift strokes he sought to turn it, till the oar brake in his hand. He strove to reach the knights on the strand, but had no other oar. Ha! how nimbly he bound it together with the thong of his shield, a narrow broidered band, and rowed to a wood down the river.

There he found his masters waiting on the beach. Many a valiant knight ran to meet him, and greeted him joyfully. But when they saw the boat full of blood from the grim wound he had given the ferryman, they began to question him.

When Gunther saw the hot blood heaving in the boat, he said quickly, "Tell me what thou hast done with the ferryman. I ween he hath fallen by thy strength."

But he answered with a lie, "I found the boat by a waste meadow, and loosed it. I have seen no ferryman this day, nor hath any suffered hurt at my hand."

Then said Sir Gernot of Burgundy, "I am heavy of my cheer because of the dear friends that must die or night, for boatmen we have none. Sorrowfully I stand, nor know how we shall win over."

But Hagen cried, "Lay down your burdens on the grass, ye squires. I was the best boatman by the Rhine, and safe, I trow, I shall bring you into Gelfrat's land."

That they might cross the quicker, they drave in the horses. These swam so well that none were drowned, albeit a few, grown weary, were borne down some length by the tide.

Then they carried their gold and harness on board, since they must needs make the passage. Hagen was the helmsman, and steered many a gallant knight to the unknown land.

First he took over a thousand, and thereto his own band of warriors. Then followed more: nine thousand squires. The knight of Trony was not idle that day. The ship was huge, strongly built and wide enow. Five hundred of their folk and more, with their meats and weapons, it carried easily at a time. Many a good warrior that day pulled sturdily at the oar.

When he had brought them safe across the water, the bold knight and good thought on the strange prophecy of the wild mermaids. Through this the king's chaplain came nigh to lose his life. He found the priest beside the sacred vessels, leaning with his hand upon the holy relics. This helped him not. When Hagen saw him, it went hard with the poor servant of God. He threw him out of the ship on the instant.

Many cried, "Stop, Hagen, stop!" Giselher, the youth, was very wroth, but Hagen ceased not, till he had done him a hurt.

Then stark Gernot of Burgundy said, "What profiteth thee the chaplain's death, Hagen? Had another done this, he had paid dear for it. What hast thou against the priest?"

The chaplain swam with all his might. He had gotten on board again had any helped him. But none could do it, for stark Hagen pushed him fiercely under. None approved his deed.

When the poor man saw that they would not aid him, he turned and made for the shore. He was in sore peril. But, albeit he could not swim, the hand of God upbore him, that he won safe to the dry land again. There he stood, and shook his clothes.

By this sign Hagen knew there was no escape from what the wild women of the sea had foretold. He thought, "These knights be all dead men."

When they had unloaded the ship, and brought all across that belonged to the three kings, Hagen brake it in pieces and threw these on the water. Much the bold knights marvelled thereat.

"Wherefore dost thou so, brother?" said Dankwart. "How shall we get over when we ride home from the Huns to the Rhine?"

Hagen told him, after, that that would never be, but for the meantime he said, "I did it a-purpose. If we have any coward with us on this journey, that would forsake us in our need, he shall die a shameful death in these waves."

They had with them one from Burgundy, a hero of great prowess, that hight Folker, and that spake with mocking words all his mind. And whatso Hagen did, this fiddler approved.

When the king's chaplain saw the ship hewn up, he cried across the water to Hagen, "What had I done to thee, false murderer, that, without cause, thou wouldst have drowned me?"

Hagen answered, "Hold thy peace. By my troth, and in sober earnest, it irketh me that thou hast escaped."

Said the poor priest, "I will praise God evermore. Little I fear thee now, rest assured. Fare forward to the Huns, and I will to the Rhine. God grant thou comest never back again. That is my prayer, for well-nigh hadst thou killed me."

But King Gunther said to his chaplain, "I will more than make good to thee what Hagen hath done in his anger, if I win back alive. Have no fear. Go home, for so it needs must be now.

Bear a greeting to my dear wife, and my other kinsfolk. Tell them the good tidings: that, so far, all is well."

The horses stood ready, the sumpters were laden. As yet they had suffered no scathe by the way, save the king's chaplain, that had to return to the Rhine afoot.

HOW DANKWART SLEW GELFRAT

HEN they were all on the shore, the king asked, "Who will show us the right way through the country, that we go not astray?"

Whereto bold Folker answered, "I will do it."

"Stop!" said Hagen, "both knights and squires. One must follow one's friends--that is plain to me, and right. But I have heavy news to tell you. Never again shall we see Burgundy. Two mermaids told me this morning early that we should win back to our home nevermore. Now follow my counsel. Arm ye, ye heroes, and guard your lives well. Stark foemen are at hand, wherefore ride as to battle. I hoped to prove the words of the wise mermaids false. They said that none save the chaplain would return. It was for that I had so gladly drowned him."

The news flew from rank to rank. Many a bold knight grew pale, and fell in fear of bitter death, whereto he journeyed. Doleful were they and dreary.

They crossed the river at Moering, where Elsy's ferryman was killed, and Hagen said further, "I have made enemies by the way, that will shortly set on us. I slew the boatman this morning;

wherefore, if Gelfrat and Elsy attack us, welcome them on such wise that it shall go hard with them. They will do it without fail, for I know them for bold men. Ride softly, that none may say we fly."

"So be it," said young Giselher. "Who will lead us through the land?"

And they answered, "Folker, the bold minstrel; he knoweth all the hills and the paths."

Or they had time to ask him, the brave fiddler stood before them, armed, with his helmet on. His harness was bright coloured, and he had bound a red pennon on his spear. Soon he came, with the kings, in great peril.

The news of his boatman's death had reached Gelfrat. Stark Elsy had heard it likewise. Wroth were they both. They summoned their knights, that were soon ready.

Straightway, as I will tell you, a mighty host, strongly armed, rode to them that had suffered scathe. To Gelfrat come more than seven hundred. When these set out to pursue their grim foemen, the leaders spurred hotly after the strangers, to be revenged. By the which they lost many friends.

Hagen of Trony had so ordered it (how could a hero guard his kinsmen better) that he brought up the rear with his vassals, and with Dankwart, his brother. It was wisely done.

The day was far spent; the light failed. He feared greatly for his comrades. They rode through Bavaria behind shields, and shortly after were set upon.

On both sides, and close behind, they heard the trample of hoofs, and spurred on. Then said bold Dankwart, "They will fall on us here. Ye did well to bind on your helmets."

So they stopped, as needs was. Then they saw the glitter of shields in the dark. Hagen held his peace longer, "Who follow us by the way?"

Gelfrat had to answer. Said the Margrave of Bavaria, "We seek our foemen and follow on their track. I know not who slew my boatman to-day. He was a valiant knight, and I grieve for his loss."

Then said Hagen of Trony, "Was the boatman thine? He would not ferry me over. The blame is mine. I slew him. Certes, I had need. I had nigh met my death at his hand. I offered him gold and raiment, Sir Knight, as his meed for rowing us into thy land. So angry was he that he struck me with his great oar, whereat I was grim enow. Then I seized my sword, and defended me from his wrath with a grisly wound, whereby the hero perished. I will answer for it as seemeth good to thee."

So they fell to fighting, for they were wroth.

"I knew well," said Gelfrat, "when Gunther crossed with his followers, that Hagen's insolence would do us some hurt. Now he shall not escape us. His death shall pay for the boatman's."

Gelfrat and Hagen couched their lances to thrust above their shields. Deadly was their hate. Elsy and Dankwart met gallantly, and proven on each other was their might. They strove grimly. How could heroes have fought better? Bold Hagen was knocked back from off his horse by a strong blow from Gelfrat's hand. The poitral brake asunder and he fell.

From the followers also rang the clash of spears. Hagen sprang up again where he had fallen on the grass from the blow; not little was his wrath against Gelfrat. I know not who held their horses.

Hagen and Gelfrat were both on the ground. They ran at each other, and their attendants helped them and fought by them. For all Hagen's fierce onset, the noble Margrave hewed an ell's length from his shield, that the sparks flew bright. Gunther's man was well-nigh slain. Then he cried aloud to Dankwart, "Help! dear brother. I perish by the hand of a hero."

Bold Dankwart answered, "I will decide between you." The knight spurred toward them, and smote Gelfrat such a blow that he fell dead.

Elsy would have avenged him, but he and his followers were overcome. His brother was slain, and he himself wounded. Full eighty of his warriors he left there with grim death; the prince had to flee before Gunther's men.

When the Bavarians gave way, there was heard the echo of grisly strokes. The men of Trony chased their foes, and they that stayed not to answer for it had little ease by the way.

But while they pursued them, Dankwart said, "Now turn we, and let them ride. They are wet with blood. Let us join our friends. Truly it were best."

When they came again where the fight had been, Hagen of Trony said, "Let us see now, ye heroes, who are amissing, and whom we have lost through Gelfrat's anger."

They had four to mourn for, that they had lost. Well they were avenged. Against these, more than an hundred of them of Bavaria lay slain. The shields of the men of Trony were dim and wet with blood.

The bright moon shone faintly through the clouds, and Hagen said, "Let none tell my dear masters what hath befallen us. Let them be free of trouble till the morrow."

When they that had fought came up with the rest, they found them overcome with weariness. "How long shall we ride?" asked many among them.

Bold Dankwart answered, "Here is no hostel. Ye must ride till it is day."

Folker, that had the charge, bade ask the marshal, "Where shall we halt for the night, that the horses and my dear masters may rest?"

But Dankwart said, "I know not. We cannot rest till the dawn. Then we shall lie down on the grass wherever we find a place." When they heard this news they were sorry enow!

Of the red blood that reeked on them nothing was said till the sun greeted the morning on the mountains with his bright beams, and the king saw that they had fought.

The knight cried angrily, "How now, friend Hagen? Wherefore didst thou scorn my help when they were wetting thy harness with blood? Who hath done it?"

Hagen answered, "It was Elsy. He fell on us by night. Because of his ferryman, he attacked us. My brother's hand slew Gelfrat. Elsy was forced to flee. An hundred of his men, and four of ours, lie dead, slain in battle."

I cannot tell you where they rested. Soon all the country folk heard that noble Uta's sons were on their way to the hightide.

They were well received at Passau. Bishop Pilgerin, the king's uncle, was well pleased that his nephews drew night with so many knights. He was not slow to give them welcome. Friends rode out to meet them on the way. When there was not room enow for all in Passau, they crossed the river to a field, and there the squires put up tents and rich pavilions.

They had to tarry there a whole day and a night. Well they were entreated! Then they rode into Rudeger's country. When Rudeger heard the news, he was glad.

When the way-weary ones had rested, and drew nigher to Rudeger's country, they found a man asleep on the marches, from whom Hagen of Trony took a stark weapon. This same good knight hight Eckewart. Right heavy was he of his cheer that he had lost his sword through the passing of the heroes. They found Rudeger's marches ill guarded.

"Woe is me for this shame!" cried Eckewart. "Sore I rue the Burgundians' journey. The day I lost Siegfried my joy was ended. Alack! Sir Rudeger, an ill turn I have done thee."

Hagen overheard all the warrior's grief, and gave him his sword again, with six red armlets. "Take them, Sir Knight, for love of me, and be my friend. Thou art a brave man to lie here all alone."

"God quit thee for thine armlets," answered Eckewart. "Yet still I must rue thy journey to the Huns. Thou slewest Siegfried, and art hated here. Look well to thyself; from true heart I warn thee."

"God must guard us," said Hagen. "No other care have these knights, the princes and their liegemen, than to find quarters, where they may tarry the night. Our horses are weary from the long way, and our provender is done. We can find none to buy. We have need of a host that, of his charity, would give us bread."

Eckewart answered, "I will show you such an host. Better welcome to his house will none give you in any land than Rudeger, if ye will go to see him. He dwelleth fast by the road, and is the best host that ever had a house. His heart blossometh with virtues, as smiling May decketh the grass with flowers. He is ever glad to serve knights."

Then said King Gunther, "Wilt thou be my envoy, and ask my dear friend Rudeger if he will keep us - me with my kinsmen and our men--till the day? I will require him as best I can."

"I will gladly be thy envoy," answered Eckewart.

He set out with good will, and told Rudeger what he had heard. Such good news had not reached him for long.

A knight was seen hasting to Bechlaren. Rudeger knew him, and said, "Here cometh Eckewart, Kriemhild's man, down the way."

He deemed that foemen had done him a hurt. He went to the door and met the envoy, that ungirded his sword and laid it down.

Rudeger said to the knight, "What hast thou heard, that thou ridest in such hot haste? Hath any done us a mischief?"

"None hath harmed us," said Eckewart straightway. "Three kings have sent me: Gunther of Burgundy, Giselher, and Gernot. Each of them commended his service to thee. The same doth Hagen from true heart, and also Folker. Further, I have to tell thee that Dankwart, the king's marshal, bade me say that the good knights have need of thy roof."

Rudeger answered with smiling face, "This is glad news, that the high kings need my service. It shall not be denied them. Right glad am I that they come to my house."

"Dankwart, the marshal, bade me tell thee who there be of them: sixty bold warriors and a thousand good knights, with nine thousand squires."

Rudeger rejoiced to hear it, and said, "Welcome are these guests--the high warriors that come to my castle, and that I so seldom have served heretofore. Ride out to meet them, my kinsmen and my vassals."

Whereat knights and squires hasted to horse. All that their lord commanded they deemed right; so they served him the better.

Gotelind, that sat in her chamber, had not heard the news.

HOW THEY CAME TO BECHLAREN

HE Margrave went to find his wife and daughter, and told them the good news that he had heard, how that their queen's brethren were coming to the house.

"Dear love," said Rudeger, "receive the high and noble kings well when they come here with their followers. Hagen, Gunther's man, thou shalt also greet fair. There is one with them that hight Dankwart; another hight Folker, a man of much worship. These six thou shalt kiss--thou and my daughter. Entreat the warriors courteously."

The women promised it, nothing loth. They took goodly apparel from their chests, wherein to meet the knights. The fair women made haste enow. Their cheeks needed little false colour. They wore fillets of bright gold on their heads, fashioned like rich wreaths, that the wind might not ruffle their beautiful hair. They were dainty and fresh.

Now leave we the women busied on this wise. There was mickle spurring across the plain among Rudeger's friends till they found the princes. These were well received in the Margrave's land. Rudeger cried joyfully as he went toward them, "Ye be welcome, ye knights, and all your men. Right glad am I to see you in my home."

The warriors thanked him with true heart void of hate. He showed them plainly they were welcome. To Hagen he gave special greeting, for he knew him from aforetime. He did the same to Folker of Burgundy. He welcomed Dankwart also.

Then said that knight, "If thou take us in, who will see to our followers from Worms beyond the Rhine?"

The Margrave answered, "Have no fear on that head. All that ye have with you, horses, silver and apparel, shall be so well guarded that ye shall not lose a single spur thereof. Pitch your tents in the fields, ye squires. Whatso ye lose here I will make good to you. Off with the bridles, and let the horses go loose."

Never before had host done this for them. Glad enow were the guests. When they had obeyed him, and the knights had ridden away, the squires laid them down on the grass over all, and took their ease. It was their softest rest on the whole journey.

The noble Margravine came out before the castle with her beautiful daughter. Lovely women and fair maids not a few stood beside her, adorned with bracelets and fine apparel. Precious stones sparked bright on their rich vesture. Goodly was their raiment.

The guests rode up and sprang to the ground. Ha! courteous men all were they of Burgundy! Six and thirty maidens and many women beside, fair to heart's desire, came forth to meet them, with bold men in plenty. The noble women welcomed them sweetly. The Margravine kissed the kings all three. Her daughter did the like.

Hagen stood by. Him also her father bade her kiss. She looked up at him, and he was so grim that she had gladly let it be. Yet must she do as the host bade her. Her colour came and went, white and red. She kissed Dankwart, too, and, after him, the fiddler. By reason of his body's strength he won this greeting.

Then the young Margravine took Giselher, the youth, of Burgundy by the hand. Her mother did the same to Gunther, and they went in merrily with the heroes.

The host led Gernot into a wide hall. There knights and ladies sat down, and good wine was poured out for the guests. Never were warriors better entreated.

The Burgundians Ride Into Bechlaren

Rudeger's daughter was looked at with loving eyes, she was so fair; and many a good knight loved her in his heart. And well they might, for she was an high-hearted maiden. But their thoughts were vain: it could not be.

They kept spying at the women, whereof many sat round. Now the fiddler was well-minded to Rudeger.

Women and knights were parted then, as was the custom, and went into separate rooms. The table was made ready in the great hall, and willing service was done to the strangers.

To show love to the guests, the Margravine went to table with them. She left her daughter with the damsels, as was seemly, albeit it irked the guests to see her no longer.

When they had all drunk and eaten, they brought the fair ones into the hall again, and there was no lack of sweet words. Folker, a knight bold and good, spake plenty of them.

This same fiddler said openly, "Great Margrave, God hath done well by thee, for He hath given thee a right beautiful wife, and happy days. Were I a king," said the minstrel, "and wore a crown, I would choose thy sweet daughter for my queen. She would be the choice of my heart, for she is fair to look upon, and, thereto, noble and good."

The Margrave answered, "How should a king covet my dear daughter? My wife and I are both strangers here, and have naught to give. What availeth then her beauty?"

But said Gernot, the courteous man, "Might I choose where I would, such a wife were my heart's desire."

Then said Hagen graciously, "It is time Giselher wedded. Of such high lineage is the noble Margravine, that we would gladly serve her, I and his men, if she wore the crown in Burgundy."

The word pleased both Rudeger and Gotelind greatly. Their hearts were uplifted. So it was agreed among the heroes that noble Giselher should take her to wife; the which a king might well do without shame.

If a thing be right, who can withstand it? They bade the maiden before them, and they swore to give her to him, whereupon he vowed to cherish her. They gave her castles and lands for her share. The king and Gernot sware with the hand that it should be even as they had promised.

Then said the Margrave, "Since I have no castles, I can only prove me your true friend evermore. I will give my daughter as much silver and gold as an hundred sumpters may carry, that ye warriors may, with honour, be content."

Then the twain were put in a circle, as the custom was. Many a young knight stood opposite in merry mood, and thought in his heart as young folk will. They asked the lovely maiden if she would have the hero. She was half sorry, yet her heart inclined to the goodly man. She was shamefast at the question, as many a maid hath been.

Rudeger her father counselled her to say "yes," and to take him gladly. Giselher, the youth, was not slow to clasp her to him with his white hands. Yet how little while she had him!

Then said the Margrave, "Great and noble kings, I will give you my child to take with you, for this were fittest, when ye ride home again into your land." And it was so agreed.

The din of tourney was bidden cease. The damsels were sent to their chambers, and the guests to sleep and to take their rest till the day. Then meats were made ready, for their host saw well to their comfort.

When they had eaten, they would have set out again for the country of the Huns, but Rudeger said, "Go not, I pray you. Tarry here yet a while, for I had never dearer guests."

Dankwart answered, "It may not be. Where couldst thou find the meat, the bread and the wine, for so many knights?"

But when the host heard him, he said, "Speak not of that. Deny me not, my dear lords. I can give you, and all them that are with you, meat for fourteen days. Little hath King Etzel ever taken of my substance."

Albeit they made excuse, they had to tarry till the fourth morning. He gave both horses and apparel so freely, that the fame of it spread abroad.

But longer than this it could not last, for they must needs forth. Rudeger was not sparing of his goods. If any craved for aught, none denied him. Each got his desire.

The attendants brought the saddled horses to the door. There many stranger knights joined them, shield in hand, to ride with them to Etzel's court. To each of the noble guests Rudeger offered a gift, or he left the hall. He had wherewithal to live in honour and give freely.

Upon Giselher he had bestowed his fair daughter. He gave to Gernot a goodly weapon enow, that he wielded well afterward in strife. The Margrave's wife grudged him not the gift, yet Rudeger, or long, was slain thereby.

To Gunther, the valiant knight, he gave a coat of mail, that did the rich king honour, albeit he seldom took gifts. He bowed before Rudeger and thanked him.

Gotelind offered Hagen a fair gift, as was fitting, since the king had taken one, that he might not fare to the hightide without a keepsake from her, but he refused.

"Naught that I ever saw would I so fain bear away with me as yonder shield on the wall. I would gladly carry it into Etzel's land."

When the Margravine heard Hagen's word, it minded her on her sorrow, and she fell to weeping. She thought sadly on the death of Nudung, that Wittich had slain; and her heart was heavy.

She said to the knight, "I will give thee the shield. Would to God he yet lived that once bore it! He died in battle. I must ever weep when I think on him, for my woman's heart is sore."

The noble Margravine rose from her seat, and took down the shield with her white hands and carried it to Hagen, that used it as a hero should.

A covering of bright stuff lay over its device. The light never shone on better shield. It was so rich with precious stones, that had any wanted to buy it, it had cost him at the least a thousand marks.

The knight bade his attendants bear it away.

Then came his brother Dankwart, to whom the Margrave's daughter gave richly broidered apparel, that afterward he wore merrily among the Huns.

None had touched any of these things but for love of the host that offered them so kindly. Yet, or long, they bare him such hate that they slew him.

Bold Folker then stepped forth with knightly bearing and stood before Gotelind with his viol. He played a sweet tune and sang her his song. Then he took his leave and left Bechlaren.

But first the Margravine bade them bring a drawer near. Of loving gifts now hear the tale. She took therefrom twelve armlets, and drew them over his hand, saying, "These shalt thou take with thee and wear for my sake at Etzel's court. When thou comest again, I will hear how thou hast served me at the hightide." Well he did her behest.

The host said to the guests, "That ye may journey the safer, I will myself escort you, and see that none fall on you by the way." And forthwith they loaded his sumpters.

He stood ready for the road with five hundred men, mounted and equipped. These he led merrily to the hightide. Not one of them came back alive to Bechlaren.

He took leave with sweet kisses. The same did Giselher, as love bade him. They took the fair women in their arms. Or long, many a damsel wept for them.

The windows were flung wide over all, for the host and his men were gotten to horse. Their hearts, I ween, foreboded their bitter woe, and many a wife and many a maiden wept sore. They sorrowed for many a dear friend that was never seen more at Bechlaren. Yet merrily they rode down the valley by the Danube into the land of the Huns.

Then said noble Rudeger to the Burgundians, "We must delay no longer to send news of our advance. Nothing could rejoice King Etzel more."

The swift envoys pressed down through Austria, and soon the folk knew, far and near, that the heroes were on their way from Worms beyond the Rhine. It was welcome news to the king's vassals. The envoys spurred forward with the tidings that the Nibelungs were come to the Huns.

"Receive them well, Kriemhild, my wife. Thy brethren are come to show thee great honour."

Kriemhild stood at a window and looked out as a friend might for friends. Many drew thither from her father's land. The king was joyful when he heard the news.

"Glad am I," said Kriemhild, "my kinsmen come with many new shields and shining bucklers. I will ever be his friend that taketh my gold and remembereth my wrong."

She thought in her heart, "Now for the reckoning! If I can contrive it, it will go hard at this hightide with him that killed all my happiness. Fain would I work his doom. I care not what may come of it: my vengeance shall fall on the hateful body of him that stole my joy from me. He shall pay dear for my sorrow."

TWENTY-EIGHTH ADVENTURE
HOW KRIEMHILD RECEIVED HAGEN

WHEN the Burgundians came into the land, old Hildebrand of Bern heard thereof, and told his master, that was grieved at the news. He bade him give hearty welcome to the valiant knights. Bold Wolfhart called for the horses, and many stark warriors rode with Dietrich to greet them on the plain, where they had pitched their goodly tents.

When Hagen of Trony saw them from afar, he spake courteously to his masters, "Arise, ye doughty heroes, and go to meet them that come to welcome you. A company of warriors that I know well draw hither--the heroes of the Amelung land. They are men of high courage. Scorn not their service."

Then, as was seemly, Dietrich, with many knights and squires, sprang to the ground. They hasted to the guests, and welcomed the heroes of Burgundy lovingly.

When Dietrich saw them, he was both glad and sorry; he knew what was toward, and grieved that they were come. He deemed that Rudeger was privy to it, and had told them. "Ye be welcome, Gunther and Giselher, Gernot and Hagen; Folker, likewise, and Dankwart the swift. Know ye not that Kriemhild still mourneth bitterly for the hero of the Nibelungs?"

"She will weep awhile," answered Hagen. "This many a year he lieth slain. She did well to comfort her with the king of the Huns. Siegfried will not come again. He is long buried."

"Enough of Siegfried's wounds. While Kriemhild, my mistress, liveth, mischief may well betide. Wherefore, hope of the Nibelungs, beware!"

So spake Dietrich of Bern.

"Wherefore should I beware?" said the king. "Etzel sent us envoys (what more could I ask?) bidding us hither to this land. My sister Kriemhild, also, sent us many greetings."

But Hagen said, "Bid Sir Dietrich and his good knights tell us further of this matter, that they may show us the mind of Kriemhild."

Then the three kings went apart: Gunther and Gernot and Dietrich.

"Now tell us, noble knight of Bern, what thou knowest of the queen's mind."

The prince of Bern answered, "What can I tell you, save that every morning I have heard Etzel's wife weeping and wailing in bitter woe to the great God of Heaven, because of stark Siegfried's death?"

Said bold Folker, the fiddler, "There is no help for it. Let us ride to the court and see what befalleth us among the Huns."

The bold Burgundians rode to the court right proudly, after the custom of their land. Many bold Huns marvelled much what manner of man Hagen of Trony might be. The folk knew well, from hearsay, that he had slain Siegfried of the Netherland, the starkest of all knights, Kriemhild's husband. Wherefore many questions were asked concerning him. The hero was of great stature; that is certain. His shoulders were broad, his hair was grisled; his legs were long, and terrible was his face. He walked with a proud gait.

Then lodging was made ready for the Burgundians. Gunther's attendants lay separate from the others. The queen, that greatly hated Gunther, had so ordered it. By this device his yeomen were slain soon after.

Dankwart, Hagen's brother, was marshal. The king commended his men earnestly to his care, that he might give them meat and drink enow, the which the bold knight did faithfully and with good will.

Kriemhild went forth with her attendants and welcomed the Nibelungs with false heart. She kissed Giselher and took him by the hand. When Hagen of Trony saw that, he bound his helmet on tighter.

"After such greeting," he said, "good knights may well take thought. The kings and their men are not all alike welcome. No good cometh of our journey to this hightide."

She answered, "Let him that is glad to see thee welcome thee. I will not greet thee as a friend. What bringest thou for me from Worms, beyond the Rhine, that thou shouldst be so greatly welcome?"

"This is news," said Hagen, "that knights should bring thee gifts. Had I thought of it, I had easily brought thee something. I am rich enow."

"Tell me what thou hast done with the Nibelung hoard. That, at the least, was mine own. Ye should have brought it with you into Etzel's land."

"By my troth, lady, I have not touched the Nibelung hoard this many a year. My masters bade me sink it in the Rhine. There it must bide till the day of doom."

Then said the queen, "I thought so. Little hast thou brought thereof, albeit it was mine own, and held by me aforetime. Many a sad day I have lived for lack of it and its lord."

"I bring thee the Devil!" cried Hagen. "My shield and my harness were enow to carry, and my bright helmet, and the sword in my hand. I have brought thee naught further."

"I speak not of my treasure, because I desire the gold. I have so much to give that I need not thy offerings. A murder and a double theft - it is these that I, unhappiest of women, would have thee make good to me."

Then said the queen to all the knights, "None shall bear weapons in this hall. Deliver them to me, ye knights, that they be taken in charge."

"Not so, by my troth," said Hagen; "I crave not the honour, great daughter of kings, to have thee bear my shield and other weapons to safe keeping. Thou art a queen here. My father taught me to guard them myself."

"Woe is me!" cried Kriemhild. "Why will not Hagen and my brother give up their shields? They are warned. If I knew him that did it, he should die."

Sir Dietrich answered wrathfully then, "I am he that warned the noble kings, and bold Hagen, the man of Burgundy. Do thy worst, thou devil's wife, I care not!"

Kriemhild was greatly ashamed, for she stood in bitter fear of Dietrich. She went from him without a word, but with swift and wrathful glances at her foes.

Then two knights clasped hands--the one was Dietrich, the other Hagen. Dietrich, the valiant warrior, said courteously, "I grieve to see thee here, since the queen hath spoken thus."

Hagen of Trony answered, "It will all come right."

So the bold men spake together, and King Etzel saw them, and asked, "I would know who yonder knight is that Dietrich welcometh so lovingly. He beareth him proudly. Howso is his father hight, he is, certes, a goodly warrior."

One of Kriemhild's men answered the king, "He was born at Trony. The name of his father was Aldrian. Albeit now he goeth gently, he is a grim man. I will prove to thee yet that I lie not."

"How shall I find him so grim?" He knew nothing, as yet, of all that the queen contrived against her kinsmen: by reason whereof not one of them escaped alive from the Huns.

"I know Hagen well. He was my vassal. Praise and mickle honour he won here by me. I made him a knight, and gave him my gold. For that he proved him faithful, I was ever kind to him.

Wherefore I may well know all about him. I brought two noble children captive to this land - him and Walter of Spain. Here they grew to manhood. Hagen I sent home again. Walter fled with Hildegund."

So he mused on the good old days, and what had happed long ago, for he had seen Hagen, that did him stark service in his youth. Yet now that he was old, he lost by him many a dear friend.

TWENTY-NINTH ADVENTURE
HOW HAGEN AND FOLKER SAT BEFORE KRIEMHILD'S HALL

HE two valiant knights, Hagen of Trony and Sir Dietrich, parted, and Gunther's man looked back for a comrade that he soon espied. He saw Folker, the cunning fiddler, by Giselher, and bade him come with him, for well he knew his grim mood. He was in all things a warrior bold and good.

The knights still stood in the court. These two alone were seen crossing the yard to a large hall at a distance. They feared no man. They sat down before the house, on a bench opposite Kriemhild's chamber. Their goodly apparel shone bright on their bodies. Not a few of them that looked were fain to know them.

The Huns gaped at the proud heroes as they had been wild beasts, and Etzel's wife saw them through a window, and was troubled anew. She thought on her old wrong, and began to weep.

Etzel's men marvelled much what had grieved her so sore. She said, "Good knights, it is Hagen that hath done it."

Then said they to the queen, "How came it to pass? A moment ago we saw thee of good cheer. There is no man so bold, had he done thee a hurt, and thou badest us avenge thee, but he should answer for it with his life."

"Him that avenged my wrong I would thank evermore. All that he asked I would give him. I fall at your feet; only avenge me on Hagen, that he lose his life."

Thereupon sixty bold men armed them swiftly, and would have gone out with one accord to slay Hagen, the bold knight, and the fiddler, for Kriemhild's sake.

But when the queen saw so small a number, she spake wrothfully to the heroes, "Think not to withstand Hagen with so few. Stark and bold as is Hagen of Trony, much starker is he that sitteth by him, Folker the fiddler by name, a wicked man. Ye shall not so lightly overcome them."

When they heard her word, four hundred knights more did on their armour, for the queen was eager to do her enemies a hurt. Soon they came in sore straits.

When she saw them well armed, she said to them, "Stand still a while and wait. I will go out to my foes with my crown on. Hearken while I upbraid Hagen of Trony, Gunther's man, with what he hath done to me. I know him for too proud a knight to deny it. After that, I care not what befalleth him."

Then the fiddler, a bold minstrel, saw the queen coming down the stair from the house, and said to his comrade, "Now see, friend Hagen, how she that hath falsely bidden us to this land, cometh toward us. Never have I beheld, with a king's wife, so many men, sword in hand, as for strife. Knowest thou, friend Hagen, that they hate thee? I counsel thee to look to thy life and thine honour. Certes, it were well. Methinketh they be wrothful of their mood. Many among them have shoulders broad enow. Who would save his life had best do it betimes. I ween they wear harness below their silk, whereof I hear none declare the meaning."

But Hagen, the bold man, answered angrily, "Well, I know that it is against me they carry their bright weapons in their hands. But, for all that, I will yet ride back to Burgundy. Now say, friend Folker, wilt thou stand by me, if Kriemhild's men fall on me? Tell me, as thou lovest me. To thy service thou wouldst bind me evermore."

"I will help thee truly," answered the minstrel; "if I saw the king coming with all his warriors, I would not, while I lived, stir a foot from thy side through fear."

"God in Heaven quit thee, noble Folker! If they fight with me, what need I more. Since thou wilt help me, as I have heard thee promise, these knights had best walk warily."

"Now rise we from our seat, and let her pass," said the minstrel. "She is a queen. Do her this honour; she is a high-born lady. Therein we honour ourselves."

"Nay, as thou lovest me!" Hagen said. "These knights might deem I did it through fear, and thought to fly. I will not rise from my seat for any of them. It beseemeth us better to sit still. Shall I show honour to her that hateth me? That I will never do, so long as I be a living man. Certes, I care little if King Etzel's wife misliketh me."

Hagen, the overweening man, laid a bright weapon across his knee, from the hilt whereof shone a flaming jasper, greener than grass. Well Kriemhild knew that it was Siegfried's.

When she saw the sword, her heart was heavy. The hilt was of gold, the scabbard of red broidered silk. It minded her on her woe, and she began to weep. Bold Hagen, I ween, had done it apurpose.

Brave Folker drew closer to him on the bench a stark fiddle-bow, mickle and long, made like a sword, sharp and broad. There sat the good knights unafraid. They deemed them too high to rise from their seat through fear of any.

Then the noble queen advanced to them and gave them angry greeting. She said, "Now tell me, Sir Hagen, who sent for thee, that thou hast dared to ride into this land? Wert thou in thy senses, thou hadst not done it."

"None sent for me," answered Hagen. "Three knights that I call master, were bidden hither. I am their liegeman, and never yet tarried behind when they rode to a hightide."

She said, "Now tell me further. Wherefore didst thou that which hath earned thee my hate? Thou slewest Siegfried, my dear husband, that I cannot mourn enow to my life's end."

He answered, "Enough! What thou hast said sufficeth. It was I, Hagen, that slew Siegfried, the hero. He paid dear for the evil words that Kriemhild spake to fair Brunhild. I deny not, mighty queen, that I am guilty, and the cause of all the mischief. Avenge it who will, man or woman. I will not lie; I have wrought thee much woe."

She said, "Ye hear him, knights! He denieth not the wrong he hath done me. I care not how he suffer for it, ye men of Etzel."

The proud warriors glanced at each other. Had there been fighting, the two comrades had come off with honour, as oft aforetime in strife. What the Huns had undertaken they durst not perform, through fear.

Then said one among them, "Why look ye at me? My word was vain; I will not lose my life for the gifts of no woman. King Etzel's wife, methinketh, would undo us."

Another said, "I am of thy mind. I would not challenge this fiddler for towers full of red gold, for much I mislike his fierce glances. This Hagen, too, I knew in his youth, and need not to be told concerning him. In two-and-twenty battles I have seen him. He hath given many a woman heart's dole. He and the knight of Spain rode on many a foray, and here, by Etzel, won many victories to the honour of the king. Wherefore none may deny him praise. In those days the knight was a child, and they that now are grey were youths. Now he is grown to a grim man. Thereto, he weareth Balmung, which he won evilly."

So they agreed that none should fight, whereat the queen grieved bitterly. The knights turned away, for the feared death from the fiddler, and were dismayed. How oft will cowards fall back when friend standeth true by friend! And he that bethinketh him betimes is delivered from many a snare.

Then said bold Folker, "Now have we seen and heard that foemen are around us. Haste we to the court, to the kings, that none dare fall upon them."

"I will follow," said Hagen.

They went where they found the knights still waiting in the courtyard; and bold Folker began to say to his masters with a loud voice, "How long will ye stand here to be jostled? Go in and hear from the king how he is minded toward you."

The knights bold and good went in pairs. The prince of Bern took great Gunther of Burgundy by the hand. Irnfried took brave Gernot, and Giselher went in with his father-in-law. Howso the others walked, Folker and Hagen parted nevermore, save once in battle, till their death; the which gave many a noble woman cause to weep.

With the kings came their followers, a thousand bold men, and, thereto, sixty warriors, brought by Hagen from his land. Hawart and Iring, two chosen knights, went after the kings, hand in hand. Dankwart and Wolfhart, a true-hearted man, bare them courteously toward them that were present.

When the prince of Rhineland came into the palace, Etzel waited no longer, but sprang up from his seat when he saw them. Never was fairer greeting between kings. "Ye be welcome, Sir Gunther and Sir Gernot, and Giselher your brother. With true heart I sent my service to you at Worms. Your knights, too, are welcome, each one. Glad are my wife and I to greet bold Folker, and also Hagen, in this land. Many a message she sent you to the Rhine."

Then said Hagen of Trony, "I heard them all. Had I not ridden hither for my masters' sake, I had come to do thee honour." Thereupon the host took his dear guests by the hand, and led them to the high seat where he himself sat. And they hasted and poured out mead, morat, and wine, for the guests, in great golden goblets, and bade the strangers heartily welcome.

Then said King Etzel, "I tell you truly that nothing in this world had pleased me better than to see you knights here. It will ease the queen of mickle heart's dole. I marvelled oft what I had done, that, among the many guests I won to my court, ye never came to my land. Glad am I to see you now."

Whereto Rudeger, the high-hearted knight, answered, "Thou rejoicest with cause, for my mistress's kinsmen are men of proven worth, and they bring many valiant knights with them."

It was on a midsummer eve that they came to Etzel's court, and seldom hath been heard such high greeting as he gave to the heroes. Then he went merrily to table with them, and no host ever entreated guests better. Meat and drink they had in plenty. All that they desired stood ready for them, for many marvels had been told of them.

The rich king had built a great castle at much cost and trouble-palaces, and towers, and chambers without number, in a big fortress, and thereto a goodly hall. He had ordered it to be built long and high and wide, by reason of the many knights that flocked to his court without cease.

Twelve great kings were his liegemen, and many warriors of much worship he had always by him, more than any king I ever heard of. He lived merrily with kinsmen and vassals round him, with the joyful tumult of good knights on every side. By reason whereof his heart was uplifted.

THIRTIETH ADVENTURE
HOW HAGEN AND FOLKER KEPT WATCH

HE day was now ended and the night drew nigh. The way-weary warriors were fain to rest, and lie down on their beds, but knew not how to compass it. Hagen asked, and brought them word. Gunther said to the host, "God have thee in His keeping. Give us leave to go and sleep. If thou desire it, we will come again early in the morning." Then Etzel parted merrily from his guests.

From all sides the folk pressed in on the strangers. Bold Folker said to the Huns, "How dare ye get before our feet? If ye void not the way, it will be the worse for you. I will give some of you a blow with this fiddle that may cause your friends to weep. Fall back from us warriors. Certes, ye had better. Ye be knights in name and naught else."

While the fiddler spake thus wrothfully, bold Hagen looked over his shoulder and said, "The minstrel giveth you good counsel. Get to your lodging, ye men of Kriemhild. This is no time for your malice. If ye would start a quarrel, come to us to-morrow early, and let us way-weary warriors lie this night in peace. I ween ye will find none readier than we are."

They led the guests to a spacious hall, where they found beds, big and costly, standing ready. Gladly had the queen worked their doom. Coverlets of bright stuffs from Arras were there, and testers of silk of Araby, the goodliest that could be, broidered and shining with gold. The bed-clothes were of ermine and black sable, for them to rest under, the night through, till the day. In such state never king lay before with his men.

"Woe is me for our lodging!" said Giselher the youth, "and for my friends that came hither with us. My sister sent us fair words, but I fear we must all soon lie dead through her."

"Grieve not," said Hagen the knight. "I will myself keep watch, and will guard thee well, I trow, till the day. Fear naught till then. After that, each shall look to himself."

They bowed to him and thanked him. They went to their beds, and, or long, the valiant men were lying soft. Then bold Hagen began to arm him.

Folker the fiddler said, "If thou scorn not my help, Hagen, I would keep watch with thee till the morning."

The hero thanked Folker, "God in Heaven quit you, dear Folker. In all my troubles and my straits I desire thee only and no other. I will do as much for thee, if death hinder it not."

They both did on their shining harness. Each took his shield in his hand, and went out before the door to keep watch over the strangers. They did it faithfully.

Brave Folker leaned his good shield against the wall, and went back and took his fiddle, and did fair and seemly service to his friends. He sat down under the lintel upon the stone. There never was a bolder minstrel. When the sweet tones sounded from his strings, the proud homeless ones all thanked him. He struck so loud that the house echoed. Great were his skill and strength both. Then he played sweeter and softer, till he had lulled many a care-worn man to sleep. When Folker found they were all asleep, he took his shield in his hand again, and went out and stood before the door, to guard his friends from Kriemhild's men.

About the middle of the night, or sooner, bold Folker saw a helmet in the distance, shining in the dark. Kriemhild's vassals were fain to do them a hurt. Or she sent them forth, she said, "For God's sake, if ye win at them, slay none save the one man, false Hagen; let the others live."

Then spake the fiddler, "Friend Hagen, we must bear this matter through together. I see armed folk before the house. I ween they come against us."

"Hold thy peace," answered Hagen. "Let them come nigher. Or they are ware of us, there will be helmets cloven by the swords in our two hands. They shall be sent back to Kriemhild in sorry plight."

One of the Hunnish knights saw that the door was guarded, and said hastily, "We cannot carry this thing through. I see the fiddler standing guard. He hath on his head a shining helmet, bright and goodly, with no dint therein, and stark thereto. The rings of his harness glow like fire. Hagen standeth by him. The strangers are well watched."

They turned without more ado. When Folker saw this, he spake angrily to his comrade, "Let me go out to these knights. I would ask Kriemhild's men a question."

"Nay, as thou lovest me," said Hagen. "If thou wentest to them, thou wouldst fall in such strait by their swords that I must help thee, though all my kinsmen perished thereby. If both the twain of us fell to fighting, two or three of them might easily spring into the house, and do such hurt to the sleepers as we could never mourn enow."

But Folker said, "Let us tell them that we have seen them, that they deny not their treachery."

Then Folker called out to them, "Why go ye there armed, valiant knights? Is it murder ye are after, ye men of Kriemhild? Take me and my comrade to help you."

None answered him. Right wroth was he.

"Shame on you, cowards! Would ye have slain us sleeping? Seldom afore hath so foul a deed been done on good knights."

The queen was heavy of her cheer when they told her that her messengers had failed. She began to contrive it otherwise, for grim was her mood, and by reason thereof many a good knight and bold soon perished.

HOW THE BURGUNDIANS WENT TO CHURCH

Y harness is grown so cold," said Folker, "that I ween the night is far spent. I feel, by the air, that it will soon be day."

Then they walked the knights that still slept.

The bright morning shone in on the warriors in the hall, and Hagen began to ask them if they would go to the minster to hear mass. The bells were ringing according to Christian custom.

The folk sang out of tune: it was not mickle wonder, when Christian and heathen sang together.

Gunther's men were minded to go to church, and rose from their beds. They did on their fine apparel - never knights brought goodlier weed into any king's land.

But Hagen was wroth, and said, "Ye did better to wear other raiment. Ye know how it standeth with us here. Instead of roses, bear weapons in your hands, and instead of jewelled caps, bright helmets. Of wicked Kriemhild's mood we are well aware. I tell you there will be fighting this day. For your silken tunics wear your hauberks, and good broad shields for rich mantels, that, if any fall on you, ye may be ready. My masters dear, my kinsmen, and my men, go to the church and bewail your sorrow and your need before great God, for know, of a surety, that death draweth nigh. Forget not wherein ye have sinned, and stand humbly before your Maker. Be warned, most noble knights. If God in Heaven help you not, ye will hear mass no more."

So the kings and their men went to the minster. Hagen bade them pause in the churchyard, that they might not be parted. He said, "None knoweth yet what the Huns may attempt on us. Lay your shields at your feet, my friends, and if any give you hostile greeting, answer him with deep wounds and deadly. That is Hagen's counsel, that ye may be found ready, as beseemeth you."

Folker and Hagen went and stood before the great minster. They did this, that the queen might be forced to push past them. Right grim was their mood.

Then came the king and his beautiful wife. Her body was adorned with rich apparel, and the knights in her train were featly clad. The dust rose high before the queen's attendants.

When the rich king saw the princes and their followers armed, he said hastily, "Why go my friends armed? By my troth it would grieve me if any had done aught to them. I will make it good to them on any wise they ask it. Hath any troubled their hearts, he shall feel my displeasure. Whatso they demand of me I will do."

Hagen answered, "None hath wrought us annoy. It is the custom of my masters to go armed at all hightides for full three days. If any did us a mischief, Etzel should hear thereof."

Right well Kriemhild heard Hagen's words. She looked at him from under her eyelids with bitter hate. Yet she told not the custom of her land, albeit she knew it well from aforetime. Howso grim and deadly the queen's anger was, none had told Etzel how it stood, else he had hindered what afterward befell. They scorned, through pride, to tell their wrong.

The queen advanced with a great crowd of folk, but the twain moved not two hands' breadth, whereat the Huns were wroth, for they had to press past the heroes. This pleased not Etzel's chamberlains, and they had gladly quarrelled with them, had they dared before the king. There was much jostling, and nothing more.

When the mass was over, many a Hun sprang to horse. With Kriemhild were also many beautiful maidens. Kriemhild sat by Etzel at a window with her women, to see the bold warriors ride, the which the king loved to do. Ha! many a stranger knight spurred below in the court!

The marshal brought out the horses. Bold Dankwart had gathered together his master's followers from Burgundy. Well-saddled horses were led up for the Nibelungs. When the kings and their men were mounted, Folker counselled them to joust after the fashion of their country. Full knightly they rode in the tourney. The counsel was welcome to all, and a mighty din and clang of arms soon arose in the great tilt-yard, while Etzel and Kriemhild looked on.

Sixty of Dietrich's knights spurred forward to meet the strangers. They were eager for the onset, had Dietrich allowed it, for goodly men were his. But it irked him when he heard thereof, and forbade them to cross lances with Gunther's warriors. He feared it might go hard with his knights.

When the knights of Bern were gone out of the yard, five hundred of Rudeger's men of Bechlaren rode up before the castle, with their shields. The Margrave had been better pleased if they had stayed away. He pressed through the crowd, and said to them that they themselves knew how that Gunther's men were wroth, and that he would have them quit the tourney.

When these also had gone back, they say that the knights of Thueringen and a thousand bold Danes rode in. Then the splinters flew from the lances. Irnfried and Hawart rode into the tourney. The Rhinelanders met them proudly. They encountered the men of Thueringen in many a joust; pierced was many a shield.

Sir Bloedel came on with three thousand. Etzel and Kriemhild saw plainly all that passed below. The queen rejoiced, by reason of the hate she bare the Burgundians. She thought in her heart, - what happed or long - "If they wounded any, the sport might turn to a battle. I would fain be revenged on my foes; certes, it would not grieve me."

Schrutan and Gibek came next, and Ramung and Hornbog, after the manner of the Huns. They all bare them boldly before the Burgundians. High over the king's palace flew the splinters. Yet all they did was but empty sound.

Gunther's men made the house and the castle ring with the clash of shields. They won great honour. So keen was their pastime that the foot-cloths ran with the sweat of the horses, as they rode proudly against the Huns.

Then said stout Folker the fiddler, "These knights dare not confront us, I ween. I have heard that they hate us. They could not have a fitter time to prove it."

"Lead the horses to their stalls," said the king. "Toward evening ye may ride again, if there be time for it. Haply the queen may then give the prize to the Burgundians."

At that moment a knight rode into the lists, prouder than any other Hun. Belike he had a dear one at the window. He was rich apparelled like a bride.

Folker said, "I cannot help it. Yonder woman's darling must have a stroke. None shall hinder me. Let him look to his life. I care not how wroth Etzel's wife may be."

"Nay now, for my sake," said the king. "The folk will blame us if we begin the fray. Let the Huns be the first. It were better so."

Still Etzel sat by the queen.

"I will join thee in the tourney," cried Hagen. "It were well that these women and these knights saw how we can ride. They give Gunther's men scant praise."

Bold Folker spurred back into the lists. Thereby many a woman won heart's dole. He stabbed the proud Hun through the body with his spear. Many a maid and many a wife was yet to weep for it. Hagen and his sixty knights followed hard on the fiddler. Etzel and Kriemhild saw it all plain.

The three kings left not the doughty minstrel alone among his foemen. A thousand knights rode to the rescue. They were haughty and overweening, and did as they would.

When the proud Hun was slain, the sound of weeping and wailing rose from his kinsmen. All asked, "Who hath done it?" and got answer, "It was Folker, the bold fiddler."

The friends of the Hunnish Margrave called straightway for their swords and their shields, that they might kill Folker. The host hasted from the window. There was a mighty uproar among the Huns. The kings and their followers alighted before the all, and beat back their horses.

Then came Etzel and began to part the fray. He seized a sharp sword out of the hand of one of the Hun's kinsmen that stood nigh, and thrust them all back.

He was greatly wroth, "Ye would have me fail in honour toward these knights! If ye had slain this minstrel, I tell you I would have hanged you all. I marked him well when he slew the Hun, and saw that it was not with intent, but that his horse stumbled. Let my guests leave the tilt-yard in peace."

He gave them escort, himself, and their horses were led to the stalls, for many varlets stood ready to serve them.

The host went with his guests into the palace, and bade the anger cease. They set the table, and brought water.

The knights of the Rhine had stark foemen enow. Though it irked Etzel, many armed knights pressed in after the kings, when they went to table, by reason of their hate. They waited a chance to avenge their kinsman.

"Ye be too unmannerly," said the host, "to sit down armed to eat. Whoso among you toucheth my guests shall pay for it with his head. I have spoken, O Huns."

It was long or the knights were all seated. Bitter was Kriemhild's wrath. She said, "Prince of Bern, I seek thy counsel and thy kind help in my sore need."

But Hildebrand, the good knight, answered, "Who slayeth the Nibelungs shall do it without me; I care not what price thou offerest. None shall essay it but he shall rue it, for never yet have these doughty knights been vanquished."

Folker Stabbeth the Hun

"I ask the death of none save Hagen, that hath wronged me. He slew Siegfried, my dear husband. He that chose him from among the others for vengeance should have my gold without stint. I were inly grieved did any suffer save Hagen."

But Hildebrand answered, "How could one slay him alone? Thou canst see for thyself, that, if he be set upon, they will all to battle, and poor and rich alike must perish."

Said Dietrich also, courteously, "Great queen, say no more. Thy kinsmen have done naught to me that I should defy them to the death. It is little to thine honour that thou wouldst compass the doom of thy kinsmen. They came hither under safe conduct, and not by the hand of Dietrich shall Siegfried be avenged."

When she found no treachery in the knight of Bern, she tempted Bloedel with the promise of a goodly estate that had been Nudung's. Dankwart slew him after, that he clean forgot the gift.

Bloedel, that sat by her, answered, "I dare not show thy kinsmen such hate, so long as my brother showeth them favour. The king would not forgive me if I defied them."

"Nay now, Sir Bloedel, I will stand by thee, and give thee silver and gold for meed, and, thereto, a beautiful woman, the widow of Nudung, that thou mayest have her to thy dear one. I will give the all, land and castles, and thou shalt live joyfully with her on the march that was Nudung's. In good sooth I will do what I promise."

When Bloedel heard the fee, and because the woman pleased him for her fairness, he resolved to win her by battle. So came he to lose his life.

He said to the queen, "Go back into the hall. Or any is ware thereof, I will raise a great tumult. Hagen shall pay for what he hath done. I will bring thee King Gunther's man bound."

"Now arm ye, my men," cried Bloedel, "and let us fall on the foemen in their lodging. King Etzel's wife giveth me no peace, and at her bidding we must risk our lives."

When the queen had left Bloedel to begin the strife, she went in to table with King Etzel and his men. She had woven an evil snare against the guests.

I will tell you how they went into the hall. Crowned kings went before her; many high princes and knights of worship attended the queen. Etzel assigned to all the guests their places, the highest and the best in the hall. Christians and heathens had their different meats, whereof they ate to the full; for so the wise king ordered it. The yeomen feasted in their own quarters, where sewers served them, that had been charged with the care of their food. But revel and merriment were soon turned to weeping.

Kriemhild's old wrong lay buried in her heart, and when the strife could not be kindled otherwise, she bade them bring Etzel's son to table. Did ever any woman so fearful a thing for vengeance? Four of Etzel's men went straightway and brought in Ortlieb, the young king, to the princes' table, where Hagen also sat. Through his murderous hate the child perished.

When Etzel saw his son, he spake kindly to his wife's brethren, "See now, my friends, that is my only son, and your sister's child. Some day he will serve you well. If he take after his kin, he will be a valiant man, rich and right noble, stark and comely. If I live, I will give him the lordship of twelve countries. Fair service ye may yet have from young Ortlieb's hand. Wherefore I pray ye, my dear friends, that, when ye ride back to the Rhine, ye take with you your sister's son, and do well by the child. Rear him in honour till he be a man, and when he is full grown, if any harry your land, he will help you to avenge it."

Kriemhild, the wife of Etzel, heard all that the king said.

Hagen answered, "If he grow to be a man, he may well help these knights. But he hath a weakly look. Methinketh I shall seldom go to Ortlieb's court."

The king eyed Hagen sternly, for his word irked him. Albeit he answered not again, he was troubled, and heavy of his cheer. Hagen was no friend to merriment.

The king and his liegemen misliked sore what Hagen had said of the child, and were wroth that they must bear it. They knew not yet what the warrior was to do after. Not a few that heard it, and that bare him hate, had gladly fallen upon him: the king also, had not honour forbidden him. Ill had Hagen sped. Yet soon he did worse: he slew his child before his eyes.

HOW BLOEDEL FOUGHT WITH DANKWART IN THE HALL

LOEDEL'S knights all stood ready. With a thousand hauberks they went where Dankwart sat at table with the yeomen. Grim was soon the hate between the heroes.

When Sir Bloedel strode up to the table, Dankwart the marshal greeted him fair. "Welcome to this house, Sir Bloedel. What news dost thou bring?"

"Greet me not," said Bloedel. "My coming meaneth thy death, because of Hagen, thy brother, that slew Siegfried. Thou and many another knight shall pay for it."

"Nay now, Sir Bloedel," said Dankwart. "So might we well rue this hightide. I was a little child when Siegfried lost his life. I know not what King Etzel's wife hath against me."

"I can tell thee nothing, save that thy kinsmen, Gunther and Hagen, did it. Now stand on your defence, ye homeless ones. Ye must die, for your lives are forfeit to Kriemhild."

"Dost thou persist?" said Dankwart. "Then it irketh me that I asked it. I had better have spared my words."

The good knight and bold sprang up from the table, and drew a sharp weapon that was mickle and long, and smote Bloedel a swift blow therewith, that his head, in its helmet, fell at their feet.

"That be thy wedding-gift to Nudung's bride, that thou thoughtest to win!" he cried. "Let them mate her to-morrow with another man; if he ask the dowry, he can have the like."

A faithful Hun had told him that morning, secretly, that the queen plotted their doom.

When Bloedel's men saw their master lying slain, they endured it no longer, but fell with drawn swords in grim wrath on the youths. Many rued it later.

Loud cried Dankwart to the squires and the yeomen, "Ye see that we are undone. Fight for your lives, ye homeless ones, that ye may lie dead without shame."

They that had not swords seized the benches, and caught up the stools from the floor. The squires of Burgundy were not slow to answer them. With these they dinted many a helmet.

The homeless youths made grim defence. They drave the armed me from the house. Yet five hundred and more lay therein dead. They were red and wet with blood.

This heave news reached Etzel's knights. Grim was their grief that Bloedel and his men were slain by the brother of Hagen, and the squires. Or Etzel knew anything of the matter, two thousand Huns or more did on their armour and hasted thither, for so it must needs be, and left not one alive. These false knights brought a mighty host before the house.

The strangers defended them well; but what availed their prowess? They had all to die. Or long the fray waxed grimmer yet.

Now shall ye list to marvels and wondrous deeds. Nine thousand squires lay dead, and twelve of Dankwart's men. He stood alone among his foes. The noise was hushed, the din had ceased. Dankwart looked over his shoulder and cried, "Woe is me for the friends I have lost! Among my foemen I stand alone."

Swords enow fell upon his body. Many a hero's wife was yet to weep for it. He raised his buckler, and lowered the thong, and wetted many a hauberk with blood.

"Woe is me for this wrong!" cried Aldrian's child. "Stand back, ye knights of Hungary, and let me to the air, that it cool a battle-weary man." Then he began, in their despite, to hew his way to the door.

When he sprang from the house, how many a sword rang on his helmet! They that had not seen the wonders of his hand fell upon him there.

"Would to God," said Dankwart, "I had a messenger to tell my brother Hagen in what peril I stand! He would help me hence, or die by me."

But the Hunnish knights answered, "Thou, thyself, shalt be the messenger, when we carry thee in dead to thy brother. So shall Gunther's man have first hear of his loss. To Etzel thou hast done grievous hurt."

He said, "Keep your threats, and stand back, or I will wet the harness of some of you. I will bear the news myself to the court, and bewail my great wrong to my masters."

He did Etzel's men such scathe, that they durst not draw against him. Then they shot so many darts into his shield that he must drop it for heaviness.

They thought to vanquish him without his shield. Ha! what deep wounds he made in their helmets! Many a bold man staggered before him. Great honour and praise were Dankwart's. From both sides they sprang at him.

I ween they were too hasty. He fought his way through his foemen like a wild boar in the forest through the hounds - bolder he could not have been. His path was ever wet anew with hot blood. When did single knight withstand foemen better? Proudly Hagen's brother went to court.

The sewers and the cup-bearers heard the clash of swords. Many dropped the drink and the meats they carried. On the stairs he found stark enemies enow.

"How now, ye sewers?" cried the weary knight; "see to the guests, and bear in the good meats to your lords, and let me take my message to my masters."

They that had the hardihood, and sprang down on him from the stairs, he smote so fiercely with his sword that they fell back for fear. With his strength he had done right wonderly.

HOW DANKWART BROUGHT THE NEWS TO HIS MASTERS

HEN bold Dankwart strode in through the door, and bade Etzel's followers void the way; all his harness was covered with blood. It was at the time they were carrying Ortlieb to and fro from table to table among the princes, and through the terrible news the child perished.

Dankwart cried aloud to one of the knights, "Thou sittest here too long, brother Hagen. To thee, and God in Heaven, I bewail our wrong. Knights and squires lie dead in our hall."

Hagen called back to him, "Who hath done it?"

"Sir Bloedel and his men. He paid for it bitterly, I can tell thee. I smote off his head with my hands."

"He hath paid too little," said Hagen, "since it can be said of him that he hath died by the hand of a hero. His womenfolk have the less cause to weep. Now tell me, dear brother; wherefore art thou so red? I ween thy wounds are deep. If he be anywhere near that hath done it, and the Devil help him not, he is a dead man."

"Unwounded I stand. My harness is wet with the blood of other men, whereof I have to-day slain so many, that I cannot swear to the number."

Hagen said, "Brother Dankwart, keep the door, and let not a single Hun out; I will speak with the knights as our wrong constraineth me. Guiltless, our followers lie dead."

"To such great kings will I gladly be chamberlain," said the bold man; "I will guard the stairs faithfully."

Kriemhild's men were sore dismayed.

"I marvel much," said Hagen, "what the Hunnish knights whisper in each other's ears. I ween they could well spare him that standeth at the door, and hath brought this court news to the Burgundians. I have long heard Kriemhild say that she could not bear her heart's dole. Now drink we to Love, and taste the king's wine. The young prince of the Huns shall be the first."

With that, Hagen slew the child Ortlieb, that the blood gushed down on his hand from his sword, and the head flew up into the queen's lap. Then a slaughter grim and great arose among the knights. He slew the child's guardian with a sword stroke from both his hands, that the head fell down before the table. It was sorry pay he gave the tutor. He saw a minstrel sitting at Etzel's table, and sprang at him in wrath, and lopped off his right hand on his viol: "Take that for the message thou broughtest to the Burgundians."

"Woe is me for my hand!" cried Werbel. "Sir Hagen of Trony, what have I done to thee? I rode with true heart to thy master's land. How shall I make my music now?"

Little recked Hagen if he never fiddled more. He quenched on Etzel's knights, in the house there, his grim lust for blood, and smote to death not a few.

Swift Folker sprang from the table; his fiddle-bow rang loud. Harsh were the tunes of Gunther's minstrel. Ha! many a foe he made among the Huns!

The three kings, too, rose hastily. They would have parted them or more harm was done. But they could not, for Folker and Hagen were beside themselves with rage.

When the King of Rhineland could not stint the strife, he, also, smote many a deep wound through the shining harness of his foemen. Well he showed his hardihood.

Then stark Gernot came into the battle, and slew many Huns with the sharp sword that Rudeger had given him. He brought many of Etzel's knights to their graves therewith.

Uta's youngest son sprang into the fray, and pierced the helmets of Etzel's knights valiantly with his weapon. Bold Giselher's hand did wonderly.

But howso valiant all the others were, the kings and their men, Folker stood up bolder than any against the foes; he was a hero; he wounded many, that they fell down in their blood.

Etzel's liegemen warded them well, but the guests hewed their way with their bright swords up and down the hall. From all sides came the sound of wailing. They that were without would gladly have won in to their friends, but could not; and they that were within would have won out, but Dankwart let none of them up the stair or down.

Then a great crowd gathered before the door, and the swords clanged loud upon the helmets, so that Dankwart came in much scathe. Hagen feared for him, as was meet, and he cried aloud to Folker, "Comrade, seest thou my brother beset by the stark blows of the Huns? Save him, friend, or we lose the warrior."

"That will I, without fail," said the minstrel; and he began to fiddle his way through the hall; it was a hard sword that rang in his hand. Great thank he won from the knights of the Rhine.

He said to Dankwart, "Thou hast toiled hard to-day. Thy brother bade me come to thy help. Do thou go without, and I will stand within."

Dankwart went outside the door and guarded the stair. Loud din made the weapons of the heroes. Inside, Folker the Burgundian did the like. The bold fiddler cried above the crowd, "The house is well warded, friend Hagen; Etzel's door is barred by the hands of two knights that have made it fast with a thousand bolts."

When Hagen saw the door secured, the famous knight and good threw back his shield, and began to avenge the death of his friend in earnest. Many a valiant knight suffered for his wrath.

When the Prince of Bern saw the wonders that Hagen wrought, and the helmets that he brake, he sprang on to a bench, and cried, "Hagen poureth out the bitterest wine of all."

The host and his wife fell in great fear. Many a dear friend was slain before their eyes. Etzel himself scarce escaped from his foemen. He sat there affrighted. What did it profit him that he was a king?

Proud Kriemhild cried to Dietrich, "Help me, noble knight, by the princely charity of an Amelung king, to come hence alive. If Hagen reach me, death standeth by my side."

"How can I help thee, noble queen? I cannot help myself. Gunther's men are so grimly wroth that I can win grace for none."

"Nay now, good Sir Dietrich, show thy mercy, and help me hence or I die. Save me and the king from this great peril."

"I will try. Albeit, for long, I have not seen good knights in such a fury. The blood gusheth from the helmets at their sword-strokes."

The chosen knight shouted with a loud voice that rang out like the blast of a buffalo horn, so that all the castle echoed with its strength, for stark and of mickle might was Dietrich.

King Gunther heard his cry above the din of strife, and hearkened. He said, "The voice of Dietrich hath reached me. I ween our knights have slain some of his men. I see him on the table, beckoning with his hand. Friends and kinsmen of Burgundy, hold, that we may learn what we have done to Dietrich's hurt."

When King Gunther had begged and prayed them, they lowered their swords. Thereby Gunther showed his might, that they smote no blow. Then he asked the Prince of Bern what he wanted. He said, "Most noble Dietrich, what hurt have my friends done thee? I will make it good. Sore grieved were I, had any done thee scathe."

But Sir Dietrich answered, "Naught hath been done against me. With thy safe-conduct let me quit this hall, and the bitter strife, with my men. For this I will ever serve thee."

"Why ask this grace?" said Wolfhart. "The fiddler hath not barred the door so fast that we cannot set it wide, and go forth."

"Hold thy peace," cried Dietrich. "Thou hast played the Devil."

Then Gunther answered, "I give thee leave. Lead forth few or many, so they be not my foemen. These shall tarry within, for great wrong have I suffered from the Huns."

When the knight of Bern heard that, he put one arm round the queen, for she was greatly affrighted, and with the other he led out Etzel. Six hundred good knights followed Dietrich.

Then said noble Rudeger, the Margrave, "If any more of them that love and would serve thee may win from this hall, let us hear it; that peace may endure, as is seemly, betwixt faithful friends."

Straightway Giselher answered his father-in-law. "Peace and love be betwixt us. Thou and thy liegemen have been ever true to us, wherefore depart with thy friends, fearing nothing."

When Sir Rudeger left the hall, five hundred or more went out with him. The Burgundian knights did honourably therein, but King Gunther suffered scathe for it after.

One of the Huns would have saved himself when he saw King Etzel go out with Dietrich, but the fiddler smote him such a blow that his head fell down at Etzel's feet.

When the king of the land was gone out from the house, he turned and looked at Folker. "Woe is me for such guests! It is a hard and bitter thing that all my knights fall dead before them! Alack! this hightide!" wailed the great king. "There is one within that hight Folker. He is liker a wild boar than a fiddler. I thank Heaven that I escaped the devil. His tunes are harsh; his bow is red. His notes smite many a hero dead. I know not what this minstrel hath against us. Never was guest so unwelcome."

The knight of Bern, and Sir Rudeger, went each to his lodging. They desired not to meddle with the strife, and they bade their men avoid the fray.

Had the guests known what hurt the twain would do them after, they had not won so lightly from the hall, but had gotten a stroke from the bold ones in passing.

All that they would let go were gone. Then arose a mighty din. The guests avenged them bitterly. Ha! many a helmet did Folker break!

King Gunther turned his ear to the noise. "Dost thou hear the tunes, Hagen, that Folker playeth yonder on the Huns, when any would win through the door? The hue of his bow is red."

"It repenteth me sore," spake Hagen, "to be parted from the knight. I was his comrade, and he mine. If we win home again, we shall ever be true friends. See now, great king, how he serveth thee. He earneth thy silver and thy gold. His fiddle-bow cleaveth the hard steel, and scattereth on the ground the bright jewels on the helmets. Never have I seen a minstrel make such stand. His measures ring through helmet and shield. Good horse shall he ride, and wear costly apparel."

Of the Huns that had been in the hall, not one was left alive. The tumult fell, for there was none to fight, and the bold warriors laid down their swords.

HOW THEY THREW DOWN THE DEAD

HE knights sat down through weariness. Folker and Hagen went out before the hall. There the overweening men leaned on their shields and spake together.

Then said Giselher of Burgundy, "Rest not yet, dear friends. Ye must carry the dead out of the house. We shall be set upon again; trow my word. These cannot lie longer among our feet. Or the Huns overcome us, we will hew many wounds; to the which I am nothing loth."

"Well for me that I have such a lord," answered Hagen. "This counsel suiteth well such a knight as our young master hath approved him this day. Ye Burgundians have cause to rejoice."

They did as he commanded, and bare the seven thousand dead bodies to the door, and threw them out. They fell down at the foot of the stair.

Then arose a great wail from their kinsmen. Some of them were so little wounded that, with softer nursing, they had come to. Now, from the fall, these died also. Their friends wept and made bitter dole.

Then said bold Folker the fiddler, "Now I perceive they spake the truth that told me the Huns were cowards. They weep like women, when they might tend these wounded bodies."

A Margrave that was there deemed he meant this truly. He saw one of his kinsmen lying in his blood, and put his arms round him to bear him away. Him the minstrel shot dead.

When the others saw this, they fled, and began to curse Folker. With that, he lifted a sharp spear and hard from the ground, that a Hun had shot at him, and hurled it strongly across the courtyard, over the heads of the folk. Etzel's men took their stand further off, for they all feared his might.

Then came Etzel with his men before the hall. Folker and Hagen began to speak out their mind to the King of the Huns. They suffered for it or all was done.

"It is well for a people when its kings fight in the forefront of the strife as doeth each of my masters. They hew the helmets, and the blood spurteth out."

Etzel was brave, and he grasped his shield.

"Have a care," cried Kriemhild, "and offer thy knights gold heaped upon the shield. If Hagen reach thee, thou hast death at thy hand."

But the king was so bold he would not stop; the which is rare enow among great princes to-day. They had to pull him back by his shield-thong; whereat grim Hagen began to mock anew.

"Siegfried's darling and Etzel's are near of kin. Siegfried had Kriemhild to wife or ever she saw thee. Coward king, thou, of all men, shouldst bear me no grudge."

When Kriemhild heard him, she was bitterly wroth that he durst mock her before Etzel's warriors, and she strove to work them woe. She said, "To him that will slay Hagen of Trony and bring me his head, I will fill Etzel's shield with red gold. Thereto, he shall have, for his meed, goodly castles and land."

"I know not why ye hang back," said the minstrel. "I never yet saw heroes stand dismayed that had the offer of such pay. Etzel hath small cause to love you. I see many cowards standing here that eat the king's bread, and fail him now in his sore need, and yet call themselves bold knights. Shame upon them!"

They Throw Down The Dead

Great Etzel was grieved enow. He wept sore for his dead men and kinsmen. Valiant warriors of many lands stood round him, and bewailed his great loss with him.

Then bold Folker mocked them again. "I see many high-born knights weeping here, that help their king little in his need. Long have they eaten his bread with shame."

The best among them thought, "He sayeth sooth."

But none mourned so inly as Iring, the hero of Denmark; the which was proven or long by his deeds.

HOW IRING WAS SLAIN

HEN cried Iring, the Margrave of Denmark, "I have long followed honour, and done not amiss in battle. Bring me my harness, and I will go up against Hagen."

"Thou hadst better not," answered Hagen, "or thy kinsmen will have more to weep for. Though ye spring up two or three together, ye would fall down the stair the worse for it."

"I care not," said Iring. "I have oft tried as hard a thing. With my single sword I would defy thee, if thou hadst done twice as much in the strife."

Sir Iring armed him straightway. Irnfried of Thuringia, likewise, a bold youth, and Hawart the stark, with a thousand men that were fain to stand by Iring.

When the fiddler saw so great an armed host with him, wearing bright helmets on their heads, he was wroth. "Behold how Iring cometh hither, that vowed to encounter thee alone. It beseemeth not a knight to lie. I blame him much. A thousand armed knights or more come with him."

"Call me no liar," said Hawart's liegeman. "I will gladly abide by my word, nor fail therein through fear. How grim soever Hagen may be, I will meet him alone."

Iring fell at the feet of his kinsmen and vassals, that they might let him defy the knight in single combat. They were loth, for they knew proud Hagen of Burgundy well. But he prayed them so long that they consented. When his followers saw that he wooed honour, they let him go. Then began a deadly strife betwixt them.

Iring of Denmark, the chosen knight, raised his spear; then he covered his body with his shield, and sprang at Hagen. The heroes made a loud din. They hurled their spears so mightily from their hands, that they pierced through the strong bucklers to the bright harness, and the shafts flew high in the air. Then the grimly bold men grasped their swords.

Hagen was strong beyond measure, yet Iring smote him, that all the house rang. Palace and tower echoed their blows. But neither had the advantage.

Iring left Hagen unwounded, and sprang at the fiddler. He thought to vanquish him by his mighty blows. But the gleeman stood well on his guard, and smote his foeman, that the steel plate of his buckler flew off. He was a terrible man.

Then Iring ran at Gunther, the King of Burgundy.

Fell enow were the twain. But though each smote fiercely at the other, they drew no blood. Their good harness shielded them.

He left Gunther, and ran at Gernot, and began to strike sparks from his mailcoat, but King Gernot of Burgundy well-nigh slew him. Then he sprang from the princes, for he was right nimble, and soon had slain four Burgundians from Worms beyond the Rhine.

Giselher was greatly wroth thereat. "Now by God, Sir Iring," he cried, "thou shalt pay for them that lie dead!" and he fell on him. He smote the Dane, that began to stagger, and dropped down among the blood, so that all deemed the doughty warrior would never strike another blow. Yet Iring lay unwounded withal before Giselher. From the noise of his helmet and the clang of the sword his wits left him, and he lay in a swoon. That had Giselher done with his strong arm.

When the noise of the blow had cleared from his brain, he thought, "I live still, and am unwounded. Now I know the strength of Giselher."

He heard his foemen on both sides. Had they been ware how it stood with him, worse had befallen him. He heard Giselher also, and he pondered by what device he might escape them. He sprang up furiously from among the blood. Well his swiftness served him. He fled from the house, past Hagen, and gave him a stout stroke as he ran.

"Ha!" thought Hagen, "Thou shalt die for this. The Devil help thee, or thou art a dead man." But Iring wounded Hagen through the helmet. He did it with Vasky, a goodly weapon.

When Hagen felt the wound, he swung his sword fiercely, that Hawart's man must needs fly. Hagen followed him down the stair. But Iring held his shield above his head. Had the stair been thrice as long, Hagen had not left him time for a single thrust. Ha! what red sparks flew from his helmet! Yet, safe withal, Iring reached his friends.

When Kriemhild heard what he had done to Hagen of Trony in the strife, she thanked him. "God quit thee, Iring, thou hero undismayed! thou hast comforted me, heart and soul, for I see Hagen's harness red with blood."

The glad queen took the shield from his hand herself.

"Stint thy thanks," said Hagen. "There is scant cause for them. If he tried it again, he were in sooth a bold man. The wound I got from him will serve thee little. The blood thou seest on my harness but urgeth me to slay the more. Only now, for the first time, I am wroth indeed. Sir Iring hath done me little hurt."

Iring of Denmark stood against the wind, and cooled him in his harness, with his helmet unlaced; and all the folk praised his hardihood, that the Margrave's heart was uplifted.

He said, "Friends, arm me anew. I will essay it again. Haply I may vanquish this overweening man." His shield was hewn in pieces; they brought him a better straight.

The warrior was soon armed, and stronger than afore. Wrothfully he seized a stark spear, wherewith he defied Hagen yet again.
He had won more profit and honour had he let it be.

Hagen waited not for his coming.   Hurling darts, and with
drawn sword, he sprang down the stairs in a fury. Iring's strength
availed him little. They smote at each other's shields, that glowed
with a fire-red wind. Through his helmet and his buckler, Hawart's
man was wounded to the death by Hagen's sword. He was never
whole again.

When Sir Iring felt the wound, he raised his shield higher
to guard his head, for he perceived that he was sore hurt.   But
Gunther's man did worse to him yet. He found a spear lying at his
feet, and hurled it at Iring, the knight of Denmark, that it stuck
out on the other side of his head. The overweening knight made a
grim end of his foeman.

Iring fell back among his friends. Or they did off his helmet,
they drew the spear out. Then death stood at hand. Loud mourned
his friends; their sorrow was bitter.

The queen came, and began to weep for stark Iring. She wept
for his wounds, and was right doleful. But the undismayed hero
spake before his kinsmen, "Weep not, noble lady. What avail thy
tears? I must die from these wounds that I have gotten. Death will
not leave me longer to thee and Etzel."

Then he said to them of Thuringia and Denmark, "See that
none of you take the gifts of the queen - her bright gold so red.
If ye fight with Hagen ye must die."

His cheek was pale; he bare death's mark. They grieved enow;
for Hawart's man would nevermore be whole.   Then they of
Denmark must needs to the fray.

Irnfried and Hawart sprang forward with a thousand knights.
The din was loud over all. Ha! what sharp spears were hurled at
the Burgundians!

Bold Irnfried ran at the gleeman, and came in scathe by his
hand. The fiddler smote the Landgrave through his strong helmet,
for he was grim enow. Then Irnfried gave Folker a blow, that the

links of his hauberk brake asunder, and his harness grew red like fire. Yet, for all, the Landgrave fell dead before the fiddler.

Hawart and Hagen closed in strife. Had any seen it, they had beheld wonders. They smote mightily with their swords. Hawart died by the knight of Burgundy.

When the Thuringians and Danes saw their masters slain, they rushed yet fiercer against the house, and grisly was the strife or they won to the door. Many a helmet and buckler were hewn in pieces.

"Give way," cried Folker, "and let them in. They shall not have their will, but, in lieu thereof, shall perish. They will earn the queen's gift with their death."

The proud warriors thronged into the hall, but many an one bowed his head, slain by swift blows. Well fought bold Gernot; the like did Giselher.

A thousand and four came in. Keen and bright flashed the swords; but all the knights died. Great wonders might be told of the Burgundians.

When the tumult fell, there was silence. Over all, the blood of the dead men trickled through the crannies into the gutters below. They of the Rhine had done this by their prowess.

Then the Burgundians sat and rested, and laid down their weapons and their shields. The bold gleeman went out before the house, and waited, lest any more should come to fight.

The king and his wife wailed loud. Maids and wives beat their breasts. I ween that Death had sworn an oath against them, for many a knight was yet to die by the hands of the strangers.

HOW THE QUEEN BAD THEM BURN DOWN THE HALL

"NOW do off your helmets," said Hagen the knight. "I and my comrade will keep watch. And if Etzel's men try it again, I will warn my masters straightway."

Then many a good warrior unlaced his helmet. They sat down on the bodies that had fallen in the blood by their hands. With bitter hate the guests were spied at by the Huns.

Before nightfall the king and queen had prevailed on the men of Hungary to dare the combat anew. Twenty thousand or more stood before them ready for battle. These hasted to fall on the strangers.

Dankwart, Hagen's brother, sprang from his masters to the foemen at the door. They thought he was slain, but he came forth alive.

The strife endured till the night. The guests, as beseemed good warriors, had defended them against Etzel's men all through the long summer day. Ha! what doughty heroes lay dead before them. It was on a midsummer that the great slaughter fell, when Kriemhild avenged her heart's dole on her nearest kinsmen, and on many another man, and all King Etzel's joy was ended. Yet she purposed not at the first to bring it to such a bloody encounter, but only to kill Hagen; but the Devil contrived it so, that they must all perish.

The day was done; they were in sore straits. They deemed a quick death had been better than long anguish. The proud knights would fain have had a truce. They asked that the king might be brought to them.

The heroes, red with blood, and blackened with the soil of their harness, stepped out of the hall with the three kings. They knew not whom to bewail their bitter woe to.

Both Etzel and Kriemhild came. The land all round was theirs, and many had joined their host.

Etzel said to the guests, "What would ye with me? Haply ye seek for peace. That can hardly be, after such wrong as ye have done me and mine. Ye shall pay for it while I have life. Because of my child that ye slew, and my many men, nor peace nor truce shall ye have."

Gunther answered, "A great wrong constrained us thereto. All my followers perished in their lodging by the hands of thy knights. What had I done to deserve that? I came to see thee in good faith, for I deemed thou wert my friend."

Then said Giselher, the youth, of Burgundy, "Ye knights of King Etzel that yet live, what have ye against me? How had I wronged you? - I that rode hither with loving heart?"

They answered, "Thy love hath filled all the castles of this country with mourning. We had gladly been spared thy journey from Worms beyond the Rhine. Thou hast orphaned the land - thou and thy brothers."

Then cried Gunther in wrath, "If ye would lay from you this stark hate against us homeless ones, it were well for both sides, for we are guiltless before Etzel."

But the host answered the guests, "My scathe is greater than thine; because of the mickle toil of the strife, and its shame, not one of you shall come forth alive."

Then said stark Gernot to the king, "Herein, at the least, incline thy heart to do mercifully with us. Stand back from the house, that we win out to you. We know that our life is forfeit; let what must come, come quickly. Thou hast many knights unwounded;

let them fall on us, and give us battle-weary ones rest. How long wouldst thou have us strive?"

King Etzel's knights would have let them forth, but when Kriemhild heard it, she was wroth, and even this boon was denied to the strangers.

"Nay now, ye Huns, I entreat you, in good faith, that ye let not these lusters after blood come out from the hall, lest thy kinsmen all perish miserably. If none of them were left alive save Uta's children, my noble brothers, and won they to the air to cool their harness, ye were lost. Bolder knights were never born into the world."

Then said young Giselher, "Fairest sister mine, right evil I deem it that thou badest me across the Rhine to this bitter woe. How have I deserved death from the Huns? I was ever true to thee, nor did thee any hurt. I rode hither, dearest sister, for that I trusted to thy love. Needs must thou show mercy."

"I will show no mercy, for I got none. Bitter wrong did Hagen of Trony to me in my home yonder, and here he hath slain my child. They that came with him must pay for it. Yet, if ye will deliver Hagen captive, I will grant your prayer, and let you live; for ye are my brothers, and the children of one mother. I will prevail upon my knights here to grant a truce."

"God in Heaven forbid!" cried Gernot. "Though we were a thousand, liefer would we all die by thy kinsmen, than give one single man for our ransom. That we will never do."

"We must perish then," said Giselher; "but we will fall as good knights. We are still here; would any fight with us? I will never do falsely by my friend."

Cried bold Dankwart too (he had done ill to hold his peace), "My brother Hagen standeth not alone. They that have denied us quarter may rue it yet. By my troth, ye will find it to your cost."

Then said the queen, "Ye heroes undismayed, go forward to the steps and avenge our wrong. I will thank you forever, and with cause. I will requite Hagen's insolence to the full. Let not one of them forth at any point, and I will let kindle the hall at its four sides. So will my heart's dole be avenged."

Etzel's knights were not loth. With darts and with blows they drave back into the house them that stood without. Loud was the din; but the princes and their men were not parted, nor failed they in faith to one another.

Etzel's wife bade the hall be kindled, and they tormented the bodies of the heroes with fire. The wind blew, and the house was soon all aflame. Folk never suffered worse, I ween. There were many that cried, "Woe is me for this pain! Liefer had we died in battle. God pity us, for we are all lost. The queen taketh bitter vengeance."

One among them wailed, "We perish by the smoke and the fire. Grim is our torment. The stark heat maketh me so athirst, that I die."

Said Hagen of Trony, "Ye noble knights and good, let any that are athirst drink the blood. In this heat it is better than wine, and there is naught sweeter here."

Then went one where he found a dead body. He knelt by the wounds, and did off his helmet, and began to drink the streaming blood. Albeit he was little used thereto, he deemed it right good.

"God quit thee, Sir Hagen!" said the weary man, "I have learned a good drink. Never did I taste better wine. If I live, I will thank thee."

When the others heard his praise, many more of them drank the blood, and their bodies were strengthened, for the which many a noble woman paid through her dear ones.

The fire-flakes fell down on them in the hall, but they warded them off with their shields. Both the smoke and the fire tormented them. Never before suffered heroes such sore pain.

Then said Hagen of Trony, "Stand fast by the wall. Let not the brands fall on your helmets. Trample them with your feet deeper in the blood. A woeful hightide is the queen's."

The night ended at last. The bold gleeman, and Hagen, his comrade, stood before the house and leaned upon their shields. They waited for further hurt from Etzel's knights. It advantaged the strangers much that the roof was vaulted. By reason thereof more were left alive. Albeit they at the windows suffered scathe, they bared them valiantly, as their bold hearts bade them.

Then said the fiddler, "Go we now into the hall, that the Huns deem we be all dead from this torment, albeit some among them shall yet feel our might."

Giselher, the youth, of Burgundy, said, "It is daybreak, I ween. A cool wind bloweth. God grant we may see happier days. My sister Kriemhild hath bidden us to a doleful hightide."

One of them spake, "I see the dawn. Since we can do no better, arm you, ye knights, for battle, that, come we never hence, we may die with honour."

Etzel deemed the guests were all dead of their travail and the stress of the fire. But six hundred bold men yet lived. Never king had better knights. They that kept ward over the strangers had seen that some were left, albeit the princes and their men had suffered loss and dole. They saw many that walked up and down in the house.

They told Kriemhild that many were left alive, but the queen answered, "It cannot be. None could live in that fire. I trow they all lie dead."

The kings and their men had still gladly asked for mercy, had there been any to show it. But there was none in the whole country of the Huns. Wherefore they avenged their death with willing hand.

They were greeted early in the morning with a fierce onslaught, and came in great scathe. Stark spears were hurled at them. Well the knights within stood on their defence.

Etzel's men were the bolder, that they might win Kriemhild's fee. Thereto, they obeyed the king gladly; but soon they looked on death.

One might tell marvels of her gifts and promises. She bade them bear forth red gold upon shields, and gave thereof to all that desired it, or would take it. So great treasure was never given against foemen.

The host of warriors came armed to the hall. The fiddler said, "We are here. I never was gladder to see any knights than those that have taken the king's gold to our hurt."

Not a few of them cried out, "Come nigher, ye heroes! Do your worst, and make an end quickly, for here are none but must die."

Soon their bucklers were filled full of darts. What shall I say more? Twelve hundred warriors strove once and again to win entrance. The guests cooled their hardihood with wounds. None could part the strife. The blood flowed from death-deep wounds. Many were slain. Each bewailed some friend. All Etzel's worthy knights perished. Their kinsmen sorrowed bitterly.

HOW RUDEGER WAS SLAIN

HE strangers did valiantly that morning. Gotelind's husband came into the courtyard and saw the heavy loss on both sides, whereat the true man wept inly.

"Woe is me," said the knight, "that ever I was born, since none can stop this strife! Fain would I have them at one again, but the king holdeth back, for he seeth always more done to his hurt."

Good Rudeger sent to Dietrich, that they might seek to move the great king. But the knight of Bern sent back answer, "Who can hinder it? King Etzel letteth none intercede."

A knight of the Huns, that had oft seen Rudeger standing with wet eyes, said to the queen, "Look how he standeth yonder, that Etzel hath raised above all others, and that hath land and folk at his service. Why hath Rudeger so many castles from the king? He hath struck no blow in this battle. I ween he careth little for our scathe, so long as he has enow for himself. They say he is bolder than any other. Ill hath he shown it in our need."

The faithful man, when he heard that word, looked angrily at the knight. He thought, "Thou shalt pay for this. Thou callest me a coward. Thou hast told thy tale too loud at court."

He clenched his fist, and ran at him, and smote the Hun so fiercely that he fell down at his feet, dead. Whereat Etzel's grief waxed anew.

"Away with thee, false babbler!" cried Rudeger. "I had trouble and sorrow enow. What was it to thee that I fought not? Good cause have I also to hate the strangers, and had done what I could against them, but that I brought them hither. I was their escort into my master's land, and may not lift my wretched hand against them."

Then said Etzel, the great king, to the Margrave, "How hast thou helped us, most noble Rudeger? We had dead men enow in the land, and needed no more. Evilly hast thou done."

But the knight answered, "He angered me, and twitted me with the honour and the wealth thou hast bestowed on me so plenteously. It hath cost the liar dear."

Then came the queen, that had seen the Hun perish by Rudeger's wrath. She mourned for him with wet eyes, and said to Rudeger, "What have we ever done to thee that thou shouldst add to our sorrow? Thou hast oft times promised, noble Rudeger, that thou wouldst risk, for our sake, both honour and life, and I have heard many warriors praise thee for thy valour. Hast thou forgotten the oath thou swearest to me with thy hand, good knight, when thou didst woo me for King Etzel--how that thou wouldst serve me till my life's end, or till thine? Never was my need greater than now."

"It is true, noble lady. I promised to risk for thee honour and life, but I sware not to lose my soul. I brought the princes to this hightide."

She said, "Remember, Rudeger, thy faith, and thine oath to avenge all my hurt and my woe."

The Margrave answered, "I have never said thee nay."

Etzel began to entreat likewise. They fell at his feet.

Sore troubled was the good Margrave. Full of grief, he cried, "Woe is me that ever I saw this hour, for God hath forsaken me. All my duty to Heaven, mine honour, my good faith, my knightliness, I must forego. God above have pity, and let me die! Whether I do this thing, or do it not, I sin. And if I take the part of neither, all the world will blame me. Let Him that made me guide me."

The King And Queen Entreat Rudeger
To Fight With The Burgundians

Still the king and his wife implored him. Whence it fell that many valiant warriors lost their lives at his hand, and the hero himself was slain.

Hear ye now the tale of his sorrow.

Well he knew he could win naught but teen and scathe. Fain had he denied the prayer of the king and queen. He feared, if he slew but one man, that the world would loathe him evermore.

Then the bold man said to the king, "Take back what thou hast given me - castles and land. Leave me nothing at all. I will go forth afoot into exile. I will take my wife and my daughter by the hand, and I will quit thy country empty, rather than I will die dishonoured. I took thy red gold to my hurt."

King Etzel answered, "Who will help me then? Land and folk I gave to thee, Rudeger, that thou mightest avenge me on my foes. Thou shalt rule with Etzel as a great king."

But Rudeger said, "How can I do it? I bade them to my house and home; I set meat and drink before them, and gave them my gifts. Shall I also smite them dead? The folk may deem me a coward. But I have always served them well. Should I fight with them now, it were ill done. Deep must I rue past friendship. I gave my daughter to Giselher. None better in this world had she found, of so great lineage and honour, and faith, and wealth. Never saw I young king so virtuous."

But Kriemhild answered, "Most noble Rudeger, take pity on us both. Bethink thee that never host had guests like these."

Then said the Margrave, "What thou and my master have given me I must pay for, this day, with my life. I shall die, and that quickly. Well I know that, or nightfall, my lands and castles will return to your keeping. To your grave I commend my wife and my child, and the homeless ones that are at Bechlaren."

"God reward thee, Rudeger," cried the king. He and the queen were both glad. "Thy folk shall be well seen to; but thou thyself, I trow, will come off scatheless."

So he put his soul and body on the hazard. Etzel's wife began to weep. He said, "I must keep my vow to thee. Woe is me for my friends, that I must fall upon in mine own despite!"

They saw him turn heavily from the king. To his knights that stood close by, he said, "Arm ye, my men all. For I must fight the Burgundians, to my sorrow." The heroes called for their harness, and the attendants brought helm and buckler. Soon the proud strangers heard the sad news.

Rudeger stood armed with five hundred men, and twelve knights that went with him, to win worship in the fray. They knew not that death was so near.

Rudeger went forth with his helmet on; his men carried sharp swords, and, thereto, broad shields and bright. The fiddler saw this, and was dismayed. But when Giselher beheld his father-in-law with his helmet on, he weened that he meant them well. The noble king was right glad.

"Well for me that I have such friends," cried Giselher, "as these we won by the way! For my wife's sake he will save us. By my faith, I am glad to be wed."

"Thy trust is vain," said the fiddler. "When ever did ye see so many knights come in peace, with helmets laced on, and with swords? Rudeger cometh to serve for his castles and his lands."

Or the fiddler had made an end of speaking, Rudeger, the noble man, stood before the house. He laid his good shield before his feet. He must needs deny greeting to his friends.

Then the Margrave shouted into the hall, "Stand on your defence, ye bold Nibelungs. I would have helped you, but must slay you. Once we were friends, but I cannot keep my faith."

The sore-tired men were dismayed at this word. Their comfort was gone, for he that they loved was come against them. From their foemen they had suffered enow.

"God in Heaven forbid," said Gunther the knight, "that thou shouldst be false to the friendship and the faith wherein we trusted. It cannot be."

"I cannot help it," said Rudeger. "I must fight with you, for I have vowed it. As ye love your lives, bold warriors, ward you well. King Etzel's wife will have it so."

"Thou turnest too late," said the king. "God reward thee, noble Rudeger, for the truth and the love thou hast shown us, if it endure but to the end. We shall ever thank and serve thee for the rich gifts thou gavest to me and my kinsmen, when thou broughtest us with true heart into Etzel's land: so thou let us live. Think well thereon, noble Rudeger."

"Gladly would I grant it," said the knight. "Might I but give thee freely, as I would, with none to chide me!"

"Give that no thought," said Gernot. "Never host entreated guests so kindly as thou us; the which will advantage thee if we live."

"Would to God, noble Gernot," cried Rudeger, "that ye were at the Rhine, and I dead with honour, since I must fight with you! Never strangers were worse entreated by friends."

"God reward thee, Sir Rudeger," answered Gernot, "for thy rich gifts. I should rue thy death, for in thee a virtuous man would fall. Behold, good knight, the sword thou gavest, in my hand. It hath never failed me in my need. Its edge hath killed many a warrior. It is finely tempered and stark, and thereto bright and good. So goodly a gift, I ween, never knight will give more. If thou forbear not, but fall upon us, and slay any of my kinsmen here, thou shalt perish by thine own sword! Much I pity thee and thy wife."

"Would to God, Sir Gernot, thou hadst thy will, and thy friends were out of peril! To thee I would entrust wife and daughter."

Then said the youngest of fair Uta's sons, "How canst thou do this thing, Sir Rudeger? All that came hither with me are thy friends. A vile deed is this. Thou makest thy daughter too soon a widow. If thou and thy knights defy us, ill am I apayed, that I trusted thee before all other men, when I won thy daughter for my wife."

"Forget not thy troth, noble king, if God send thee hence," answered Rudeger. "Let not the maiden suffer for my sin. By thine own princely virtue, withdraw not thy favour from her."

"Fain would I promise it," said Giselher the youth. "Yet if my high-born kinsmen perish here by thy hand, my love for thee and thy daughter must perish also."

"Then God have mercy!" cried the brave man; whereat he lifted his shield, and would have fallen upon the guests in Kriemhild's hall.

But Hagen called out to him from the stairhead, "Tarry awhile, noble Rudeger. Let me and my masters speak with thee yet awhile in our need. What shall it profit Etzel if we knights die in a strange land? I am in evil case," said Hagen. "The shield that Gotelind gave me to carry, the Huns have hewn from my hand. In good faith I bore it hither. Would to God I had such a shield as thou hast, noble Rudeger! A better I would not ask for in the battle."

"I would gladly give thee my shield, durst I offer it before Kriemhild. Yet take it, Hagen, and wear it. Ha! mightest thou but win with it to Burgundy!"

When they saw him give the shield so readily, there were eyes enow red with hot tears. It was the last gift that Rudeger of Bechlaren ever gave.

Albeit Hagen was grim and stern, he was melted by the gift that the good knight, so night to his end, had given him. And many a warrior mourned with him.

"Now God reward thee, noble Rudeger; there will never be thy like again for giving freely to homeless knights. May the fame of thy charity live for ever. Sad news hast thou brought me. We had trouble enow. God pity us if we must fight with friends."

The Margrave answered, "Thou grievest not more than I."

"I will requite thee for thy gift, brave Rudeger. Whatever betide thee from these knights, my hand will not touch thee - not if thou slewest every man of Burgundy."

Rudeger bowed, and thanked him. All the folk wept. Sore pity it was that none could stay the strife. The father of all virtue lay dead in Rudeger.

Then Folker the fiddler went to the door and said, "Since my comrade Hagen hath sworn peace, thou shalt have it also from my hand. Well didst thou earn it when we came first into this country. Noble Margrave, be my envoy. The Margravine gave me these red bracelets to war at the hightide. See them now, and bear witness that I did it."

"Would to God that the Margravine might give thee more! Doubt not but I shall tell my dear one, if I ever see her alive."

When he had promised that, Rudeger lifted up his shield; he waxed fierce, and tarried no longer. Like a knight he fell upon the guests. Many a swift blow he smote. Folker and Hagen stood back, for they had vowed it. But so many bold men stood by the door that Rudeger came in great scathe.

Athirst for blood, Gunther and Gernot let him pass in. Certes, they were heroes. Giselher drew back sorrowing. He hoped to live yet awhile; wherefore he avoided Rudeger in the strife.

Then the Margrave's men ran at their foemen, and followed their master like good knights. They carried sharp weapons, wherewith they clove many a helmet and buckler. The weary ones answered the men of Bechlaren with swift blows that pierced deep and straight through their harness to their life's blood. They did wonderly in the battle.

All the warriors were now in the hall. Folker and Hagen fell on them, for they had sworn to spare none save the one man. Their hands struck blood from the helmets. Right grim was the clash of swords! Many a shield-plate sprang in sunder, and the precious stones were scattered among the blood. So fiercely none will fight again. The prince of Bechlaren hewed a path right and left, as one acquainted with battle.

Well did Rudeger approve him that day a bold and blameless knight.

Gunther and Gernot smote many heroes dead. Giselher and Dankwart laid about them, fearing naught, and sent many a man to his doom. Rudeger approved him stark enow, bold and well armed. Ha! many a knight he slew! One of the Burgundians saw this, and was wroth; whereat Rudeger's death drew nigh.

Gernot cried out to the Margrave, "Noble Rudeger; thou leavest none of my men alive. It irketh me sore; I will bear it no longer. I will turn thy gift against thee, for thou hast taken many friends from me. Come hither, thou bold man. What thou gavest me I will earn to the uttermost."

Or the Margrave had fought his way to him, bright bucklers grew dim with blood. Then, greedy of fame, the men ran at each other, and began to ward off the deadly wounds. But their swords were so sharp that nothing could withstand them.

Rudeger the knight smote Gernot through his flint-hard helmet, that the blood brake out. Soon the good warrior was avenged. He swung Rudeger's gift on high, and, albeit he was wounded to the death, he smote him through his good shield and his helmet, that Gotelind's husband died. So rich a gift was never worse requited. So they fell in the strife - Gernot and Rudeger - slain by each other's hand.

Thereat Hagen waxed grimmer than afore. The hero of Trony said, "Great woe is ours. None can ever make good to their folk and their land the loss of these two knights. Rudeger's men shall pay for it."

They gave no quarter. Many were struck down unwounded that had come to, but that they were drowned in the blood.

"Woe is me for my brother, fallen dead! Each hour bringeth fresh dole. For my father-in-law, Rudeger, I grieve also. Twofold is my loss and my sorrow."

When Giselher saw his brother slain, they that were in the hall suffered for it. Death lagged not behind. Of the men of Bechlaren there was left not a living soul. Gunther and Giselher, and eke Hagen, Dankwart and Folker, the good knights, went where the two warriors lay, and there the heroes wept piteously.

"Death hath despoiled us sore," said Giselher the youth. "Stop your weeping, and go out to the air, that we strife-weary ones may cool our harness. God will not let us live longer, I ween."

They that were without saw them sitting, or leaning and taking their rest. Rudeger's men were all slain; the din was hushed.

The silence endured so long that Etzel was angered, and the king's wife cried, "Woe is me for this treason. They speak too long. The bodies of our foemen are left unscathed by Rudeger's hand. He plotteth to guide them back to Burgundy. What doth it profit us, King Etzel, that we have shared all our wealth with him? The knight hath done falsely. He that should have avenged us cometh to terms with them."

But Folker, the valiant warrior, answered her, "Alack! it is not so, noble queen. If I might give the lie to one so high-born as thou art, thou hast foully slandered Rudeger. Sorry terms have he and his knights made with us. With such good will he did the king's bidding, that he and his men all lie dead. Look round thee for another, Kriemhild, to obey thee. Rudeger served thee till his death. If thou doubtest, thou mayest see for thyself."

To her grief they did it. They brought the mangled hero where Etzel saw him. Never were Etzel's knights so doleful. When the dead Margrave was held up before them, none could write or tell all the bitter wailing whereby women and men alike uttered their heart's dole. Etzel's woe was so great that the sound of his lamentation was as a lion's roar. Loud wept his wife. They mourned good Rudeger bitterly.

HOW DIETRICH'S KNIGHTS WERE ALL SLAIN

SO loud they wept on all sides, that palace and towers echoed with the sound. One of Dietrich's men of Bern heard it, and hasted with the news.

He said to the prince, "Hearken, Sir Dietrich. Never in my life heard I such wail as this. Methinketh the king himself hath joined the high-tide. How else should all the folk make such dole. Either the king or Kriemhild - one of them at the least - have the guests killed through hate. The valiant warriors weep bitterly."

The prince of Bern answered, "Judge not so hastily, my good men. What the stranger knights have done, sore peril hath constrained them to. Let it boot them now that I sware peace to them."

But bold Wolfhart said, "I will go and ask what they have done, and will tell thee, dear master, when I know the truth." Sir Dietrich answered, "When a knight is wroth, if one question him roughly, his anger is soon kindled. I would not have thee meddle therein, Wolfhart."

He bade Helfrich haste thither, and find out from Etzel's men, or from the guests, what had happed, for he had never heard folk wail so loud.

The messenger asked, "What aileth you all?"

One among them answered, "Joy is fled from the land of the Huns. Rudeger lieth slain by the men of Burgundy. Of them that entered in with him, not one is left alive."

Helfrich was sore grieved. He had never told so sad a tale, and went back weeping.

"What news?" cried Dietrich. "Why weepest thou so bitterly, Sir Helfrich?"

The knight answered, "I may well mourn. The Burgundians have slain Rudeger."

But the prince of Bern said, "God forbid! That were stark vengeance and devil's sport. What had Rudeger done to deserve it? Well I know he was their friend."

Wolfhart answered, "If they have done this, their life shall pay for it. It were shameful to endure it. For oft hath Rudeger's hand served us."

The prince of Amelung bade them inquire further. He sat down at a window sore troubled, and bade Hildebrand go to the guests, and ask them what had happened.

Master Hildebrand, bold in strife, took with him neither shield nor sword, and would have gone to them on peaceful wise. But his sister's child chid him.

Grim Wolfhart cried, "Why goest thou naked? If they revile thee, thou wilt have the worst of the quarrel, and return shamed. If thou goest armed, none will withstand thee."

The old man armed him as the youth had counselled. Or he had ended, all Dietrich's knights stood in their harness, sword in hand. It irked the warrior, and he had gladly turned them from their purpose. He asked their intent.

"We would follow thee," they answered. "What if Hagen of Trony, as his wont is, mock thee?" Whereupon Hildebrand consented.

When bold Folker saw the knights of Bern, Dietrich's men, girt with swords, and coming armed, with shields in their hands, he told his masters of Burgundy.

He said, "Dietrich's men draw nigh like foemen, armed, and in helmets. They come to defy us. I ween it will go hard with us forlorn ones."

Hildebrand came up while he spake. He laid his shield at his feet, and said to Gunther's men, "Alack! ye good knights! What have ye done to Rudeger? Dietrich, my master, sent me hither to ask if any here slew the good Margrave, as they tell us. We could ill endure such loss."

Hagen of Trony answered, "The news is true. Glad were I had the messenger lied to thee, for Rudeger's sake, and that he lived still. Both men and women must evermore bewail him."

When they heard he was dead in sooth, all the warriors wept, as was meet. Down beard and chin ran the tears of Dietrich's men. Right heavy were they and doleful.

A duke of Bern that hight Siegstab, cried, "Now is ended all the loving kindness wherewith Rudeger cheered our sad days. Ye have slain, in Rudeger, the friend of all homeless knights."

Sir Wolfwine of Amelung said, "I had not grieved more this day to see my father dead. Woe is me! Who will comfort the good Margravine?"

Sir Wolfhart cried angrily, "Who will lead the warriors forth to battle now, as Rudeger so oft hath done. Woe is me for brave Rudeger! We have lost him!"

Wolfbrand and Helfrich and eke Helmnot wept for his death with all their friends.

Hildebrand could ask no more for grief. He said, "Grant now, ye warriors, that for which my master sent me. Give us dead Rudeger from out the hall, with whom all our joy hath perished, and let us requite him for all the kindness he hath shown to us and many another. Like him we are homeless. Why tarry ye? Let us bear him hence, and serve him dead, as we had gladly served him living."

Then said King Gunther, "No service is better than that of friends to a dead friend. I approve the true hearth of him that doeth it. Ye have cause to praise him. He hath shown you much love."

"How long shall we entreat?" cried Wolfhart. "Sith ye have slain our joy, and we can have him no more, let us bear him hence to bury him."

But Folker answered, "Ye shall get him from none here. Come and take him out of the house, where he lieth with his death-wounds in the blood. So shall ye serve Rudeger truly."

Cried bold Wolfhart, "God knoweth, sir fiddler, thou dost wrong to provoke us further; thou hast done us hurt enow. If I dared before my master, it would go hard with thee. We may not fight; he hath forbidden it."

The fiddler said, "He that avoideth all that is forbidden is over fearful. He hath not the right hero's heart."

Hagen approved the word of his comrade. But Wolfhart cried, "Give over mocking, or I will put thy fiddle-strings out of tune, that thou mayest have somewhat to tell, if ever thou ridest again to Burgundy. I can no longer, with honour, endure thine insolence."

The fiddler answered, "If thou spoilest my strings, my hand will dim thy helmet afore I ride back to Burgundy."

Wolfhart would have run at him, but his uncle, Hildebrand, held him fast and would not let him. "Thou art mad in thy foolish wrath. We should come in disgrace forever with my master."

"Let loose the lion that is so grim, sir knight. But if he fall into my hand," said Folker, "I will slay him, though he had laid the whole world dead. There will be an end of his hot answers."

Wolfhart fell in a fury thereat. He lifted his shield and sprang at him like a wild lion. His friends followed after. But, quick though he was, old Hildebrand came before any to the stair-way, that he might not be second in the fight. They found plenty to meet them among the strangers.

Hagen leapt upon Master Hildebrand. The weapons rang loud in their hands, for it was well seen they were wroth. A fire-red wind blew from their swords. But they were parted in the fray by the knights of Bern, that pressed in amain. So Master Hildebrand turned away from Hagen.

Stark Wolfhart ran at Folker. He smote the fiddler on his helmet, that the sword's edge cut into the beaver. The bold fiddler struck him such a blow that the sparks flew from his harness. Deadly was their hate. Then Sir Wolfwine parted them. If he was not a hero, there never was one.

Gunther, the noble king, met the famed Amelung knights with ready hand. Sir Giselher made many a polished helmet red and wet with blood. Dankwart, Hagen's brother, was a grim man. All that he had done afore to Etzel's warriors was but a wind to what he did now; fell and furious was Aldrian's child. Ritschart and Gerbart, Helfrich and Wichart, had never spared themselves in battle, the which they let Gunther's men see.

Wolfbrand was undaunted in the strife. Old Hildebrand fought as he were mad. Many a good knight fell dead in the blood before the sword of Wolfhart. Rudeger was well avenged. Sir Siegstab did right valiantly. Ha! how many hard helmets Dietrich's sister's son brake to his foemen. Bolder in battle he could not have been.

When stark Folker saw that Siegstab struck blood from the hauberks, he was wroth, and leapt upon him and slew him. Such proof of his skill gave the fiddler that Siegstab died.

Hildebrand avenged him as beseemed his might. "Woe is me for my dear lord, that lieth slain by Folker's hand! Bitterly shall the fiddler pay for it."

Certes, Hildebrand was grim enow. He smote Folker, that the gleeman's shield and helmet flew in splinters across the hall. That was an end of stark Folker.

Then Dietrich's men rushed in from all sides. They smote till the links of their foemen's mail whistled asunder, and their broken sword-points flew on high. They struck hot-flowing streams from the helmets.

When Hagen of Trony saw Folker dead, he grieved more bitterly than he had done yet, all the hightide, for kinsman or vassal. Alack! how grimly he began to avenge him!

"Old Hildebrand shall not go scatheless, for his hand hath slain my friend, the best comrade I ever had."

He raised his shield, and hewed his way right and left.

Helfrich slew stark Dankwart. Doleful enow were Gunther and Giselher when they saw him fall in his bitter pains. Yet he had well avenged his death with his own hand.

Albeit many mighty princes of many lands were gathered there against the little band, their prowess had brought them forth alive, had not the Christian folk turned foemen.

Meantime, Wolfhart went to and fro, and hewed down Gunther's men. He cut his way round the hall thrice. Many a knight fell before him.

Then cried stark Giselher to Wolfhart, "Woe is me, that I have so grim a foe! Come hither, bold warrior, and I will make an end of this. Longer it shall not endure."

Wolfhart turned to Giselher in the strife. They gave one another wide wounds. So fiercely Wolfhart sprang at him that the blood under his feet spurted over his head.

Fair Uta's child welcomed Wolfhart, the bold knight, with swift blows. Albeit the warrior was mighty, he perished. Never king so young was so valiant. He smote Wolfhart through his goodly harness, that blood flowed down from the gash: he wounded Dietrich's man to the death. None save a hero had done it.

When Wolfhart felt the sword-cut, he threw away his shield, and lifted a mighty and sharp weapon, wherewith, through helmet and harness, he slew Giselher. They gave each other a grim death, for Dietrich's man fell likewise.

Old Hildebrand grieved sore when he saw Wolfhart fall. All Gunther's men and Dietrich's were dead, and he went where Wolfhart lay in the blood, and put his arm round him to bear him away out of the house. But he was too heavy, so he must needs let him lie.

Then the deadly wounded man looked up from among the blood, and saw that his uncle would have helped him, and he said, "Dearest uncle, no help availeth me. Thou didest better to beware of Hagen, for grim and fell is his heart. And if my kinsmen, my nearest and my best, mourn for me hereafter, say that they weep

Hildebrand Fleeth From Hagen

without cause, for that I died gloriously by the hand of a king. In the fight I have so well avenged me that many a warrior's wife shall wail. If any question thee, tell him straight that, with my single hand, I slew an hundred."

Then Hagen thought on the fiddler that old Hildebrand had slain, and he said to the knight, "Thou shalt pay for my teen. Thou hast robbed us of many a good warrior."

He smote Hildebrand, that Balmung, the sword he had taken from Siegfried when he slew him, rang loud. But the old man stood boldly on his defence. He brought his sharp-edged sword down on Hagen, but could not wound him. Then Hagen pierced him through his good harness.

When Master Hildebrand felt the wound, he feared more scathe from Hagen, so he threw his shield over his back and fled. Now, of all the knights, none were left alive save two, Gunther and Hagen.

Old Hildebrand, covered with blood, ran with the news to Dietrich, that he saw sitting sadly where he had left him. Soon the prince had more cause for woe. When he saw Hildebrand in his bloody harness, he asked fearfully for his tale.

"Now tell me, Master Hildebrand, why thou art so wet with thy life's blood? Who did it? I ween thou hast fought with the guests in the hall, albeit I so sternly forbade it. Thou hadst better have forborne."

Hildebrand answered his master, "Hagen did it. He gave me this wound in the hall when I turned to flee from him. I scarce escaped the devil with my life."

Said the prince of Bern, "Thou art rightly served. Thou heardest me vow friendship to the knights, and thou hast broken the peace I gave them. Were it not that I shame me to slay thee, thy life were forfeit."

"Be not so wroth, my lord Dietrich. Enough woe hath befallen me and mine. We would have borne away Rudeger's body, but Gunther's men denied it."

"Woe is me for this wrong! Is Rudeger then dead? That is the bitterest of my dole. Noble Gotelind is my cousin's child. Alack! The poor orphans of Bechlaren!"

With ruth and sorrow he wept for Rudeger. "Woe is me for the true comrade I have lost. I must mourn Etzel's liegeman forever. Canst thou tell me, Master Hildebrand, who slew him?"

Hildebrand answered, "It was stark Gernot, but the hero fell by Rudeger's hand."

Said Dietrich, "Bid my men arm them, for I will thither straightway. Send me my shining harness. I, myself, will question the knights of Burgundy."

But Master Hildebrand answered, "Who is there to call? Thy sole living liegeman standeth here. I am the only one. The rest are dead."

Dietrich trembled at the news, and was passing doleful, for never in this world had he known such woe. He cried, "Are all my men slain? then God hath forgotten poor Dietrich! I was a great king, rich and proud. Yet how could they all die, these valiant heroes, by foemen so battle-weary and sore beset? Death had spared them, but that I am doomed to sorrow. Since this hard fate is needs mine, tell me if any of the guests be left alive."

Hildebrand answered, "None save Hagen, and Gunther, the king. God knoweth I say sooth."

"Woe is me, dear Wolfhart, if I have lost thee! It were better I had never been born. Siegstab and Wolfwine and Wolfbrand: who is there then left to help me in the land of the Amelungs? Is bold Gelfrich slain also? And Gerbart and Wichart? When shall I have done weeping? This day hath ended all my joy. Alack! that none may die of grief!"

HOW GUNTHER, HAGEN, AND KRIEMHILD WERE SLAIN

HEREUPON Sir Dietrich went and got his harness himself. Old Hildebrand helped to arm him. The strong man wept so loud that the house rang with his voice. But soon he was of stout heart again, as beseemed a hero. He did on his armour in wrath. He took a fine-tempered shield in his hand, and they hasted to the place - he and Master Hildebrand.

Then said Hagen of Trony, "I see Sir Dietrich yonder. He cometh to avenge his great loss. This day will show which of us twain is the better man. Howso stark of body and grim Sir Dietrich may deem him, I doubt not but I shall stand against him, if he seek vengeance." So spake Hagen.

Dietrich, that was with Hildebrand, heard him. He came where both the knights stood outside the house, leaning against the wall. Good Dietrich laid down his shield, and, moved with deep woe, he said, "Why hast thou so entreated a homeless knight? What had I done to thee? Thou hast ended all my joy. Thou deemedst it too little to have slain Rudeger to our scathe; now thou hast robbed me of all my men. I had never done the like to you, O knights. Think on yourselves and your loss - the death of your friends, and your travail. By reason thereof are ye not heavy of your cheer? Alack! how bitter to me is Rudeger's death! There was never such woe in this world. Ye have done evilly by me and by yourselves. All the joy I had ye have slain. How shall I ever mourn enow for all my kinsmen?"

"We are not alone to blame," answered Hagen. "Your knights came hither armed and ready, with a great host. Methinketh the tale hath not been told thee aright."

"What shall I believe then? Hildebrand said that when my knights of Amelung begged you to give them Rudeger's body, ye answered mockingly, as they stood below."

Then said the prince of the Rhineland. "They told me they were come to bear Rudeger hence. I denied them, not to anger thy men, but to grieve Etzel withal. Whereat Wolfhart flew in a passion."

Said the prince of Bern, "There is nothing for it. Of thy knightliness, atone to me for the wrong thou hast done me, and I will avenge it no further. Yield thee captive, thee and thy man, and I will defend thee to the uttermost against the wrath of the Huns. Thou wilt find me faithful and true."

"God in Heaven forbid," cried Hagen, "that two knights, armed as we are for battle, should yield them to thee! I would hold it a great shame, and ill done."

"Deny me not," said Dietrich. "Ye have made me heavy-hearted enow, O Gunther and Hagen; and it is no more than just, that ye make it good. I swear to you, and give you my hand thereon, that I will ride back with you to your own country. I will bring you safely thither, or die with you, and forget my great wrong for your sakes."

"Ask us no more," said Hagen. "It were a shameful tale to tell of us, that two such bold men yielded them captive. I see none save Hildebrand by thy side."

Hildebrand answered, "Ye would do well to take my master's terms; the hour will come, or long, when ye would gladly take them, but may not have them."

"Certes, I had liefer do it," said Hagen, "than flee mine adversary like a coward, as thou didst, Master Hildebrand. By my troth, I deemed thou hadst withstood a foeman better."

Cried Hildebrand, "Thou needest not to twit me. Who was it that, by the wask-stone, sat upon his shield when Walter of Spain slew so many of his kinsmen? Thou, thyself, art not void of blame."

Said Sir Dietrich then, "It beseemeth not warriors to fight with words like old women. I forbid thee, Master Hildebrand, to say more. Homeless knight that I am, I have grief enow. Tell me now, Sir Hagen, what ye good knights said when ye saw me coming around. Was it not that thou alone wouldst defy me?"

"Thou hast guessed rightly," answered Hagen. "I am ready to prove it with swift blows, if my Nibelung sword break not. I am wroth that ye would have had us yield us captive."

When Dietrich heard grim Hagen's mind, he caught up his shield, and sprang up the steps. The Nibelung sword rang loud on his mail. Sir Dietrich knew well that the bold man was fierce. The prince of Bern warded off the strokes. He needed not to learn that Hagen was a valiant knight. Thereto, he feared stark Balmung. But ever and anon he struck out warily, till he had overcome Hagen in the strife. He gave him a wound that was deep and wide.

Then thought Sir Dietrich, "Thy long travail hath made thee weak. I had little honour in thy death. Liefer will I take thee captive."

Not lightly did he prevail. He threw down his shield. He was stark and bold, and he caught Hagen of Trony in his arms. So the valiant man was vanquished. King Gunther grieved sore.

Dietrich bound Hagen, and led him to the queen, and delivered into her hand the boldest knight that ever bare a sword. After her bitter dole, she was glad enow. She bowed before the knight for joy. "Blest be thou in soul and body. Thou hast made good to me all my woe. I will thank thee till my dying day."

Then said Dietrich, "Let him live, noble queen. His service may yet atone to thee for what he hath done to thy hurt. Take not vengeance on him for that he is bound."

She bade them lead Hagen to a dungeon. There he lay locked up, and none saw him.

Then King Gunther called aloud, "Where is the hero of Bern? He hath done me a grievous wrong."

Sir Dietrich went to meet him. Gunther was a man of might. He tarried not, but ran toward him from the hall. Loud was the din of their swords.

Howso famed Dietrich was from aforetime, Gunther was so wroth and so fell, and so bitterly his foemen, by reason of the wrong he had endured, that it was a marvel Sir Dietrich came off alive. They were stark and mighty men both. Palace and towers echoed with their blows, as their swift swords hewed their good helmets. A high-hearted king was Gunther.

But the knight of Bern overcame him, as he had done Hagen. His blood gushed from his harness by reason of the good sword that Dietrich carried. Yet Gunther had defended him well, for all he was so weary.

The knight was bound by Dietrich's hand, albeit a king should never wear such bonds. Dietrich deemed, if he left Gunther and his man free, they would kill all they met.

He took him by the hand, and let him before Kriemhild. Her sorrow was lighter when she saw him. She said, "Thou art welcome, King Gunther."

He answered, "I would thank thee, dear sister, if thy greeting were in love. But I know thy fierce mind, and that thou mockest me and Hagen."

Then said the prince of Bern, "Most high queen, there were never nobler captives than these I have delivered here into thy hands. Let the homeless knights live for my sake."

She promised him she would do it gladly, and good Dietrich went forth weeping. Yet soon Etzel's wife took grim vengeance, by reason thereof both the valiant men perished. She kept them in dungeons, apart, that neither saw the other again till she bore her brother's head to Hagen. Certes, Kriemhild's vengeance was bitter.

The queen went to Hagen, and spake angrily to the knight. "Give me back what thou hast taken from me, and ye may both win back alive to Burgundy."

But grim Hagen answered, "Thy words are wasted, noble queen. I have sworn to show the hoard to none. While one of my masters liveth, none other shall have it."

"I will end the matter," said the queen. Then she bade them slay her brother, and they smote off his head. She carried it by the hair to the knight of Trony.

He was grieved enow.

When the sorrowful man saw his master's head, he cried to Kriemhild, "Thou hast wrought all thy will. It hath fallen out as I deemed it must. The noble King of Burgundy is dead, and Giselher the youth, and eke Gernot. None knoweth of the treasure now save God and me. Thou shalt never see it, devil that thou art."

She said, "I come off ill in the reckoning. I will keep Siegfried's sword at the least. My true love wore it when I saw him last. My bitterest heart's dole was for him."

She drew it from the sheath. He could not hinder it. She purposed to slay the knight. She lifted it high with both hands, and smote off his head.

King Etzel saw it, and sorrowed. "Alack!" cried the king, "The best warrior that ever rode to battle, or bore a shield, hath fallen by the hand of a woman! Albeit I was his foeman, I must grieve."

Then said Master Hildebrand, "His death shall not profit her. I care not what come of it. Though I came in scathe by him myself, I will avenge the death of the bold knight of Trony."

Hildebrand sprang fiercely at Kriemhild, and slew her with his sword. She suffered sore by his anger. Her loud cry helped her not.

Dead bodies lay stretched all over. The queen was hewn in pieces. Etzel and Dietrich began to weep. They wailed piteously for kinsmen and vassals. Mickle valour lay there slain. The folk were doleful and dreary.

The end of the king's hightide was woe, even as, at the last, all joy turneth to sorrow.

Kriemhild With The Head Of Gunther

I know not what fell after. Christian and heathen, wife, man, and maid, were seen weeping and mourning for their friends.

I WILL TELL YOU NO MORE. LET THE DEAD LIE.
HOWEVER IT FARED AFTER WITH THE HUNS,
MY TALE IS ENDED. THIS IS THE
SONG OF THE NIBELUNGS.

GLOSSARY

Abate: Lessen, decrease, subtract something from. *'Show the over-weening man he did well (he would do well) to abate his pride.'*

Abide, to: To live, stay, remain

Aforetime: Formerly

Albeit: Although. *'Albeit now there is no time for more word thereof.'*

Amiss: Faulty, out of order; improper;. *'Nor did these find the fair youth amiss.'*

Apparel: Clothing

Beseem, to: To be fitting or becoming. *'That I and my fellows may have raiment beseeming proud knights.'*

Behove, to: To be necessary or fitting for. *'It behoved the knights...'*

Belike: Probably; perhaps. *"Belike thou sayest sooth.*

Betide: Happen. *'From both I will keep me, that evil betide not.'*

Betwixt: Between

Bid, to: To command, to direct. *'They sat down as they were bidden.'*

Brach: A bitch hound.

Buckler: A small shield. *'He raised his buckler, and lowered the thong, and wetted many a hauberk with blood.'*

Carve at the board, to: The man who carves the meat at the 'board', or table, holds a place of high distinction in a household.

Certes: Certainly

Cleave, to: To split or sever. *'His fiddle-bow cleaveth the hard steel.'*

Comely: Pleasant to look at; attractive.

Deem, to: To think, consider, reckon, suppose, regard.

Dight, to: To make ready for a use or purpose; prepare:

Do off, to: To remove one;s garments. Later abbreviated to 'doff'.

Do on, to: To put on, as in putting on one's garments. 'Do on' was later abbreviated to 'don'.

Dole: Sadness

Doughty: Steadfastly courageous and resolute; valiant.

Draw nigh, to: To approach, to come near.

Dub, to: To give a name or a title to someone. *'To be dubbed a knight.'*

Durst, to: To dare. *'Nor durst any chide him, for from the day he bare arms he rested not from strife.'*

Enfeoff, to: To invest with a feudal estate or fee. *'The king enfeoffed Siegfried with lands and castles.'*

Enow: Enough

Gleeman: An entertainer, often travelling between towns, villages, inns and taverns.

Goodly: Attractive, excellent, or admirable.

Guerdon: A reward or recompense.

Had: (in context) : Would have. *'There many a Bavarian robber had gladly plundered them on the road.'*

Hardihood: Audacity, hardiness, boldness, courage, daring.

Harness: battle-armour

Hauberk: a shirt of mail.

Hie, to: To go quickly; hasten.

Hight, to: To be named, to be called.

Hightide: A feast, a celebration.

Hither: To or toward this place

Homage: A show or demonstration of respect or dedication to someone or something. *'Many youths there, afraid of the man and his sword, did homage for castles and land.'*

Howso: howsoever, regardless of how. *'Howsoever his his father hight, he is, certes, a goodly warrior.'*

I'faith: In faith; indeed; truly.

Inly: Inwardly; thoroughly

Irk, to: To be irritated or vexed by. *'It irked him that none knew it.'*

Kinsman: a person of the same nationality or ethnic group.

Knightly: Chivalric; characteristic of a knight; noble, courageous. *'Knightly he standeth there as for the onset.'*

Leman: A paramour, a lover, especially one in an adulterous relationship.

Liefer: Readily; willingly. *'Though we were a thousand, liefer would we all die by thy kinsmen.'*

Liegeman: The subject of a sovereign or feudal lord; vassal.

Limehound: A dog used in hunting the wild boar.

Loth: To be: to be reluctant, unwilling . *'He was little loth thereto.'*

Mailcoat: A corselet of scales, a cuirass formed of pieces of metal overlapping each other, like fish-scales. *'. . . and began to strike sparks from his mailcoat.'*

Massy: Consisting of a large mass; bulky; massive.

Meed: Merited gift or wage. *'The meed of love is sorrow.'*

Meet: Appropriate. *'It is not meet that all Etzel's men be greeted on like manner.' 'Meet is it that the old help the young, even as they in their day were holpen.'*

Methinketh: I believe; I think.

Mickle: Much.

Minster: Church.

Misproud: Wrongly or unreasonably proud, arrogant.

Naught: Nothing.

Needs must: Of necessity; necessarily: *'We must needs go.'* *'Needs made they dole, for they were sorrowful.'*

On like manner: In the same way. *'It is not meet that all Etzel's men be greeted on like manner.'*

On this wise: In this way/manner.

Onset: A military attack. *'Knightly he standeth there as for the onset.'*

Or: Before.

Overweening: Showing excessive confidence or pride. 'Show the overweening man he did well to abate his pride.'

Poitrel: The breastplate for a horse.

Prowest: Superlative form of prow, 'foremost'. *'There dwell the prowest ever sworn to king.'*

Raiment: Clothing, garments. *'. . . that I and my fellows may have raiment beseeming proud knights.'*

Reck, to: To heed, to be concerned by. *'Little recked Siegfried of heart's dole.'*

Rue, to: To regret.

Scathe: Injury. '*I shall be without scathe among foemen*'

Seemly: Conforming to accepted notions of propriety or good taste; decorous. '*Never knights were in seemlier trim.*'

Sennight: An abbreviation of 'seven-night' - a fortnight.

Shamefast: Bashful, modest; shy.

Slay, to: To kill.

Smite, to: To strike with a firm blow. '*He smote the two kings dead.*'

Somewhat: Something

Sooth: Truth. 'Belike thou sayest sooth.'

Sore/sorely: To a very high degree or level of intensity (especially of an unwelcome or unpleasant state or emotion).

Stark: Strong

Stint, to: To supply an ungenerous or inadequate amount of something.

Suffer, to: To permit (someone to do something). '*Without guards he was suffered not to ride abroad.*'

Sumpter: A pack animal, such as a horse or mule.

Tarnkappe: Siegfried's magical cloak that made the wearer invisible

Tarry: Stay longer than intended; delay leaving a place:

Teen: Misery; grief.

Therein: In that place, document, or respect. *'I will further thee therein as I best can.'*

Thereof: Of the thing just mentioned; of that:

Thereto: To that, this, or it.

Thong: A narrow strip of leather or other material, used esp. as a fastening or as the lash of a whip.

Tidings: News.

Tilt, to: To aim or thrust (a lance) in a joust. *'Then the king bade stay the tilting.'*

Tourney, to: To take part in a tournament.

Troth: Faith or loyalty when pledged in a solemn agreement or undertaking. *'By my troth'*

Trow, to: To think or believe.

Turned, to be: To allow oneself to be persuaded otherwise. *'Since thou wilt not be turned...'*

Twain: Two

Upbear: To lift up.

Vassal: A person who holds land from a feudal lord and receives protection in return for homage and allegiance.

Vaunt, to: To boast about or praise(something), especially excessively.

Versed, to be: To be acquainted through study or experience. *'Wise men versed in honour.'*

Vesture: Clothing; dress.

Vouch, to: To give personal assurances; give a guarantee.

Wax red or white, to: To blush or turn pale.

Wax, to: To grow, become. The opposite of 'to wane', which is 'to decrease'. *'He waxed in goodliness and honour.'*

Weal: Injury

Ween, to: To think; suppose. *'Of no king, I ween, is it told, that he held a longer marriage feast.'*

Weighed with: Compared to *'Weighed with him all other suitors were as wind.'*

Well minded, to be: To feel tempted or inclined to. *'The rich lords were well minded to have Siegfried to their prince.'*

Would: I would like. *'I would have raiment for so many.'*

Wrest, to: To forcibly pull (something) from a person's grasp.

Wot, to: To know.

Wroth, to be: To be angry.

Some titles in the Professor's Bookshelf series

THE
ILL-MADE
MUTE

CECILIA
DART-THORNTON

Cecilia Dart-Thornton

THE ILL-MADE MUTE
Book I of The Bitterbynde Trilogy

The Stormriders land their splendid winged stallions on the airy battlements of Isse Tower. Far below, the superstitious servants who dwell in the fortress' lower depths tell frightening tales of wicked creatures inhabiting the world outside, a world they have only glimpsed. Yet it is the least of the lowly, a mute, scarred, and utterly despised foundling, who dares to scale the Tower, stow away aboard a Windship, and then dive from the sky.

The fugitive is rescued by a kind-hearted adventurer, who bestows a name, the gift of communicating by handspeak, and an amazing truth never before guessed. Now the foundling begins a journey to distant Caermelor, to seek a wise woman whose skills may prove life-changing.

Along the way, this shunned outsider with an angel's soul and a gargoyle's face must survive in a wilderness of extraordinary danger. And as the challenges grow more deadly Imrhien learns something more terrifying than all the evil eldritch wights combined . . .

In a thrilling debut combining storytelling mastery with a treasure trove of folklore, Cecilia Dart-Thornton creates an exceptional epic adventure.

'Not since Tolkien's *The Fellowship of the Ring*... have I been so impressed by a beautifully spun fantasy.'
ANDRE NORTON, GRAND MASTER OF SCIENCE FICTION.

THE PROFESSOR'S BOOKSHELF

Stories that inspired Professor JRR Tolkien,
author of 'The Lord of the Rings'.'

www.professorsbookshelf.com

www.ingramcontent.com/pod-product-compliance
Lightning Source LLC
Chambersburg PA
CBHW060946030726
47503CB00003B/753